PAYBACK IN
PLEASANT
PASTURES

A PASTOR JOHN AND WENDY NOVEL

Greg Chantler

Contents

Prologue

NICK SALERNO SAT IN HIS OPULENTLY FUR-
nished office, located in one of his popular nightclubs
in downtown Chicago. His three nightclubs had rapidly
expanded since becoming topless venues, and Nick was enjoying his
success. The money was pouring in, and the customers couldn't seem
to get enough of what he offered.

Nick had tried to break into the prostitution racket, but that had
gone sideways on him. He had attempted to launch this new business
endeavor with his most popular dancer, but she got scared off and fled
the scene for parts unknown. Nick knew that his idea to use some of
his most popular dancers in this new endeavor was priceless. He could

only imagine what some of his wealthier customers would pay for a little extra time with their favorite dancer. That was sure to be a gold mine. And, in fact, it wouldn't it just be profitable for him, imagine what it could do for his girls. They'd be making more money than most of these girls could ever have dreamed of. If he was to be really honest, Nick saw himself as a savior, of sorts. Most of these girls who danced for him would have never had the opportunities he offered them.

His mind wandered back to Wendy, his most popular dancer. He gave her a chance when she was at her lowest. He even paid for her son to go to that exclusive private school, which all the rich schmucks were trying to get their kids into. Well, it took a little persuasion for the school officials to finally get her kid enrolled. In addition to that little favor, Nick also picked up the tab. He had done a lot for that gal and her kid. And how does she repay him? She split the scene and left him high and dry.

And, the thing that really bothered him was that she owed him. He had done her a huge favor by getting her out of that dump of a diner, where she was making peanuts, and getting her the dancing gig that brought big bucks her way. True, he had upped the ante a bit when he transformed his clubs into topless venues, but hey, they were well compensated for it. And, when he took it a step beyond that, with his idea to turn them into professional escorts for gentlemen who were willing to open their wallets to, shall we say, experience a more private rendezvous with their favorite dancer, everybody was going to win.

But a week ago, she upped and took off on him. He had no idea where she and the kid had gone; they could be anywhere. He had tried to shake down her mother for information, but her mom was as clueless as he was. He even tried to squeeze some information out of that old lady babysitter, Mrs. York. But she didn't know anything either. He considered getting a bit rough with the two broads, but what good would that do? They had no idea where Wendy was, and all the muscle would've done was gotten him in trouble with the law. And that was something Nick wanted no part of. He had known too many guys from the old neighborhood who spent time in the slammer, and according to them, it's not a place you wanted to be. Spending years in an 8 x 10 box would drive you crazy, if you could even survive long enough to lose your marbles.

No, Nick realized he'd been lucky. His clubs were all legit, and his other escort enterprise hadn't gotten off the ground yet. And when it did, he'd make sure that his lawyers hid the true nature of the business in pages of legal jargon that nobody could understand. But roughing up a couple of ladies could draw unwanted attention to himself, and that's the last thing Nick needed.

Still, the fact that Wendy walked out on him and left for who knows where, didn't sit well with Nick. She owed him. He did her a huge favor that not only cost him time, but it also cost him a bundle. That private school didn't come cheap. He'd invested a lot of his own money in a girl that he thought would be a top moneymaker, and then poof, she vanished without a trace. Just the thought of that made him furious. She owes me, Nick thought, and she's gonna pay me back.

Just then, two of Nick's "associates" knocked on the door and entered, when Nick gave the okay. Ed and Louie walked in and sank deep into the two, overstuffed leather chairs, sitting in front of Nick's enormous Cherrywood desk. They looked uncomfortable, and Nick knew they had something on their minds. Nobody said anything for a few seconds; they just sat and stared at each other. Finally, Nick broke the ice and said, "Okay guys, you look like a bunch of sad sacks. What's going on - I haven't got all day." Louie, who was the spokesman for this two-person mob, spoke up and told Nick that the word on the street was that he was going soft. Other guys in the business had heard about the gal who'd run out on Nick, leaving him in a lurch. She owed him, and he let her get away. "That's bad for your rep, boss," Louie declared. "You can't let her get away with that - otherwise your cred winds up in the toilet. And that's bad for business, you know that. So how we gonna to fix this?"

Nick looked at Louie and began a slow burn that was growing in intensity with each second. He didn't like having his faults pointed out to him. He had enough of that when he attended that Catholic school in his old Italian neighborhood. The nuns were always getting on his back about something, and he couldn't stand it. Why should he listen to some old biddy, who couldn't bag a husband, and gave the dumb excuse that she was married to the church? Who gets married to a building? That's crazy; Nick wasn't buying it. And so, he dropped out after sixth grade and went to public school. It was rough at first, but it wasn't long before his fists, and fiery temper, earned him the reputation that Nick Salerno was nobody to mess with. And sure enough, all the way through school, Nick was untouchable.

But now his hard-earned reputation was on the line. He took a few moments to let the anger die down, and then he spoke quietly, and calmly. He'd learned a very valuable lesson years before. He'd learned that you can get much more accomplished by exuding a quiet and controlled demeanor. It was quiet and controlled, but when necessary, the voice would slowly rise in intensity, and with each volume progression, the meaning behind his words became increasingly clear. Though he was quietly controlled, there was no missing the underlying strength and power. Nick was going to get what Nick wanted.

He looked at Ed and Louie, two of his closest childhood friends from the neighborhood, and gave them his instructions. She'd been gone less than a week. She was driving a silver Buick Skylark, with a black vinyl top. She'd have a young boy with her, about eight years old. She always talked about wanting to live in a warmer climate, because she was tired of the harsh Chicago winters. Right away Louie pipes up and makes the expected observation that she probably vanished to Florida, or at least to somewhere in the South. Nick looked at Ed and Louie shrewdly and said, "Yeah, that's what you'd think, wouldn't you? But if you really want to disappear, would you be so obvious about it? Nah. My money's on the northwest: Montana-Idaho-Washington-Oregon, maybe even Canada, the Vancouver area. I'd start there, boys. I want you to do some checking. I want you to find that girl, and when you do, I just want you to sit on the information and not tell anyone, but me. Don't try to settle things yourself. I want to take care of it personally. Is that understood? Are we perfectly clear on that fellas?" Ed and Louie indicated they understood the assignment and would get right on it. One way or the other, they were going to find Wendy Baker.

Four months later, they were back in Nick's office. Nick looked up at them, raised his eyebrows and asked, "Well?" Louie looked at Nick with an evil grin, and said, "We found her."

Chapter 1

THE BRIGHT EASTERN WASHINGTON SUN WAS streaming in through the partially opened curtains of the parsonage. Wendy's eyes were beginning to flutter in an attempt to get used to the daylight, after a long night of sleep. The temperature had cooled off enough that she had slept very comfortably, as always, on her left side, with her arm tucked under her pillow, to give a little more support for her head.

She yawned and stretched, so that every muscle in her body became taut, from her shoulders, all the way down to her feet. Waking up was one of her favorite times of the day; she'd always been a morning person and could never understand how people could sleep half the day away. Even when you didn't have that much on your plate for the day, to sleep much past 7 o'clock, which was late for her, just seemed odd. But, of course, other people thought she was strange for being so perky at the crack of dawn.

Fortunately, her husband John was an early riser too. Her husband, John. It still had a great ring to it; the term hadn't lost its freshness yet. Wendy had only been Mrs. John Larson for a little over two weeks now, and her new name was just beginning to feel real. Mr. and Mrs. John Larson, sounded so nice, and looked so natural, when she'd first seen it in print on the hotel bill from the Sheraton in Maui, where they'd spent a portion of their honeymoon. It was new, and yet somehow felt so natural. She knew beyond a shadow of a doubt, that her marriage to this wonderful man was on the order of the miraculous. I suppose some might question her use of the term miraculous, but those who knew their story never would. There was no missing God's hand in the events that led up to their marriage. Wendy would cherish that certainty for the rest of her life.

Wendy turned over to her right side, and pushed her body up against the huge lump in bed, next to her. That lump was her new husband, who was still snoring. He must've been pretty tired last night, since he was usually the one to wake up first. Of course, John is a stomach sleeper and didn't have the sun pouring in the window and directly into his eyes. How he could sleep on his stomach, and not wake up with a crink in his neck, or a seriously sore back, she'd never know. He challenged her to try it once, but she gave it up after about 30 minutes. She knew that if she laid like that much longer, she'd be as stiff as an arthritic, 90-year-old lady, and she didn't need that right now.

She snuggled up to John, as much as she could with him lying flat on his face, and he did what she hoped he'd do. He turned over on his side, away from her, and she, in turn, scooted over and formed herself around his body, spoon-like. That had become her all-time favorite position, both when going to sleep and waking up. They couldn't sleep like that all night; they'd always drift to their usual positions while they were sleeping. But starting out that way was always good and, in fact, it was more than good, it was a must.

You see, going to sleep like that, except in reverse, gave her a wonderful sense of security, of closeness, of protection. When John would snuggle up to her and lay his arm on the top of her body, putting his hand over hers, and drawing her close to him, it was the best feeling in the world. There's no place else she'd rather be than safely tucked into his arms, knowing that they had a lifetime of this to look forward to.

Mr. and Mrs. John Larson. John and Wendy Larson. Both of these phrasings sounded so good and made her feel alive with joy and excitement. But Pastor and Mrs. John Larson? Now, that's the one that she still had a difficult time believing. She loved it, and was truly looking forward to all that it would mean, but it still was a bit intimidating. I mean, think about it. Just a few short months ago her life was a mess, but now it felt like she had died and gone to heaven. The only problem was that she wasn't quite sure how to act in heaven.

Wendy understood that she was going to have to grow into her new position as the pastor's wife. How was she going to do that? They certainly didn't offer a class on that at the community college, and none of her friends in Pleasant Pastures had been in that position. And she obviously didn't have anybody back home who could coach her. What a joke. If some of her fellow dancers at the nightclub where she worked in Chicago could see her now, they'd faint from shock. What topless dancer becomes a pastor's wife? It sounds too weird to even be the plot of a B-movie, let alone a smash hit.

Well, wherever she got it, she was going to have to find someone who could coach her on some of the finer points of being in ministry, hand-in-hand, with her husband. Wendy wasn't really worried about it because it was something God obviously had planned when she and John first met. And if this was all part of His plans and goals for their life together, things would work out fine. It's just that being new to this whole spiritual scene made the idea a bit daunting - not scary, exactly - just different enough to give her a bit of a pause. But I guess that's what keeps life kind of interesting; definite direction, interspersed with seasons of the unknown.

John began to stir a bit as she snuggled to his back, and then he slowly turned over and drew Wendy into his arms. He held her close and squeezed her gently, as if he wasn't ever going to let her go. And that was fine with her. She realized, just then, that she had to adjust her ratings of feel-good embraces. This was number one and spoons was number two. There was nothing like the feeling of being held in John's strong arms, looking at each other, in the dawn of a new day. Yeah, this was right at the top, for sure.

John muffled a yawn and stretched his six-foot- two-inch frame, until his feet hung over the end of the bed. He was a pretty tall guy, a little less than a foot taller than Wendy. When she wore heels, the height difference wasn't quite so noticeable, but when she was in her bare feet, it was pretty obvious. But Wendy liked it; she liked the fact that John was tall and in good shape. She knew that staying in shape was important to John - the whole "your body is a temple" thing. Well, whatever his motivation, it was fine with her. She didn't mind if he and The Tanks hit the gym together a couple two or three times a week to lift weights, or box a few rounds, or engage in some wrestling moves. But by John's own admission, wrestling The Tanks, Max and Ryan, who were 6'6" and 300 pounds and 6'8" and 350 pounds, respectively, he usually came out on the losing end. He could hold his own in boxing because he was faster, but wrestling these two giant brothers was a whole different story.

As they lay on their backs together, John's arm around her shoulders, they talked about the events of the past couple of weeks. They both expressed delight to be able to finally, after three months, wake up in each other's arms. They talked about their amazing honeymoon that was a total surprise for them. It was still mind-boggling to them how kind and generous their congregation at Pleasant Pastures Community Church had been. Not only had they warmly, and lovingly embraced Wendy, after hearing her story of a life lived in chaos, dysfunction and poor choices - some hers, and some by others - they then surprised them with a two-week honeymoon to the Hawaiian Islands. As much as they wanted to go, they just couldn't swing it financially. Well, the good and generous folks at church decided to make their dream honeymoon come true. It was a totally unexpected gift, one that left John and Wendy humbled, but grateful, beyond words. But as wonderful as the honeymoon was, as they got to about day 12, both John and Wendy started getting a little bit antsy, admitting they were ready to get home to the real world and start their life together. Besides, they were missing Travis, their eight-year-old son. They weren't worried about him, because they knew he was being well cared for by Maggie, who was kind of like a grandma to Travis. Maggie was the owner and operator of Maggie's Country Diner, and had given Wendy her first job when she and Travis had come to Pleasant Pastures. Maggie could tell that Wendy had a story, a past, but wasn't about to push for info; that would come out if, and when, Wendy was ready. But at the moment Wendy showed up, with Travis in tow, Maggie desperately needed a good waitress. Well, it was a match made in heaven, for both of them. And during those first few days, Wendy learned a lot about Maggie, but especially about her strong faith.

Wendy hadn't just been running from a toxic and dangerous situation in Chicago, she was also running from God – a God she wasn't even sure existed. But if He did, she wanted nothing to do with Him. In her estimation He had bailed on her when she needed Him most. But Maggie, very gently, and with no preaching, helped bring her around to another view.

Of course, the first step in the turnaround was introducing her to John, who Wendy came to find out a few minutes later, was the pastor of the church Maggie had invited her to. Wow! She sure didn't see that coming. But the obvious attraction was there, and like they say, the rest is history. After a fairly fast, whirlwind courtship, not without its struggles, by the way, here they both were lying in each other's arms, talking about their new life together.

Wendy found John to be a wonderfully kind and thoughtful man. He seemed to have a genuine love for people, especially those in his congregation, and he'd go out of his way to help folks in need, in whatever way he possibly could. She had watched John and The Tanks put on their work clothes and go out to the home of an older parishioner, and help with some project that desperately needed to be done, and yet the funds were lacking. In the same way, they'd help out a single mom who was all but going crazy, with absolutely zero adult contact or time for herself. She watched as they lined up some of the ladies of the church to help this harried single mom with a few hours of childcare, just to give her a break; perhaps a trip to the beauty parlor to get her hair and nails done. She'd even seen the guys take some of the older kids and get them out on one of the many trails in the area for a good hike, a chance to burn off some of that youthful energy. And when she saw or heard about these kinds of things that John and The Tanks did, she'd often think to herself "what kinds of guys do this?" She'd never met guys like that, not in her former life.

She felt very blessed to be where she was at this time in her life. In fact, there were times that she felt totally unworthy of all that had taken place, over the last four months. But every time she voiced this, John would gently remind her that that none of us deserve that, or are worthy of that on our own. All of these good gifts were from the hand of a very loving God, who cared for His children greatly. In the beginning, she'd argue with John a bit and say things like, "Yeah, but where was God when all the bad things were happening to me? If He's so powerful, and supposedly in control, why did He make all that stuff happen?" And John would gently remind her, that most of those bad things that happen to us are the result of bad and selfish choices, either someone else's, or our own. God didn't cause them; it was a matter of freewill. And when the natural consequences of those bad choices played themselves out, He was weeping right along with us. John always reminded her, that when her view of God got a little bit skewered by some nasty circumstances, she should just look at Jesus. One of John's favorite lines was, "If you want to know what God is truly like, study the life of Jesus, and get to know Him intimately. Jesus is God, in the flesh. So, if you see Jesus, you're seeing God. And if you know Jesus, you're knowing God."

Well, Wendy couldn't argue with that, it made perfect sense. But as she continued to grow, by leaps and bounds in her faith, she came to know just how true and valuable John's counsel was. It may have sounded a bit theological and preacher-esque, but there was no doubt as to its effectiveness in shaping her worldview. She'd always be grateful for a husband who knew a lot about Jesus and the Bible, and yet was always willing to listen to her questions and concerns, even admitting, at times, that he didn't know the answers to something she had brought up. But, neither did he seem particularly concerned when she stumped him. He'd just smile, and say something to the effect, that he never figured that one out, and if Wendy ever did, he would be eternally grateful to know the answer. Because in all 2000 years of Christianity, nobody else has ever conclusively figured it out either. She loved that about John. He was smart, knowledgeable and articulate. But he was also honest enough to know when he was stumped, and he was humble enough to admit it. What a guy!

So, as they lay there in bed, intertwined in each other's arms, she wondered once again, what adventures this new life had for them. What kind of an impact would they have together both in their church, and in the small town they now called home? What was God up to that would make a real difference in people's lives? Would ministry just wind up being business as usual? Not that there was anything wrong with that. Holding services and recruiting people to run different programs for children and youth, as well as the sizable group of senior citizens - Goldenaires, as they preferred to be called - all of that was great, and very necessary. So that was fine; business as usual was vastly important.

But then Wendy began to think about the life she had left behind in Chicago. What about that? What about some of her dancer friends whose lives were on a fast-track to nowhere but destruction? What happens to people like that? And what about Nick, her former boss? What he tried to do with her was horrible - it was disgusting. And, as much as she hated what he had tried to do with her, and was now, no doubt, doing to the other girls - as much as she hated his actions, she didn't hate him. What if he didn't know any other way to live? What if nobody had ever told him that there's a better way?

And, talking about Chicago and her former life, what about her mom? She never really had a good relationship with her and found herself quite angry at times for the way her mom had raised her; guys coming in and out of the home – her mom's endless quest for her knight-in-shining-armor. Her mom's knight never showed up, by the way. Her mom wasn't exactly nurturing and caring, but then again, neither was *her* mom. So, what if her mom didn't mess things up on purpose? What if her mom just didn't know any better, simply because she'd never been introduced to a better way to live? Why couldn't God change her mom too? In fact, why couldn't God change all of them? If He could do it for her, He could certainly do it for them.

Wendy thought about all of these things as she lay there, feeling safe and secure in the arms of the man she loved. Business as usual is fine Lord, it really is. But Father, I just want you to know that I'm willing to step out of the quiet life in Pleasant Pastures, if you want me to, and I know John is with me, all the way. Take us further than we could ever possibly imagine. We will follow you anywhere and do anything that's on your heart. And thank you Lord, that we have a congregation that's pumped up and ready to make the journey with us. Help us – me especially – in this first full week of ministering together as husband and wife. I love you, Jesus. Amen.

Just as Wendy finished praying about launching their new ministry for the week, John told her that he had a marvelous idea. Why don't they both get up and go brush their teeth. Wendy smiled, knowing right away where this was going. I guess ministry would have to wait a while.

Chapter 2

NICK SAT IN HIS LEATHER CHAIR BEHIND HIS desk and pondered what Ed and Louie had told him. When he looked at his clock he was shocked to see that 30 minutes had gone by. He'd spent 30 minutes thinking about Wendy Baker, the girl he once thought was going to make him a ton of money. He thought long and hard about that, because the fact was, he already had a ton of money. He certainly had more money stashed here and there than he ever thought he would when he was a kid, growing up in a tough, Italian neighborhood.

His clubs had been successful and had netted him a handsome profit within just a few months of opening. It was a little touch and go on his first one, and he remembered the days of pacing his office floor, wondering how this was all going to turn around. Waking up at 3 o'clock every morning, with the headaches and worries of owning his own business began to take its toll on him, after a while. He popped Tums on a regular basis, just to keep his stomach from churning and gurgling. The heartburn was a drag, but he supposed it was just part of the price he paid for wanting to be successful.

But sure enough, Nick kept going, working long hours, and finally his first club began to turn around and show profit. In fact, he'd made enough profit eventually to open another club, several miles away. This club was designed to reach a wealthier segment of society in Chicago's nightlife. His first club catered to the average working stiff who just wanted to unwind after a hard day's work at the factory, or driving that truck, or building the latest skyscraper that changed the Chicago skyline. These guys would come in after work and spend hours sitting at the table that surrounded the circular stage - a stage full of good-looking girls, dressed in bikinis, and dancing to the latest sounds of the 70's disco scene. They'd drink and watch the dancers for hours, each one of them escaping from whatever pathetic existence they called life. Even though Nick owned the club, and even though the customers were paying for his new home and big, gold Cadillac, it was still a pretty sorry way to live your life. Still, that wasn't his problem; he was just trying to make life a little more interesting for them. So, in essence, this club was doing them a service. It was putting a little zip, a little flash, into their otherwise bleak existence.

So, his first club had become successful after several months of hand-wringing and sleepless nights. But the second club took off like a shot, mainly because he had jumped on the bandwagon and gone with topless dancers. Plus, he had opened his club in a swanky part of town, where gentlemen came out of their offices, having spent their day negotiating huge business deals. They were exhausted, and looking forward to a brief time of R and R. Then they'd go home to their wife and kids and assume the roles expected of them. The difference between his first club and this one, his second endeavor, is that this one was profitable from the very start - very profitable, in fact. The drinks, and therefore the money, flowed freely every night, and pretty soon Nick found himself with more money than he knew what to do with.

The only thing that was giving him a little concern was this dancer that disappeared on him. It really wasn't that big of a deal to him, because after all, girls are a dime a dozen, and in Nick's way of thinking, they were just a commodity. You kept them around to serve your purposes, and when you were done with them, you discarded them. You kicked them to the curb. Wasn't anything personal, it was just good business. If they weren't producing, if they weren't drawing the guys in, they'd be out on their ear, no doubt about it, and no second chances.

But this gal Wendy was different. She was a top moneymaker and could have gone far, which would have benefited not only Nick, but herself. At least that's the way Nick thought about it. So, when she walked out on him, it was a huge shock and disappointment, but hey, he'd just have to find another Wendy. The only problem was that bit of scuttlebutt on the street that Nick Salerno was going soft and breaking a kind of unspoken creed among guys in the business - someone owes you, you're going to collect, one way or the other. And so, when Ed and Louie reported back to Nick that they had found the dancer who had gone AWOL on him, he knew he had to act fast. And he needed to do it personally, so that everyone would realize that you can't put something over on Nick Salerno and get away with it.

As he sat there pondering the situation, a plan began to come together. Ed and Louie had reported that after four months of looking under every rock they could think of, they finally got a tip from one of their cousins who worked in the DMV. A car with her license plate had been registered in Washington State, in a small town, east of the Cascade Mountain Range. And sure enough, the registered owner of the car was Wendy Baker, the runaway dancer.

So, as Nick formulated his plan, he decided to take care of the situation personally. He'd never had a break. In 10 years of owning clubs, he had never taken a vacation, a getaway. He had no family, no wife and kids, and so work was his life. But hey, everybody needs a break, right? Maybe he should take that little vacation now and use it to refresh himself, get the old spark back. And if, in the process of vacationing, he just happens to run into one Wendy Baker, a gal from the old neighborhood, how could he be accused of anything underhanded or illegal? If you're on vacation and happen to come across a former acquaintance, that's not stalking, that's just coincidence.

The question in his mind though, was what should he do when he finds her? I mean, there were several ways this could go down. He might meet her accidentally, in a public place, and inquire how she and that kid of hers were doing. If she's living in some rat-infested slum, making peanuts as a waitress at some dump that the Public Health Department should've shut down long ago, maybe she'd come back with him. And when the guys would question Nick as to why he let her come back, he'd use his favorite line from The Godfather - "I made her an offer she couldn't refuse." They'd all laugh, and nod with the understanding of those in the business. The offer she couldn't refuse basically meant, in her case, that she had one of two choices. Either come back with me and pay back what you owe, or get ready for a long nap in the local bone-yard, pushing up daisies.

Another option is that he could sweet-talk her, and try to convince her how much he really cared about her. Nick was a good-looking guy, with a ton of charisma. That's one of the things that made him the successful businessman that he was. Maybe he'd just have to whisper a few endearing words in her ear that would convince her that he cared for her, in a personal way. Maybe he's realized, over the months, that what he thought was a business relationship, was actually love. It took him these four months of separation for him to see that, but would she consider coming back with him, not as an employee, but as his girlfriend? Now, that plan would serve two purposes. It would get his top dancer back, his gold mine, the one all the guys paid big bucks to see. And more importantly, it would allow him to save face with the other guys in the business - guys whose opinions meant something, and carried real weight. They'd look at this new relationship and realize that she didn't break a business deal when she ran out on Nick; she was just reacting to a lover's quarrel. Everybody understood the crazy actions that come when you're involved in a lovers' spat. Everybody understands, because they've all been there. So great! No harm, no foul. The lovers are back together again, and they're on their way to living happily ever after.

Of course, there was a third option, one that made Nick feel a little queasy. She could refuse and fight him on everything he was trying to do. And then he'd be out of options. The only thing he could do then would be to get rid of her. Now, Nick didn't want to do that. Nick knew something, deep inside, that nobody else knew. He knew that he came across as strong and tough - he came across as someone you never wanted to mess with - and to a certain extent, that was true.

But what people didn't realize was, that as many fights as Nick had gotten into growing up, and despite the fact that by the public opinion of the day, he had won every fight, the fact was, Nick had never seriously injured anyone. There was a bloody nose here and there, and a black eye occasionally, but nothing that was life-threatening or permanently damaging. Nick just wasn't sure he had the stomach to follow through on his occasional threat. If he could maintain his no-nonsense reputation, he'd never have to worry about it, and he wouldn't have to try to win it back again.

And so, after going over his options, he decided to take a little vacation to Eastern Washington, which, according to the travel books he had picked up, was a place of comfortable 80° temperatures in September. That sounded pretty good to him after the sweltering heat and humidity of the Chicago summer. Besides, he'd never been to that part of the country and was looking forward to getting out of his hometown, something he'd rarely experienced. He'd also heard that Seattle had quite the nightlife. Maybe he could kill two birds with one stone and make some valuable connections out there.

He picked up the phone and called his cousin Big Joey Martelli. Big Joey was a nickname that stuck with him since high school. It was one of those names that was meant to be a joke. Big Joey was about 5'2", but he was built like a fireplug. Guys who made fun of Joey's size in high school did it once, and never again. He may have been short on height, but he was long on toughness. Joey, and his cousin Nick, soon earned the reputation that made bigger, and supposedly tougher guys, shake in their boots. Nobody messed with the cousins.

Nick had asked Big Joey to be his partner years ago and he had jumped at the chance. Nick came to find out that his cousin had a pretty good head for business; he knew that he'd have had no problem covering for Nick when he was gone for a few weeks of vacation. Nick called Big Joey and told him about his plans to take a vacation, a getaway of sorts, but Joey knew there was more to the story. However, he'd also learned a long time ago not to ask too many questions. Sometimes it's just better not to know the details.

As they were about to hang up, Big Joey asked him what airlines he was going to fly, and Nick surprised him. He told Joey he wasn't going to fly. Instead he was going to drive across the country in his big, gold Cadillac. Maybe it would give the local-yokels out there a thrill to see that kind of a machine. It was pretty impressive, even by Chicago standards. He could only imagine how it would look in some podunk town in Eastern Washington. If nothing else, at least it would make a statement. The owner of this big, gold Cadillac is powerful, successful, and rich, so you'd better pay attention.

Nick packed up, took care of a few last-minute details and hit the road, with a full tank of gas, a wad of cash in his pocket, and a destination in his mind. Lookout Pleasant Pastures - Nick Salerno's coming to town.

Chapter 3

IT'D BEEN A PRETTY GOOD FIRST WEEK BACK FOR John and Wendy. Sometimes coming back from a vacation can be kind of rough - re-entry seems to take a while to get used to - especially when you're coming from a Hawaiian paradise. But John and Wendy were actually anxious to get home and start life for real. Honeymoons are wonderful, but eventually life needs to get back to some semblance of normal. The romance certainly should remain, but it has to be in the midst of the real world of work and relationships, of household chores and car maintenance; all the normal, everyday activities that are part of life.

John had gone into his office that first day back, and as much is he missed the soft sand and beautiful sunsets along the Ka'anapali coast in Maui, he had to admit that it felt good to be back. Re-entry isn't so tough when you enjoy your job. Of course, he also knew that unlike just a few weeks ago, before the wedding, he wouldn't be going home to an empty parsonage. Now, at the end of the day, he'll go home to Wendy and Travis. John still couldn't get over the fact that he had a family. Something stirred within him when he thought about it. He felt warm inside, and very grateful for God's provision of these two wonderful people he had come to love with his whole heart.

John was jarred out of his familial reverie by the ringing of his office phone. It was about 8:00 AM and he was the only one in the office. He picked up the receiver, wondering who would be calling this early on a Friday morning. The voice, on the other end of the line, belonged to Fred Winters who had been a member of Pleasant Pastures Community Church for about five years now. Fred worked as a landscaper in and around the Leavenworth/Wenatchee area. The majority of his work came through a couple of local contractors who built homes in the area. Part of the appeal to their new home-buyers was that when they built the house, they also had the yard landscaped, so that the house would be complete. The new owner didn't have to worry about putting in the yard, it was already finished.

When he heard Fred's voice, he knew something was wrong. Fred was usually a pretty light-hearted kind of guy, always quick with a joke or a funny story on the tip of his tongue. But he sounded pretty serious and so John inquired as to how he was doing. Fred told John that his mother, Irma, who was living in a nursing home in Wenatchee, wasn't doing too well. She had begun to slip a few years ago and had to leave her home to go to an assisted living facility, and eventually, into the nursing home itself. She'd been pretty good up until about a day or two ago. She had quit eating and it had become increasingly difficult to wake her up. They called her doctor in, who, after examining her, felt that her body, at age 96, was just wearing out, and it wouldn't be long.

John sat there and listened to Fred, whose voice was shaky with emotion. Irma had lived a good, long life, and had been a faithful Christian for about 70 years, having come to Christ at about the age of 26. Fred was thankful for all the years he had her, but he knew that was coming to an end. As a Christian, Fred knew that "to be absent from the body, was to be present with the Lord." The Apostle Paul had encouraged believers with those wonderful words for the last 2000 years, but as wonderful as that was, death still hurt; not for the believer who died, but for those left behind. No matter how strong a person's faith, death of a loved one still takes its toll.

John gently asked Fred if he'd like him to come over to his house for a few minutes so that they could talk and pray together. Fred told John that, yeah, he'd really appreciate it, he was feeling pretty low. John told him he'd be over in a few minutes, said goodbye and hung up the phone. Fred just lived a few blocks from the church, so rather than drive, he just decided to walk. It was a beautiful day in early September, and he knew the warm days were soon going to give way to the crispness of fall, and then progress to the winter snow. He'd better enjoy these warm temperatures while they were still around. Of course, coming from Duluth, Minnesota, where winter temperatures could go to 20° below zero, he wasn't too worried about his first winter in Eastern Washington. He was pretty confident he'd survive. Compared to Duluth, winters here would be a piece of cake.

John started out to walk the few blocks to Fred's house and as he walked, he prayed. Truth be told, this was one part of the ministry that he found quite difficult. Now, the people he was ministering to in their grief wouldn't know that. John was always warm, and yet professional, but in all honesty, it took its toll on him. It was very difficult to always be with people in the midst of their grief - their crying - their pain. On the one hand, he felt privileged to be there with them and help them to navigate the pain of death. On the other hand, he always walked away struggling with the thought that maybe he could have done more to alleviate their suffering. Maybe he didn't say the right words. Maybe he didn't read the right scriptures, or enough scriptures. Or maybe he read too *many* scriptures and he should've just talked with them more. Or maybe he talked too much, and should've just shut up and let them do all the talking. John always second-guessed himself in those situations. He supposed that it would get easier the older he got, and the longer he was in ministry, but he wasn't sure about that. Death is painful - and always would be.

He got to Fred's house, knocked on the door, and Fred answered a few seconds later. Fred told him that he was going to be leaving in a few minutes to go up and see his mom, even though she wasn't responding and was comatose. But he wanted to see her, particularly since she seemed to be slipping pretty fast. John asked if Fred would like him to go with him when he went. Fred was thoughtful for a minute or two, and finally said, "Oh, thanks pastor, that's very kind of you. But I think I'd rather just go by myself. There are a few things I'd like to say to my mom that are kind of personal. I've always heard that the hearing is the last sense to go, so I'm going to talk with her and just trust that she's hearing me."

John encouraged Fred to carry through with his plan. And then, as a way of encouraging Fred further, John told him of the experience he had when he was at his former church, First Baptist, and he went to the bedside of a dying church member, who also was in a coma. She wasn't expected to live more than an hour or two. John read her the scriptures and offered a short prayer, asking the Lord to take her home peacefully. And then he left, already beginning to plan her memorial service in his mind. Well, was he ever surprised when he got a call from this woman's daughter, telling him that her mom was sitting up in bed and eating her lunch. She had snapped out of the coma and went on to live another four years. But the thing that most surprised John was when he went to visit her the next day. He happened to mention that he had seen her, just a few hours before she was supposedly going to die. She blew him away when she said, "Oh yes, pastor, I knew you were here. You read the 23rd Psalm and John 14, and then you prayed for the Lord to take me peacefully. Well, I guess the Lord said no! He wasn't taking me peacefully, or any other way. He wasn't done with me, and so here I am." Huh? So how do you argue with that?

John and Fred talked for about a half hour about his mom, and his growing up years. His dad had passed away several years ago and that was hard, but not unexpected. His dad's medical problems struck pretty early on with a heart attack at age 58. And, even though he lived another 10 years, he just wasn't the same active, energetic guy Fred had known all his life. That was hard on everybody and yet, by God's grace, they made it. And even with the medical problems hanging over their heads, life was still precious and good.

They finished up their talk and made plans to meet when Fred's mom finally passed on. John didn't really know her, but was happy to be a part of the process with Fred. He was a great guy, and John felt honored to be available at this very difficult time in Fred's life. He just hoped and prayed that being a part of this season of Fred's life would bring him a measure of comfort and a sense of community - a sense that he's not alone in this.

John left and started walking back to the church, enjoying the warm sun, and thinking about how precious life is. Just as he was starting to get into the deep theological meanderings on the nature of death and how it relates to a Christian, he heard someone calling his name. He looked around and saw Virginia Crupp step out of the "Fishers Five and Dime," - a small family-owned store that specialized in low-priced items; anything from toys to toiletries - from candy to crayons. She came up to John and asked if he'd heard about Dave and Heather? No, he hadn't heard anything yet; he'd been in a meeting. He figured he knew what she was going to say, but waited for Virginia to tell him the news that was getting her worked up, in a good way. Virginia broke out in a broad smile and joyfully announced that Dave and Heather, one of Pleasant Pastures young married couples, had just had their baby, not more than an hour ago. They were up at the small hospital in Leavenworth and everything had gone very well. Virginia always loved to see young couples come to church and become a part of the community there. It gave her a reassuring sense of hope that when some of the original members of the church passed on, it would still be a shining light for decades to come.

Dave and Heather had come to Pleasant Pastures when Dave had accepted a summer job as a guide for a river-rafting business that had started up a few months ago. "Extreme Adventures," as the new business was known, grew in popularity very rapidly. People would come from miles around to ride the rapids and enjoy the beauty and adventure of Eastern Washington. It was pretty good pay, and Dave thoroughly enjoyed meeting people and guiding them into some adventures they'd remember for years to come. And then, in the fall and winter months, when the river-rafting shut down for the season, he would take groups of winter tourists on snow-shoeing and cross-country skiing expeditions. All in all, it was the perfect way to earn a living, doing what he loved to do, and had been doing most of his life. But now, he was getting paid to do it. Kind of hard to beat a job like that.

But today his mind wasn't on the river, or the coming fall and winter activities. Now David's mind was with Heather, and their brand-new 8 lbs. 10 oz. baby boy, Christopher. Christopher Stephen Lewiston. That's a strong sounding name and reminded John of one of his favorite authors: C. S. Lewis. Who knows, maybe Christopher will take after the famous author with the strikingly similar name. Well, whatever happens, it'll be fun to watch how God leads in this young child's life. Both Dave and Heather had a strong faith and he knew they would raise Christopher in the ways of the Lord.

John went back to his office, grabbed his car keys and took off for the hospital. On the way, he stopped at the Safeway store in Leavenworth and picked up a little bud vase, with three roses. He went to the hospital and inquired as to Heather's room. The nurse at the front desk asked if he was family, and he told them that he was their pastor. That got him in the door right away, and after knocking and asking if Heather was decent, he was invited in. When he entered the room, the first thing he saw was a very tired, but happy couple. Tired, because Heather had been up all night in labor, with Dave right alongside coaching her. And then he saw the little bundle in Heather's arms, sleeping so peacefully. He crept over silently, not wanting to wake the little one. Heather lifted the blanket that was placed gently over his eyes, and he saw a beautiful, baby boy, with an amazing amount of hair and striking blue eyes. He didn't know if those blue eyes were going to change, as they usually did, but regardless, he was a cute little boy. His parents were beaming, and Dave especially was so proud. He told John how rough the night had been on him, while Heather just rolled her eyes and said, "Right Dave, it was so rough on you, while I just breezed right on through." David laughed, and admitted that, yeah, maybe it was actually a little tougher on Heather. They all laughed and began to talk about how this would change their lives, but in a very good way.

John expressed his happiness for them, and then asked if he could pray for them. They said yes, of course, and so John prayed that God would bless and protect this little family and reveal His plans and goals for their lives. They chatted for just a few minutes about possible dates for a child dedication service at church. But then John told them to just settle in, and when things seemed to be in a pretty good routine, to give him a call and they'd set a date. They agreed, and said good-bye. John hugged them both and kissed the top of Christopher's head, before going out to his car.

As he drove home from Leavenworth, he was pondering about what his day had been like. He had met with Fred, who was going through the grief of losing his mom. He was grieving, and she wasn't even gone yet, but by all indications she would be very soon. The grief process had started, and would continue, John knew, for quite some time. Fred would make it through, but it was going to be rough going for a little while.

And then, on the other hand, you had Dave and Heather, with little new born Christopher Stephen. Little Christopher had only been in this world a few hours, and yet had impacted his parents' life, probably more than they understood at this moment. John knew the sobering fact that when you're a parent, you're a parent for life. Just because your kids turn 18 and get out on their own, doesn't mean you quit feeling responsible or you quit being concerned. As near as he could figure, and after having talked with many folks who had raised their families, this parenting gig changed you forever. He'd only been a dad to Travis for what, three weeks now? Not too long, but long enough to feel the weight of the responsibility. It was good - it really was - but it was still quite daunting, quite challenging. He knew, with God's help, he'd be up to the challenge, but he figured his prayer life was going to have to ratchet up a bit if he was going to be a good father.

So, John pondered the cycle of life. Babies are born, and old people die. It happens every day, just like clockwork. I guess the thing to center in on isn't so much the birth and death aspects of the cycle. Maybe the thing to center in on is the time in between; what we do with those years in between birth and death? I guess that's where the real difference is made, John thought. So, Lord, let our lives make a difference; may every moment, every hour, be yours to do with, what you will. That's what real living…genuine living, is all about anyway, isn't it? You're the boss! Do what you will.

John drove into the little town he'd come to call home, over the last several months. He'd come to know the people in his church, and looked forward to knowing each of them on a deeper level. He'd also gotten to know the little town itself - the stores and restaurants - the specialty shops and office buildings - even the cars that were parked on the street each day were beginning to look familiar. Lots of jeeps and other four-wheel-drive vehicles, that were so necessary in an area that almost always got a few feet of snow over the winter. Pleasant Pastures wasn't a large town, maybe just a few thousand, but it was a wonderful place to call home, and raise a family. He was looking forward to getting to know the people better, not just in his church, but in the town in general. He felt he had a pretty good start on that. Like he'd thought before: I think I'm actually getting to recognize the cars, for heaven sake - the make and the model - where they're parked - and who owns them. I guess that's a good sign that I'm getting pretty acclimated.

As he was driving down Main Street, toward the church, he saw something out of the corner of his eye that caught his attention. He saw a nice-looking gentleman in conversation with Floyd Weatherby, the owner of "Floyd's Service Station and Mini-Mart" - the only gas station in town. The idea that they were having a conversation didn't attract John's attention. It was a well-known fact that Floyd could talk to anybody, and usually did. And if you talked to the Floyd long enough, chances were very good that you'd wind up in his Mini-Mart, buying something. Floyd had the gift of gab. He could probably bottle water, sell it to the masses, and make a killing. In fact, John often thought that it was too bad Floyd didn't come to church. He could put him in charge of the church financial budget and they'd probably never have a shortfall. Anyway, maybe someday Floyd would come and join them.

But again, it wasn't the fact that Floyd was having a pleasant conversation, with a good-looking stranger in town that caught John's attention. It's just that John wasn't used to seeing anything but jeeps and trucks, or some other rugged, four-wheel drive vehicles. But the car that Floyd was filling up with gas just didn't look like it belonged here. It was beautiful…impressive really. John wondered what kind of a car it was; maybe it was some kind of an exotic, foreign model. But as he got closer and could get a better look, he saw that the car was as American as they came. It was a big, shiny, gold Cadillac.

Chapter 4

WENDY WAS SLAMMED AT THE DINER FOR the Friday lunch hour. She didn't know why everybody and their brother just decided to go out for lunch, all on the same day, at the same time. But she liked the hustle and bustle of it, finding it both tiring, yet energizing at the same time. Being a waitress was a job she had been doing since she was 15 and now, 14 years later, she was still doing it. Sometimes she wondered if she'd be doing this all of her life.

Maggie was a wonderful boss to work for. She'd been encouraging from the very beginning. And Wendy knew that she was also a blessing to Maggie, because not only was she a hard worker, she was also friendly to everyone who came through the doors. Wendy had learned a long time ago that when people felt welcomed, and genuinely cared for, they'd be back. And so, Wendy knew that Maggie's business would just continue to pick up, as the service remained top-notch.

So, all in all, Wendy enjoyed her job. But something was kind of nagging at her. And it wasn't until this morning that she'd been able to put her finger on it. Although she couldn't quite articulate what she was feeling, she knew enough that she recognized a restlessness of sorts. And that made her a little nervous, because she wasn't quite sure what the restlessness was, and where it was coming from.

It certainly wasn't about her personal life; that was going great. She had more than she could have ever possibly imagined. She had a brand-new marriage to an exceptionally wonderful husband, who was head over heels in love with her, by the way, and treated her like a queen. If you would've told her six months ago that this was what life was going to be like, she would've looked at you like you were crazy. Her life had changed so dramatically these last months; she still had to pinch herself to see if she was dreaming. So, no, the restlessness wasn't from the fact that she was a newlywed. In fact, that was a major source of peace and tranquility. Everything was right on in that department.

And then there was her son Travis who'd been the light of her life for the past eight years. And even when Wendy got off track and started going down some dark paths, Travis still had brought so much joy into her heart, it was almost painful, in a good sort of way. It almost felt that it was Travis who'd given her life meaning. Now, Wendy was smart enough to know that relying on your eight-year-old son to be the total source of meaning in your life wasn't really all that healthy, but at the same time, that's all she'd had.

John and Wendy had just enrolled Travis in the elementary school in Pleasant Pastures, and he would be starting that next week. The school did some preliminary testing and discovered – no surprise to John and Wendy – that Travis was quite a bit ahead of the typical fourth-grader. They knew Travis was very smart and that he picked things up quite quickly. Their greatest concern was that Travis might be bored with school; that it wouldn't be enough of a challenge for him. Even the counselors at his school were a little concerned about that and suggested that, perhaps, they should skip him to the next highest grade. But both John and Wendy wanted to give his own grade level a try first, particularly for the socialization with kids his own age.

They had noticed that Travis was very advanced when it came to talking with adults. In fact, since Wendy had arrived in Pleasant Pastures five months ago, Travis had pretty much been around adults the entire summer. He had developed a great relationship with Maggie, of course; she was a kind of grandma to him. And he really enjoyed Terry, the cook at the diner, who had taken him under his wing since the very first day. And, of course, there were The Tanks, who had taken John and Travis up into the woods and taught them a little bit about the logging business, as well as the importance of having a real reverence for the beauty of God's creation.

So, most of the time Travis had been with adults and that was fine with him and actually opened his eyes to new worlds. But he hadn't really made many friends his own age yet, and that was a bit of a concern to John and Wendy. So, they decided to keep him in his grade level to see if that would work out for him. Ms. Connors, his new fourth grade teacher, was aware of his test scores, but felt that, with a little extra time spent with him, she could challenge him with some personal high-achievement assignments, as well as giving him some extra tasks that would put his gifts to use. And then, if that didn't work, they could always either skip him, or enroll him in the private school for gifted children located near Wenatchee. That would mean a long bus ride every day, but that could be managed.

As Wendy thought about her restlessness, trying to determine the source of it, she knew, for sure, that it wasn't her new marriage - as Mary Poppins would say...it was *practically perfect in every way* - nor was it with Travis and his situation. It might have been a bit of a challenge having a son who was so advanced, but it certainly wasn't the source of restlessness. No, Wendy decided, the restlessness was inside of her. It had to do with her.

She mulled that over in her mind for several days, finally coming to the conclusion that it had to do with her new-found faith in the Lord. God had become number one in her life, and every time she thought about His goodness and grace, she'd well up with tears. She felt so undeserving in one way and yet so very grateful in other ways. But the thing that was beginning to eat away at her a bit was the use of her time. And the question that kept coming over and over to her mind was: Am I using my time in the best way possible for God? In other words: Is there another way I could serve you better, Lord?

As Wendy pondered these questions in the middle of serving breakfast and lunch to her customers, it finally hit her. As a waitress, she was serving food to people that nourished their bodies in such a way that they'd leave satisfied. And as a waitress, that's exactly what she wanted to do, and truthfully, did quite well. But the restlessness she was feeling was tied into that somehow. It had to do with her job, and the result of her job; the result of her hours of serving people who left feeling full and satisfied.

The thing that finally struck Wendy, like a ton of bricks, was that she continued to want to serve people food, until they were full and satisfied and nourished. But now, she wanted to serve them a different kind of food; a food where they'd be full and satisfied and nourished in a whole new way - a permanent way. She wanted to somehow serve spiritual food that comes from the hand of God. She wanted to be able to serve people in a way that nourished them spiritually. She wanted to serve them food that would stick with them and not leave them hungry a few hours later. That, she realized, was the source of her restlessness. She felt that God was drawing her into a different line of service. And though she wasn't sure what that would be, she told the Lord that when it was time, she was open and available to His leading. She wasn't sure where His leading would take her, but wherever she went, whatever the destination, she knew it would be good.

She had talked to John about her growing restlessness, just last night. They tossed several scenarios back-and-forth; ways in which God might use her in some new opportunities. One of the scenarios had to do with her position as the pastor's wife. That alone would open doors for ministry in the church, and they both agreed that was a real option and would definitely factor in.

But she also felt that there was another aspect to it, something that included personal growth, which she, in turn, could use to nourish others. She told John about how when she was first thinking about her role as a pastor's wife, she hoped that she could find someone who could show her the ropes, so to speak. But she wasn't really sure how that would come about, or who it could possibly be. John had suggested that he could ask his friends at the monthly Pastors Prayer Fellowship if any of their wives would be willing to mentor her, but after talking about it a bit more, they just decided to relax, and see how God would lead. John had learned a long time ago, that sometimes trying to force a good thing isn't the best way to achieve the goal. God has plenty of ways to accomplish His purposes. So, with that being said, they decided to wait a bit and give God time to do what He wants.

Well, that conversation last night helped her to relax somewhat, although she was still excited about what lay ahead. Just as Wendy was thinking about this, and as the noon rush began to die down, a nice-looking, older couple walked in and sat in the booth, near the door. Wendy couldn't recall seeing them before and so she approached them with a bright smile, and welcomed them to Maggie's Country Diner. They returned her pleasant smile, and said that they lived just outside of Wenatchee, but they were out exploring for the day. They were relatively new to the area, only having been here about six months. They'd been so busy settling in, after moving up from Oregon, getting their house set up, and spending long hours at work, that this was actually their first full day off, so they decided to look around at some of the different little towns nearby. They also said that one of the fun things they liked to do when they're in a new town, particularly a smaller one like this, is to try a local diner or restaurant. None of those chain restaurants for them; they wanted something unique to this particular town.

Wendy laughed and said, "Well, you can't get much more unique than Maggie's. She'd never let a big chain come in and tell her how to run her diner. That would *never* fly with her. I think you'll enjoy the food. And I think you'll enjoy Maggie too. I'll bring her over, if she ever gets free, and introduce you." They agreed to that idea and then set about ordering dinner salads and a Reuben sandwich, with fries to share. Wendy affirmed their choice and told them that the Reuben was a good one to share, because it was huge. A few minutes later she brought their salads, and about 10 minutes after that, she produced the

Reuben, split onto two separate plates. And sure enough, they both exclaimed that it was really a good thing they shared. That sandwich could feed an army.

Wendy told them she knew they were going to enjoy it and then turned around to walk away. She got a few feet from the table and remembered that she didn't ask them if they wanted catsup with their fries. She turned around and was just ready to speak, when she saw their heads bowed and their hands clasped, praying over their meal. She waited until they had finished praying and then approached them about the catsup. They said that yes, catsup would be great, and a little tartar sauce for the fries also, if they had it. Wendy assured them that she would be back with the condiments in just a minute.

When she came back with the catsup and the tartar sauce, she was just about ready to turn around, when a thought struck her. She said, "I don't want to intrude in your private life, but I saw you praying and I was just wondering if you're believers?" They smiled and said, "Oh yeah, we've been walking with the Lord our whole married life now. In fact, it's been 40 years, this coming November." Wendy offered her congratulations and then asked them if they had found a church in the area, because if not, she'd like to invite them to her church, where her husband is the pastor. They look delighted at hearing this and said, "Oh, so you're a pastor's wife?" And Wendy replied, "Yeah, for all of three weeks now. This is so new to me; I'm not even sure what I'm supposed to do. I'm afraid I'm going to do the wrong thing, or say something the wrong way, or voice my opinion, when it would be just better to listen. It's tricky, but God's leading, I guess - and they haven't kicked me out yet." They all laughed, and agreed that she was probably safe - at least for now. They all laughed again, and then Wendy asked what they did. They smiled and said, "Well, we pastor the Assembly of

God church, on the outskirts of Wenatchee. We've been in the ministry now about 35 years full-time, and five years part-time, before that. We've lived all over the country and have pastored several churches, some big, some small. We know some of the challenges you and your husband face, if not now, maybe in the future. But even though we've been through some tough things, in a few churches that weren't what you would call healthy, by the time we left, God had turned them around and brought real ministry there. We wouldn't trade the last 40 years for anything."

Wendy told them how reassuring that was to a young pastor's wife, with zero experience, and they expressed joy at being able to encourage her. She apologized for interrupting their meal and turned to take care of three guys who looked like they'd just come off a construction site, and needed a big lunch to see them through the rest of the day.

After about 10 minutes, she returned to the table of the pastor and his wife, offering refills on their coffee. They told Wendy that they really enjoyed the conversation and then introduced themselves. They were Ken and Barbie Stockton, originally from Portland, Oregon. Wendy looked at them and grinned and said, "You're kidding me, aren't you? Ken and Barbie?" They assured her that they weren't kidding; those were their real names, and they were sticking with them. Besides, when you're doing the children's sermon and the girls hear that Ken and Barbie are going to be preaching, that gets a pretty good crowd of little girls. Of course, when they see that Ken and Barbie look like their grandparents, it kind of takes away some of the excitement, but they usually come around in a few minutes anyway. Kids like grandma and grandpa types too.

They asked Wendy her name, and she automatically said Wendy Baker. And then she blushed, and said that she hadn't gotten used to her new married name yet. Her name is Wendy Larson, and her husband is John, and pastors the Pleasant Pastures Community Church, down at the end of Main Street. They all smiled at her mistake, Barbie acknowledging she had done the same thing her first month of being married. And then Barbie took Wendy's hand and she said, "Wendy, I have an idea. What would you think of you and me spending a little time together? We could talk about what it means to be a pastor's wife, and how you navigate the church politics, and various personality quirks of your members. Because believe me, you'll run into that. Take it from me; I've seen all kinds."

Wendy was shocked, but delighted at the same time. She told Barbie that she'd love to do that and asked her when, where, and how. Barbie laughed and asked, "What's a good time for you?" Wendy told her that Mondays were always good for her, anytime. So, they set a date to meet that next Monday at 10 o'clock in the morning, at the Pancake House in Leavenworth, which was about halfway between their two homes. They both looked excited and re-confirmed the time and place. They all said goodbye and expressed how nice it was to meet one another.

When they walked out the door, Wendy smiled and thought to herself, Ken and Barbie? Wait'll I tell John; he won't believe that one.

Wendy got home about 5 o'clock and John was already setting up the grill for hamburgers and grilled corn on the cob. Travis was in washing lettuce and slicing tomatoes and onions. It's pretty nice to have a son who'd spent four months living in a diner, learning how to prepare ingredients and then turn them into something delicious. The other good thing is that she didn't even have to force him to help in the kitchen. Travis loved it and helped whenever he could.

They enjoyed a wonderful meal together, and then Travis asked if he could ride around town a bit on his bicycle to see if he could meet some other kids that go to his school. He figured it might be good to get a jump on that, with school starting next Monday. They were a little surprised at that, but thought that was a good thing. Travis was trying to be a little more social with kids his own age. Well, let's pray he'll meet some good kids who can become close friends.

After Travis left, and the dishes had been done, John and Wendy sat down to talk about their day. John told Wendy to go first and so she launched into an hour by hour description of her day at the diner. She talked about how The Tanks came in at about 7:00 AM and both ordered a huge platter of pancakes, along with eggs and sausage on the side. She didn't think it was possible to eat that much in one sitting; that would've lasted her a week. They made her laugh when she went to pick up their plates, and both had a piece of pancake, the size of a quarter left behind. They looked at her, with all seriousness and said, "We just couldn't eat another bite." And when she looked surprised and started to say something, they cracked up, each taking their fork, stabbing the last piece and scarfing it down. They laughed and said, "Come on Wendy, you know there's never too much food with us. We could eat everybody in town under the table!" And with that, they paid their check and left, still laughing at their little joke.

John was laughing too and then asked if there was anything else that made her day special. Wendy got that excited, sparkly look in her eyes that John loved, and told him about her meeting with Ken and Barbie. He started to question the names also, but she shushed him and said, "Yes, that's their real names. But that's not the exciting part. Listen to this." And then she went on to tell him about their conversation, and their 40 years in ministry. But the truly exciting part was that she and Barbie were going to meet together on a regular basis, so that, in Wendy's words, "I can learn what in the world I'm doing." John was pleased to hear about that and thought that was a pretty quick answer from the Lord. They had just prayed the night before about her sense of restlessness, and now maybe this was going to help her with that.

Wendy asked John about his day, and he told her about going over to Fred Winters and spending a little time with him, while he talked and grieved about the imminent death of his mother. He then became a little more upbeat about Dave and Heather's new baby, Christopher Stephen. So, all in all, it was a good day, although he'd much rather do a visit on new parents, then with a grieving son. Both were necessary, and both ministered, but John supposed he was like anybody else; he'd rather talk about life, than death.

Wendy asked him if anything else happened. John thought for a minute and said, "Oh yeah. You know how I always tell you that it would be fun to get a new car, something small and fast, like a Triumph or a Porsche? Or, something big and luxurious, with plush, leather bucket seats, and electric windows, and air conditioning. You know, all the bells and whistles?" Wendy told him that she knew what he was talking about, but she really hoped he hadn't gone out and made a spur-of-the-moment purchase, and there was a brand-new sports car sitting in their garage, even now. He assured her that there wasn't, but that he'd seen a beautiful car and sure wouldn't mind owning one like it someday. She asked him what kind of a car it was and he told her it was a big, gold Cadillac. He went on to describe it in detail and as Wendy tried to listen, her stomach gave just a little lurch. So many memories - none of them pleasant. After a while, she relaxed and realized how irrational her fear had been. Just let John enjoy his story. That car, and all that it represents, was a lifetime ago. Wendy knew this. But still…

Chapter 5

S ATURDAY MORNING DAWNED BRIGHT AND
sunny, with clear blue skies, and a promise of a comfortably
warm day. The temperature was forecasted to be 80°; perfect
weather for outdoor activities - not too hot - not too cold - just right.
Good weather was crucial to the success of the event that was planned
at the church today. If the weather was bad, it would definitely affect
the outcome.

Today was the much-anticipated Pleasant Pastures Community
Church Garage Sale. The church began holding a yearly sale about
five years ago, and it had grown in its scope from a small event, with a

few tables of household items and two or three racks of clothing, to the biggest and best garage sale in town.

The money, this year, was going to be going towards the purchase of a home that could be used to house women and children who were in need of a place to live. They'd become homeless, for any number of reasons. Some had been through the pain of divorce and had never recovered financially. Their ex-husbands had not only run off with some young, blonde floozy, they had also moved far away and just stopped their court-ordered child support. It wasn't fair, but there was really no way to track them down and force them to pay what they owed. That, of course, took its toll on single moms who had two or three kids to care for. Many of those moms weren't trained in any kind of a trade or profession, and so the only jobs they could get were for minimum wage. The hard reality was that by the time they paid for child care, their minuscule paycheck would be eaten up, and they'd have very little left over for rent, and food, and transportation, and so on. It was a very sad situation, but was actually becoming disturbingly common.

The other problem that plummeted some of these ladies into homelessness, was drug abuse. The really scary thing was that drug abuse was becoming a major social problem, especially among the younger generation of folks, coming out of the 60s. Pot smoking was rampant and acceptable as a harmless way to relax and mellow out, very much like a person would experience drinking wine or other forms of alcohol. But the folks who studied this trend were very worried that marijuana was a pretty dangerous gateway drug. In other words, pot was seen as a gateway that opened up into much more serious forms of drug abuse.

Well, regardless of how it all happened, the fact was that there were women out there who needed help, and government social programs could only go so far. Besides, as a church, the folks at Pleasant Pastures had to deal with the classic question, "What would Jesus do?" It certainly didn't take a highly educated theologian to read through the Gospels and come to the conclusion that Jesus would help them. He would bring them hope, in the midst of their desperation, and He would bring them healing in the midst of their pain. And so, the church decided that if that's what Jesus would do, then that's what they were going to do.

And one of the most effective ways to do that, would be to open a home for women who found themselves in dire straits. This home would be a haven for those who, for whatever reason, found themselves without a place to call their own. There would be no judgment, no condemnation. The home would be there to provide food and shelter, as well as other basic necessities of life. But it would also offer something else. It would offer them a second chance - a second chance at life itself.

A plan had been drawn up that included strategies for getting help for those who were addicted to drugs and alcohol. The women would also be encouraged to take training in various trades or professions that would allow them to make enough money to be self-supporting. A childcare co-op would be set up so that moms could go to school, or hold a job, all the while knowing that their children would be well cared for. And the women would agree that whatever money they made, a financial advisor, provided by the church, would make sure that the majority of their money would be placed into a savings account that was only accessible by two signatures, the mom, and the financial advisor. This would ensure that when the mom finally left the Home, she would have a nest egg with which to start over.

The plans looked so good on paper and everybody was excited to be able to get the home up and going. There were women and children out there who needed help, not just in the big cities like Seattle, but also in smaller places like Wenatchee and Leavenworth and Cle Elum. And who knows? Maybe there was that kind of need right here in Pleasant Pastures. The town was small, and seemed to be a very happy and well-adjusted place to live. But you really didn't know what went on behind closed doors, or what might be boiling below the surface, just waiting to erupt.

The plans were in place and the excitement was growing. But they were still a long way from being financially able to make the dream become a reality. Purchasing a home of this nature would cost money, and that didn't even take into consideration what running a home would cost on a monthly basis. They'd also need to find a loving, but highly disciplined woman who could act as the "House Mother," to make sure that everything stayed on track. You get upwards to 10 women and children, from all walks of life, living in the same house, and that could be a recipe for disaster. But with the right combination of love and grace, as well as a good dose of discipline and structure mixed in, the congregation at Pleasant Pastures Community Church was confident that it would be successful. They really wanted to be a part of transforming the lives of women and children.

They were all very excited about this particular garage sale. The perfect house had just come on the market and they wanted to come up with enough money to put a down payment on it. They would then organize a capital funds campaign to try to secure pledges that would allow them to make the monthly payments, while at the same time, adding more each month to reduce the principle faster. The goal was to have the house up and running in the next six months, and be totally paid off in five years.

The house that had just become available was the old Sinclair mansion. Charles Sinclair and his family had lived in Pleasant Pastures since its beginning over 50 years ago. They were a wealthy family who had made their money in the wheat farms of Eastern Washington. After they grew weary of the long hours, and the volatility of the markets, they decided to sell everything and move to this new start-up town, near the foothills of the Cascades. Well, pretty soon the town grew up around them and now the house was pretty much in the middle of Pleasant Pastures. It wasn't located on Main Street, but it was close.

Charles Sinclair, and his wife Marjorie, raised their family there until their deaths in 1960, at the ages of 91 and 92, respectively. Their kids had all grown up and moved away, but when the parents died within just a month of each other, they came back to begin sorting through all the belongings, and navigating the legal details. All the grown children, eventually, had to get back to their lives in various parts of the country, where their jobs were located. But their oldest son, Bradley, was at a place in his life where he was free to re-locate. So, Bradley came back to Pleasant Pastures, having recently retired from banking, at the age of 60. Even though he was well off financially, he still chose to deal in the stock markets occasionally, and made sure his investments were secure and growing.

Bradley died at the age of 78, just a few months ago and his one remaining sibling came out to act as the executor of his will. Being the only surviving sibling, he inherited everything, including the house. But it certainly wasn't going to be feasible to move from his home in New York, and come and live in the house. Neither did he want the hassle of trying to rent it, especially when he saw the shape it was in. Oh, the structure was sound enough, and would certainly stand for years to come. But cosmetically, it needed a lot of work. It was apparent that as Bradley had aged, his eyesight had grown dim. There was an obvious lack of upkeep – paint – wallpaper - cracks in the ceiling - roof tiles missing - fence needing repair - driveway with cracks, needing to be redone - all kinds of things that needed fixing. Not difficult necessarily, but definitely a bit costly, and time consuming.

When the folks at church saw that the house was on the market, they knew that this would be a perfect home for their "Safe Haven" house. It was huge and had six bedrooms and four bathrooms. It was in a great location for moms who maybe had to walk to work, as well as kids who needed to get to school. It was also located far away from the bigger cities that, perhaps, could be sources of temptation for the women to go back to the former lifestyle they had left, some of them being fairly damaged.

It was the perfect place, and everyone knew that the success of this garage sale was crucial. If they could get enough for a down payment, they could secure the purchase and then start on the rather herculean task of raising a significant amount of funds, over and above the regular, on-going church budget. So, this year's garage sale was going to really outshine all the others. They had contacted each group in the church to see what unique service they could provide. And as it turned out, all ages and stages were excited and on board to help. For example:

1: The men of the church were going to provide the muscle. They would be in charge of lifting and moving the heavier items from the storage room in the basement, to the circular driveway in front of the church. And if a large item, such as a washer or mattress or refrigerator, needed to be delivered, some of the guys would lift it onto a pickup truck, jump in, and deliver it right to the purchaser's home.

2: The women of the Martha Circle, headed up by Virginia Crupp, were in charge of pricing. Now, that was a bit tricky. You had to price things low enough that people thought they were getting a good deal. But, on the other hand, you couldn't price them so low that you wouldn't make a profit. Well, nobody was better at pricing than Virginia and her team of bargain hunters. They really knew their merchandise.

3: The senior group, the Goldenaires, decided to sell reasonably priced snack items, such as home-made cookies and brownies, as well as slices of home-made pies - everything from apple, berry, cherry, peach and even lemon meringue. People were more than happy to part with their money for these kinds of home-made treats.

4: The children of the church decided to host a lemonade stand, right nearby where the baked goods were being sold. Their moms had helped them come up with several flavors of lemonade, including raspberry, peach, strawberry, and of course, plain lemon. It was a nice pleasant 80°, but after standing in the warm sunshine, a glass of ice cold lemonade hit the spot.

5: The final group was the teenagers who comprised the Pleasant Pastures youth group. They decided to host some carnival-type games to occupy the kids while their parents shopped. They set up booths with simple games such as the Ring Toss, or the Basketball Throw, or the Dime-in-the-Dish, Pin the Tail on the Donkey and many others. They even got "Fishers Five and Dime" to donate inexpensive little trinkets for prizes, after promising that they would display a prominent sign thanking the store for their generous donation.

Well, people came to the garage sale in droves. As John and Wendy worked the tables, and helped count back change, as well as carrying items to the various car trunks, their excitement about the project grew. It had been a dream of the church before John had come as their pastor, but when he heard about it, he marveled at their vision, and their progress, so far, in planning. When they asked him what he thought he said, "I think Jesus is smiling down on this one. It's exactly the kind of thing He's called us to do. I'm with you, 100%."

And as Wendy looked at all the activity going on around her, she was very happy to be part of it. She loved the excitement when people ran across something they'd been looking for and would let out a cry of delight. She loved the laughter of the little children as they played the carnival games and won their cheap trinkets, treating them like they were their newest, most prized possessions. And she loved watching the Goldenaires standing at the snack table, listening to people marvel at the various home-made baked goods. She laughed, as she saw one man come back four times for a piece of pie, a different one each time. "His wife probably doesn't bake," Wendy thought, "and he's stocking up while he's got the chance."

Everybody was having a wonderful time in the festive atmosphere. Not only were they excited about the deals they were getting, or the snacks they were consuming, or the games they were playing; perhaps the real source of excitement was about the purpose of the garage sale. The "Safe Haven" home for women and children was foremost in everybody's mind. That's why some people, when told the price of an item, declared, quite authoritatively, that it wasn't enough and then handed over three times the asking price. When Wendy witnessed that, she teared up and thanked the Lord for His goodness and for the generosity of the folks in Pleasant Pastures.

It was obvious that everyone was enjoying the excitement of the crowd and the fun of participating. But off on a side street, a half block over, sat a lone gentleman, carefully watching what was going on. He had heard about the garage sale when he stopped for gas at "Floyd's Service Station and Mini-Mart." He had met the owner Floyd, who turned out to be quite the talker. When he had asked the gentleman if there was anything exciting going on in town that weekend, Floyd had told him about the garage sale, down at the church. He almost laughed in the man's face. Since when did having a garage sale become the major social event of a weekend? But that's a small-podunk town for you – about as exciting as sitting there watching paint dry. But then Floyd said something that caught the man's attention. He told him that the garage sale was sponsored by the little white church at the end of Main Street. The pastor was this new guy from Minnesota, and he had just gotten married to a pretty, young gal, by the name of Wendy.

Nick sat in his car, a half block over from the church and thought things over. How was he going to play this? What would his next move be?

Chapter 6

JOHN AND WENDY WOKE UP ABOUT 6:30 AM ON Sunday morning, the day after the garage sale. They slept a little later than normal, mainly because they had come home fairly exhausted after working the sale from 7 o'clock in the morning, helping with setup, until 8:00 PM, taking everything down. Tables had to be broken down and stored - signs had to be removed from around the neighborhood - miscellaneous items had to either be re-stored in the church basement, or bagged up to be taken to the Goodwill in Leavenworth, on Monday.

There was a lot to do in putting on a garage sale, but it was always fun to work on a project with the other members of the church.

It had a way of drawing everybody together for a common purpose, a common goal, and that was always healthy for any community.

Even Travis had enjoyed the social interaction with the other kids working the lemonade stand. He was right there with his folks and also wound up spending the entire day, helping wherever he could. He particularly enjoyed engaging the adults in conversation. He'd always been good at talking with adults and didn't seem to have a shy bone in his body when it came to interacting with them. He was a bit shyer around his own peers, but Saturday, at the garage sale, had really helped him with that. In fact, some kids from the neighborhood, who Travis had met while riding his bike on the streets of the town, came by and asked if they could help also. Of course, they were welcome to jump in and help the cause, along with everybody else. They weren't members of the church, or the children's program there, but maybe this would draw them in. Well, whatever happened next, Travis was happy to work alongside of them and make friends. School was starting on Monday, and it would go a lot easier on the first day, the more kids he already knew.

The garage sale had been a huge success on many different levels. It had certainly drawn the church folks together around a common cause and helped to further solidify their already close bond with each other. It also, as in the case of the kids, brought other adults along who offered to help. Everyone who expressed an interest in helping was given a task to do, and were later thanked profusely for their willingness to step in. Not only did that help the sale to be more effective, and lighten the load for everybody else, it also had another unexpected, but pleasant result. Those who volunteered to work also wound up hearing more about the "Safe Haven" home for women and children. And just hearing more about it got them excited about being a part of such a wonderful project.

John and Wendy, of course, made sure that they got around to all the folks who had just joined in on-the-spot to help. They introduced themselves to the few they didn't know, either from the diner, or just in the community in general. And then they also told them that the financial team was going to be doing a final count that night, after the sale, and the results would be shared and celebrated during the church service tomorrow morning. They told the folks that they'd sure be welcome to come and join in the celebration with the rest of the folk's tomorrow morning at 11:00 AM. Everyone was pretty excited to see if their goal had been met. After having received John and Wendy's invitation, several promised they'd be there - they wouldn't miss it.

The home was huge, and if it had been in perfect repair, it would've probably been listed at about $20,000 more. But in order to facilitate a quick sale, and realizing that the home was in need of a cosmetic fix in several areas, the normally $75,000 home was listed at $60,000. That was still a pretty hefty price and left John wondering what houses would cost in the coming decade of the 80's. Well, he wasn't going to worry about that now. All he was concerned about was whether or not they were going to raise enough to make the 10% down payment. If they could make the down payment, the house would be theirs, and then they could raise funds in the coming months. But the down payment was crucial in order to secure the house.

However, after everything was added up from the money boxes and the donation basket, it came up to $4009.35. That was a great deal of money to raise in just a day-long garage sale. And John marveled at the generosity of some of the folks who donated big-ticket items to be sold, as well as those who went through their closets and garages for other smaller items, that someone else would consider an amazing find. In fact, Wendy was still amazed at what some people found that delighted them to no end. To be honest, it kind of looked like junk to Wendy, but to someone else it was pure gold. Oh well, to each his own.

The garage sale was very successful and left everyone feeling tired and worn out, but in a good way. It felt good to work hard for such a worthy cause. The only difficulty now was to have to tell the folks that we hadn't reached the goal yet, but let's not give up. We're two thirds of the way to our 10% down payment. The house is still available, and if God wants us to have it, He'll show us a way to get it. John wasn't exactly sure how that was going to happen, but he'd seen God do some pretty miraculous things in the past, and he felt that this might wind up being one of those God-things. This might be another example of God's miracle-math which He was so known for. John and Wendy prayed about it as they were having a cup of coffee and a light breakfast before leaving for church the next day. They weren't sure how it was all going to come together, but they had faith that God would lead every step of the way. Even as they had been in the bedroom getting dressed for church, they tossed around different ideas to make the extra $2000 that was needed, but nothing seemed to really jump out and grab them.

They walked next door to the church and headed to the adult Sunday school class that was always taught by the various class members who felt comfortable taking a turn. John liked to run a Sunday school class that gave different folks the opportunity to dig into the topic, do some real research, and then present their findings to the class. Now, some folks who volunteered were quite good, and seemed to really enjoy the process. But some of the other folks were outstanding, and revealed a tremendous gift for breaking open the word of God, helping people's minds come alive to the biblical text, and what it would have meant to the readers in that time and culture. And then they had the ability to take those ancient truths, and present them to a whole new audience, 2000 years later, in a way that made sense and was relevant to modern-day life. And that was a very special gift.

All the way through the class, however, John's mind was still on how he was going to present the results to his church body. They'd been so excited about making, or possibly even breaking the goal. They were positive that they were going to see God do something amazing. And John felt that He did, even though they didn't reach the goal. You see the one thing that kept encouraging John, even though the goal wasn't reached, at least not yet, was the fact that, no getting around it, $4000 was a lot of money to be raised in one single day. John knew that the folks at his church weren't exactly wealthy. Now, he had pastor friends in larger churches that had a few members who were very wealthy, and when they had a special need, or project, the pastor could always go to them, present the need, and could pretty much be assured of a hefty donation. And John thought that was just fine. People who were quite wealthy, and loved the Lord with their whole heart, oftentimes also had the gift of giving. They just flat-out loved to give to the Lord's work. It brought them great joy to see the work of God go forth, and so they gave joyfully and generously, and most often, anonymously.

Now, in John and Wendy's church, as far as they knew, they didn't really have any wealthy members. Everyone seemed to be doing fine, sure, but it was pretty much just the normal crowd of folks with typical incomes. Now, the interesting thing however, is how many people, though they weren't wealthy, still had the gift of giving and took great delight in giving at least a 10% tithe of their income to the Lord. And, in special cases, they gave offerings above their usual giving. The gift of giving wasn't as much about the condition of a person's bank account, as much as it was the condition of their heart. The gift of giving was actually more centered in the heart than in the wallet.

These thoughts were still going through both John and Wendy's minds as they finished up the Sunday school class and headed for the 11:00 AM service. The children's program had been suspended for the day so that the kids themselves could be in the service to celebrate what the Lord had done with the garage sale. They were an important part of the success and needed to be with the rest of the body.

The service started out as usual with a grand hymn, "Great Is Thy Faithfulness," and then continued with some well-known worship choruses that were currently popular in Christian circles. The Johnson sisters, three teenage girls from a very musical family, sang the special music that morning and did a beautiful, acappella version of the old hymn, "My Jesus I Love Thee." John was once again so inspired by both the tone quality of their voices and their flawless blend, not to mention the dynamics of their rendition. It was just beautiful and John wondered what God might have in store for them musically, in the coming years.

The ushers came forward to the front of the sanctuary, and after a brief prayer, thanking God for his goodness, the plates were passed up and down the aisles, as people put in their weekly tithes and offerings. John found himself thanking God once again for the faithful and generous giving of this wonderful congregation. As he sat there, truly thankful for all they had given, he was still struggling with how to present the final numbers from the garage sale.

As the offertory came to a close, John stood up and thanked the folks for all their hard work. He commended them for the outstanding job they had done, from setting up to taking down, and everything in between. He then thanked and acknowledged their special guests from the community who jumped in to help yesterday and were in the church service celebrating with them. The folks began to clap and cheer for the visitors and John found himself smiling. He hoped that he hadn't embarrassed any of them, but then thought, hey, look at it this way: Where else can you go and have people applaud and cheer you? That's pretty good.

He then gave all the facts and figures and told the folks gathered there that they were two thirds of the way towards the goal. That's phenomenal - to be able to raise $4000 in one day - he's never experienced anything like that. And then, on the spur-of-the-moment, John encouraged the congregation to give God a round of applause, in praise and thanksgiving for what He had accomplished. The applause went on for several seconds. John finally broke in as it began to die down and said that now we're just excited to see how God's going to bring the rest of the money in. If this is God's idea, if this is on His heart, that money is going to come in, someway, somehow. Let's be praying and trusting Him for it.

And then John asked the folks to turn to the biblical text, in preparation for the sermon. But just as John was going to begin, someone from the congregation spoke up and said, "Pastor, can I say something?" John looked out and saw that it was their newest member, Vern Hodges, who had asked the question. John said, "Well, of course Vern, let me bring you the mic." John stepped off the platform and came to Vern, who was sitting on the end of the pew. Vern stood up and said, "As most of you know I'm kinda new to this Christian thing, and so I don't know as much as y'all do, but it's just occurred to me that maybe God's answer to bringing the rest of the down payment, is actually right here in this room. Maybe God wants to bring the rest of it through our gifts, our sacrifice, and not by another bake-sale or car-wash. Now, those of you who know me have probably always known my well-deserved reputation for being a cranky, old tightwad. (That received a good laugh.) But God's been changing me lately, and now I find that the offering time is my favorite part of the worship service. I'm finally giving back to God just a little of what He's given me over the years. Anyway, I'm not rich by any means, and I'm not sure you are either. Now, I've been sitting here doing a headcount, and as near as I can figure, we've got about 200 people here, give or take a few. It suddenly hit me that if every one of us gave $10 today, right now, in a special offering, we'd have the money we need. Now, some folks might not be able to do that, but others might be able to give more. I guess what I'm asking, pastor, is could we take up another special offering, specifically for the "Safe Haven" house? I'd really like to see that happen soon. I just filled out a check, and I'd like to be the first one to start the offering. Can we do that pastor - or am I breaking some rule, or some Bible verse, I don't know about?" At that, the people laughed long and hard, and John said, "Well Vern, I don't know any verse that tells us *not* to give, so I guess it's okay. What do you think, Church? That was met with a chorus of amens and more applause.

John asked Max Sherman and Virginia Crupp to lead the congregation in prayers of faith, as the ushers brought the plates around again. He asked the Johnson sisters if they would mind singing their song, one more time, because he couldn't think of a more fitting song for what they were about to do than "My Jesus I Love Thee." This special offering was all about loving Jesus. So, the Johnson sisters came and sang, once again doing a beautiful job. After the offering John told them that they'd announce the results at the end of the service. And then John launched into his sermon, with much passion and fervor, closing after 30 minutes. He then asked the head of the financial team to bring him the results of the special offering.

John read the slip of paper silently to himself and felt tears willing up in his eyes. He then called Wendy to the front, so that they could give the announcement together. Wendy saw the slip of paper and also began to feel the tears start to flow. They needed to reach that crucial $2000 mark if they were going to purchase the home on Monday morning. John said, "Wendy, why don't you read the amount?" Wendy looked at the congregation, with deep love and admiration, and then announced, "The total received in our special offering this morning was $3120!" The audience gasped and then, simultaneously, broke out in applause, with shouts of Amen and Hallelujah ringing through the rafters of the little church. They had exceeded the goal by $1120. The "Safe Haven" house would be theirs by Monday morning.

Seated in the back row, behind a church lady with a huge, flamboyant hat, taking it all in, was Nick. This is all very interesting, he mused to himself. What kind of a racket have they got going here? How did Wendy fall into something like this? Somebody who really knew money, and had just the right amount of charisma, could really cash in on something like this. I've got to find out a little more about this scam they've got going here. In fact, I've got to find out a *lot* more.

Chapter 7

AFTER THE APPLAUSE AND EXUBERANT CELE-bration had calmed down, Pastor John had Harley Logan come to lead the closing hymn. Harley picked up his guitar and told the congregation that he was going to change the closing hymn, to something he felt might be more appropriate for the occasion. He talked about how one day Jesus reached down and touched him, taking his sin away and lifting the heavy burden off his back. And that's what the Lord was going to do with the women and children who would come to "Safe Haven." He was going to touch the lives of so many women in the next several years, and they were going to be made whole.

He then invited the congregation to stand and sing the powerful gospel song, "He Touched Me." It was one of Harley's favorite songs and he had led the folks in it many times before, and so most everyone gathered there knew it by heart. Harley began, with a few strums on his guitar, and the folks stood to sing this well-loved song, that suddenly had taken on new meaning for them.

As Wendy stood up on the platform with John, still overcome by all that God had done, she looked out over the congregation and thanked God for this new and exciting season of ministry they were heading into as a church. "Safe Haven" truly was going to be a very effective and Holy Spirit-anointed ministry that was going to change the lives of so many.

As the congregation began to sing those first few words, Wendy joined right in, knowing how deeply those words spoke of her own testimony. She looked out at the last couple of pews and saw some movement that caught her attention. Melverna Berglund bent down to get a Kleenex out of her purse, and Wendy grinned when she saw the huge, spectacular hat she was wearing. There are all kinds of people that come to church, Wendy thought, and Melverna and her hats testified to that. She was a bit of a character, and everybody wondered where in the world she got those hats, but in spite of her unique taste in clothes, or maybe *because* of it, she was well loved and appreciated by everyone.

But something else grabbed Wendy's attention and made her catch her breath. Directly in back of Melverna, no longer hidden by her hat, sat Nick Salerno. Wendy's heart stopped and panic began to flood in like a raging river. She felt like she could barely breathe. It *was* his gold Cadillac that John had seen after all. Nick was the man who John had seen at Floyd's Service Station on Friday - the man with the sharp car John had admired. Wendy recalled her few seconds of panic when John innocently described it to her, but she put the thought out of her mind as being ridiculous. What would Nick be doing out in this area? He never left Chicago; he was a home-town boy, through and through.

And yet, here he was, big as life. She turned to John and whispered in his ear, telling him to look at the back row, right where Melverna had been sitting. John looked back for a second or two before Melverna stood back up again. He saw a visitor he didn't know and hadn't met before the service. He was a visitor, and yet, somehow, his face looked familiar. And then he remembered - that was the guy with the gold Cadillac he had seen at the gas station. He leaned over and whispered in Wendy's ear that he's the guy who'd been at Floyd's, thinking she was simply pointing out a visitor to him, so that they could be sure to greet him afterwards. Wendy leaned over to John, and in a voice that was breaking with fear, told him that the man was Nick - Nick Salerno, her former boss from Chicago. John's heart skipped a beat and he said, "Wendy, I want you to slip out the side door when I give the closing prayer and I want you to go home. You let me handle this and don't worry. I've got The Tanks for backup. She told John to be careful, and when he began to pray, she looked at Nick, out of half-closed eyes and noticed that he was looking around the room, his eyes diverted from the platform. She quickly slipped out the side door and walked down the hallway.

As she was heading out of the church by the other door, closest to the parsonage, she ran into Max Sherman. Max and Ryan usually left during the last hymn to get into position at the doors in order to thank the folks for coming. They actually stood outside the doors, allowing people enough room to make their exit, rather than having to squeeze by these two huge men. As Wendy saw Max, she breathed a prayer of thanks and quickly gave Max a heads-up on what was happening. He assured Wendy that both he and Ryan would keep an eye on the situation, from a distance, and step in, if it seemed necessary. Since nobody knew what Nick's intentions were, they wanted to be careful not to escalate the situation. Wendy thanked Max profusely and then left to go home.

John, in the meantime, debated about how to handle the situation, trying to decide whether to just let it play out, or to take a more aggressive approach. He decided to hit the situation pro-actively, head on. And so, as John prayed, he knew what he was going to do. He finished the benediction and encouraged people to attend the coffee hour in the fellowship hall. There were leftover cookies and brownies from the garage sale. There might even be a few samples of pie that had been cut into bite-size pieces, from the slices remaining after the sale. A murmur of anticipation went up from the crowd and John had a fleeting thought - this group of folks sure liked their food.

As he was dismissing them, he also reminded them that they had quite a few visitors today who'd come to find out the results of the garage sale. So, come on Church, don't let them walk out the door without being greeted. If you see somebody you don't know, stop and introduce yourself and make sure they feel welcomed. And, with that, the organist began to play the postlude and the sanctuary began to come alive with movement and the buzz of conversations. He did a quick glance toward the back row and saw that his plan had worked. Several people had cornered Nick, making it impossible for him to leave, and were shaking his hand, welcoming him to church.

John made his way up the side of the sanctuary and away from the congested middle aisle. He casually walked over to Nick and stood there, as the others finished their greetings and left for the fellowship hall, knowing that the visitor was in good hands with their pastor. If anybody was concerned or worried, thinking something wasn't quite right, it certainly didn't show. The folks were just happy to see all the visitors who came to celebrate this momentous day.

The sanctuary quickly emptied until it was just John and Nick standing there. The two men looked at each other and sized one another other up. John felt something he wasn't used to - anger. He looked at the man who had used Wendy when she was at her most vulnerable, and he felt anger. He shot up a quick prayer, asking the Lord to help him, because what he was feeling at this moment wasn't in keeping with his Christian testimony, or with his position as pastor. To be perfectly honest, John wanted to take Nick and give him the thrashing of his life. But John also knew that wouldn't end well at all; nor would it accomplish anything. Nick would get hurt and John would feel badly afterwards, all from the comfort of a jail cell in Wenatchee. Think it through John, and don't do anything stupid.

John looked at the man standing in front of him with a smirk on his face, and said, "Hi Nick - what are you doing here?" Nick looked surprised for a minute, and then realized that Wendy must've seen him when hat-lady reached for her purse. Nick looked at John and told him he was just out here on a little vacation and happened to stop by this charming little town, on his way to Seattle. He could hardly believe it when he found out his old friend and employee, Wendy Baker, actually lived here. What a coincidence - never thought that could happen in a million years.

John fought the urge to smack that smirk right off Nick's face and calmly said, "Hey Nick, you and I both know that's a bunch of baloney. You didn't just happen by here; you came here for a reason.

What? Have you been stalking Wendy? Are you here to try to make good on your threat to kill her, if she didn't do what you wanted her too? Is that why you're here?" Nick looked at John and said, "Oh, so you know about that, huh? She told you? Why would she tell you about that? Did she tell you everything about her past; how she made a living, and what she was planning to do before she split? I find it pretty hard to believe that she'd tell a preacher what her life was like back in Chicago. I doubt you know it all; otherwise there's no way you would've hooked up with her. You don't know the whole story, buddy. If you did, she'd be out on her ear."

John looked at Nick and again prayed for control, and told him the truth. He said, "Well Nick, I think I know most of the gory details of what you did to her. The short version is that you hired her as a go-go dancer, and then decided you could make more money if your clubs went topless. The money really began pouring in and Wendy was your most popular dancer. You then came up with a brilliant plan to try to prostitute her to some of your wealthiest and most discerning customers. You, in essence, would then act as a pimp with your very own high-priced call girl. You threatened her life if she didn't follow through. But guess what? Somebody told her to run fast and she did - away from you and your sleazy business."

Nick looked puzzled and angrily demanded to know who told her to run. John smiled and said, "Well Nick, normally I would keep something like that to myself, because I wouldn't want you to go after the one who gave her that very sound piece of advice. But, in this case, I think that person's pretty safe. He's got it handled. It was God who spoke to her Nick. It was God who told her to run. And it was God who guided her out here to Pleasant Pastures. And it was God who brought her and I together, all the while changing her into the woman she is today. And Nick, I'll tell you one more thing. Even though you took advantage of a vulnerable, and pretty damaged young woman, all for your own selfish benefit, God did what He always does. He's brought good out of this very raunchy and evil situation. So, Nick, I'm really not too worried about God in this. I think even a tough guy like you wouldn't be any match for the Almighty - what do you think?"

Nick looked at John and said, "Okay, all that may be true preacher, but I'm just wondering what your congregation of do-gooders would think if they knew all about the wife of their pastor. I bet they really wouldn't be too happy to know about her dancing naked, night after night, in front of a room full of men. And I can pretty much bet they'd be shocked and disgusted if they knew about her appointment that last night."

"Oh, you mean the appointment she didn't keep?"

"Yeah, but she made it, and was planning to follow through with it."

"Maybe, but she didn't follow through, did she Nick? No, she listened to God and ran."

"Maybe so, but I bet your congregation of little old church ladies wouldn't find the story much to their liking. What do you think, John? You think I ought to clue them in on their sweet and innocent pastor's wife?"

"Well, you could do that Nick, I suppose. But that wouldn't get the response you'd be expecting. You see, Wendy already told her story to the entire congregation. She came clean Nick, and everybody loves her for that. That's what we do, Nick. We take broken people and shower them with God's grace and love - something that you obviously know nothing about."

Nick didn't know what to say. Threatening to tell the entire church had been a major part of his plan. He figured Wendy, and her preacher-husband, would give him back the money he'd spent on that exclusive school for Travis. They'd pay him back for his silence. He would get what he felt she owed him, and his reputation would remain intact. They, on the other hand, could go on with their perfect little lives and everybody would be happy as clams. The only thing that bothered Nick was thinking that maybe they should pay him a little more than that. He figured to put the heat on them to pay a modest, monthly charge for his silence. I mean, look at the money scam they've got going here. They make 4 grand at a garage sale, put on by the members. Zero money out of their pockets - all profit. The next day in church, he watched as people put checks and cash into the offering plates, and though he didn't know the exact amounts, he was pretty sure it added up to quite a bit. And, on top of that, this old guy gets up and challenges the folks to give even more money, to whatever cause they got going on, and he gives the first check. He was a plant, if Nick ever saw one, and the town people all followed along, like dumb sheep. John and Wendy had probably paid the old guy a few bucks to play on the emotions of the people and get the ball rolling. Yeah, they got a pretty sweet deal going on here; they can afford a grand a month.

That's what Nick was planning, even as he sat through the long service that seemed to take forever. That was a great plan! But now, with the revelation that she's already told her whole story to the church, that wasn't going to work. Well, whatever the case, he had to be paid back or his reputation would be in the toilet. Nick would have a new rep all right - soft and easily suckered. Can't let it happen, Nick thought to himself.

Nick stared at John and said, "Look, I'm tired of messing around with you and this one-horse-town you call home. I put out 6 grand for that kid to go to school and I want every penny back, with interest. And so, because I've got a fairly steep interest rate, based on Nick Salerno's way of doing finances, I figure you owe me about 12 grand. You pay me that and I'll disappear. You don't, and we're gonna have trouble."

John watched Nick carefully, waiting for him to make a move. John stared at Nick and said, "Pal, you're not getting one dime from us. The agreement was that she'd dance for your clubs, and as a bonus for being your top dancer, her son could go to school. You kept your end of the bargain, and she kept hers. It's complete, Nick. Nothing else to discuss. We're done here."

As John started to move away, Nick grabbed him roughly by the arm and said, "We're not done, until I say we're done." And just at that moment, two of the biggest guys Nick had ever seen, walked in and said, "Everything all right here, fellas? Seems like there's a little tension in the air. Pastor John, who might this visitor be?" John smiled at Max and said, "Max and Ryan, I'd like you to meet Nick." Max looked at Nick and said, "Oh my gracious, not *the* Nick - not Chicago Nick - not gangster Nick? Why, whatever are you doing out here in our neck of the woods? Did you come for the fall colors? It's such a lovely time of year."

Nick stared at these two giants and tried to calculate his chances in a fight. He wisely decided that he'd lose big-time, and so he chose to put off any further confrontation until later. But he looked at John and said, "Okay, preacher man. You think you're going to get away with this, don't you? You think I'm gonna go back to Chicago with my tail between my legs, just because you called your goons?" Max looked at Ryan and said, "Little brother, I think Nick here just called us a couple of goons." And Ryan, all 6'8" and 350 pounds of him, stood up to Nick and said, "Why Nick, that hurts our feelings. We're not a couple of goons, we're a couple of deacons, and there's usually a vast difference."

Nick stared at the three men and retorted, "You might think this is funny - a real joke. But one of these days, preacher, I'm going to find you alone and I'll let my fists do the talking. You mark my words."

Max and Ryan looked at each other and begin to shake their heads. Max said, "Oh Nick, buddy, I don't think you want to make threats like that. That just wouldn't be good, on so many different levels. It just might be better if you took that fancy car of yours and headed back to Chicago, of course, enjoying the lovely sights along the way." Nick looked at them and said, "Okay you clowns, we're done for now." Ryan said, "Max, now he called us clowns. What did we ever do to him?" Max just shrugged and shook his head.

"You better watch yourself, preacher, they won't always be around," Nick said calmly. And then he walked out.

The preacher and his deacons stood looking at each other, until Max smiled and said, "That fellow there seems to have some real anger issues." John laughed and said, "Gee Max, do you really think so?" They all cracked up for a few seconds, until Ryan said, "Yeah, but maybe we still ought to pray for him." They all agreed to commit Nick, and the whole situation to prayer. It seemed a little complicated right now, but nothing God couldn't handle. John was just anxious to see how He was going to do it and what the eventual outcome would be.

John expressed his gratefulness to The Tanks for stepping in, and then took off for home, looking forward to hugging his wife and son.

Chapter 8

THAT WAS AN UNUSUAL WAY TO END A SUNDAY morning, John thought to himself. The confrontation with Nick and The Tanks, who stepped in at just the right time and launched into their "sophisticated logger" routine, wasn't something John was used to. He had never been one who relished confrontation, with the exception of sports. It's one thing to be going head-to-head in the ring, or on the wrestling mats, but confrontation of that nature in church, just wasn't something you'd expect to encounter after an inspiring worship service. On the other hand, people are people, and you never know what's going to set them off.

As John walked around the church, locking up and making sure everything was secure, he thought more about Nick and his threat. He'd made it pretty clear that he didn't consider the matter closed, by any means. John wasn't quite sure what that meant, or if it was just an empty threat from a guy who had to put on a show of bravado, but John came to the conclusion that he should probably stay vigilant, without slipping into paranoia. He prayed for a hedge of protection to surround everyone concerned, but especially he and Wendy, who seemed to be the targets of Nick's anger and frustration. John didn't know Nick, other than what Wendy had told him, and so he really wasn't too sure what to think. But whatever might be brewing in that mind of his, John determined that he would keep his guard up until some kind of a resolution came about.

John finished closing up and then began walking next door to the parsonage. He was very anxious to go inside and hold Wendy and Travis close. He was going to be honest with Wendy about what happened, while at the same time, trying to keep from alarming her. And in terms of Travis, he wanted to keep the whole situation quiet so as not to scare him, or take away his excitement of the first day of school tomorrow. Travis was nervous enough; he didn't need the added stress of knowing that his folks were involved in a potentially dangerous situation.

Just as he was about to walk in the front door, he had a thought. He turned around and went back to the church and into his office. He picked up his personal phone directory, and looked up the number of an old friend from Duluth. He and Bill had gone to school together, from elementary, right on through high school, and had been good friends the whole time. They even went to the same church together and so shared a common faith in Christ. He was hoping that Bill could help him out a bit, and bring a little clarification to the situation.

He picked up the receiver and began to dial the number, noting that it would be about 3 o'clock in the afternoon in Duluth, due to the time zones. The phone rang three times, and then Bill's deep, resonant, bass voice came on the line. John often wondered why Bill hadn't gone in for broadcasting, because he definitely had the voice for it. But John remembered how Bill knew from the time he hit junior high, what he wanted to do in life, and sure enough, his dream had come true.

Bill had graduated from high school and had done a two-year stint in the Army, courtesy of the draft. He thought for sure he would be heading to Vietnam as a grunt, but the Army surprised him. When he was inducted, he was given a battery of tests that measured his aptitudes and interests. He was also given an opportunity to request an MOS, in other words, a particular job he'd like to do. Some guys wanted to be mechanics and work on trucks and tanks and other motorized vehicles. Other guys wanted to serve in artillery, or supply, or food services. Some wanted to go to OCS, Officer Candidate School, and come out as a second lieutenant and be in command of people, at some point. The Army had every job you could possibly think of, so the sky was the limit. Theoretically.

But, in actuality, the Army put you pretty much where they wanted to. Your desire for a particular job in which you'd spend your two years of service, was a nice thought, but in most cases, it was highly unlikely to happen. The job you got assigned to was pretty much determined by what the Army needed at the time, to fill the slots. Bill, much to his surprise, knew guys in basic training who were already highly qualified in a variety of trades, and even professions. But the Army seemed to pay little attention to what you did as a civilian.

If they needed cooks at the time, they'd take a guy who was a licensed truck driver in civilian life, and make him a cook. If they needed mechanics at the time, they'd take a guy who was a successful chef in civilian life, and make him a mechanic. Bill even knew a couple of guys who'd gone to college for four years, and then three years of law school, and graduated at the age of 26. They passed the bar exam and were ready to practice law, but being that they were still 26, which was the age limit of the draft, they wound up being called to service. But in both cases, they sent the two lawyers into the infantry. You could turn that into a great lawyer joke, except in their cases, it was true.

But, in Bill's case, he actually got what he signed up for. For as long as John could remember, Bill wanted to be a cop. He wanted to go into law enforcement. In fact, his desire was so strong, that John had never known Bill to veer off his dream. Most guys, John included, looked at all kinds of options while growing up, and changed their minds at least a dozen times, but not Bill. When he was drafted, Bill put down that he wanted to be a Military Policeman. After hearing other stories from his fellow basic training recruits, who'd gotten orders for AIT, which was short for *advanced individual training*, and realizing that the future training had nothing to do whatsoever with their requests, he just figured his was a hopeless cause, and he'd be stuck peeling potatoes or working in a supply depot. But, lo and behold, when he got his orders, he was astonished to see that they had actually given him what he wanted. He was going to be undergoing training as an MP-Military Police.

Well, Bill passed his training with flying colors and wondered where they would send him. He thought of all the exotic places they could send him for his last 20 months of service – Germany - South Korea – Japan – Alaska - sunny Vietnam - any number of exciting locales. But when he got his orders, he found that he was assigned to Fort Lewis, Washington. He was going to spend his entire tour of duty in a city where it was reported to be gray and rainy, all day, every day. Some of his buddies told him that people in Tacoma got so much rain, that they actually were growing webbed feet, a truly evolutionary wonder. Of course, he knew they were kidding, but he wondered what duty would be like there. But as he went and got used to the place, he found that the Tacoma/Fort Lewis area was actually pretty nice. There *were* a lot of gray days of drizzle, but on those rare days when the sun was shining, and the blue skies were as clear as anything you'd ever seen, you couldn't find a more beautiful area of the country. A 90-minute ride east and you could be in the rugged Cascade Mountains. A 90-minute ride west and you could be at the ocean, going salmon fishing on a charter boat. A 90-minute ride north and you could be in a whole different country: Vancouver, Canada. And from there, you could take a short jaunt on a ferry to the little English town of Victoria. So much to do, so much to see. It was actually pretty good duty and he thoroughly enjoyed it.

He especially enjoyed being an MP. The only time when things got a little awkward was when they did a traffic stop, for example, and the person behind the wheel turned out to be an officer. It was pretty intimidating for Private First Class Bill Parker to stop Major Lead-Foot for speeding. Most of the time he let them go with a warning to slow it down, but other times he and his partner couldn't just let it go. Bill recalled the few times he had to pull somebody over for "driving while intoxicated," and would then find out that the person driving was an officer. And even though he hated to do it, knowing that it could ruin the officer's career, he had no choice but to arrest the driver and take him to the brig. To do anything less would have endangered many others on the road. So, he and his partner would make the arrest and thoroughly document everything, including the procedures used, the conversations, and the attitude and actions of the driver. Those kinds of situations were uncomfortable, but they had to be done. Bill also knew he'd run into those kinds of awkward situations when he was a civilian police officer also, so he figured it was just good training for the future.

Finally, after serving two years at the request of Uncle Sam, Bill returned home to Duluth and applied to the police academy, where he was accepted immediately. The fact that he had served his country with honor and integrity, plus the fact that he was already trained as an MP, made him an ideal candidate for a career in law enforcement in his home state of Minnesota.

So, when John heard Bill's voice on the other end of the line, all of that history came flooding back, and he hoped that his friend could help him out. John told Bill the shortened version of he and Wendy's story, including her past and the threat by Nick to kill her. Bill listened to the story and then observed that the tale of John and Wendy would make a great movie. John laughed and agreed that it would, indeed, hold an audience's attention. But then he asked Bill if there was any way that he could help them. The threat against both he and Wendy had left him a bit nervous, understandably so. He wasn't scared necessarily, but he had learned a long time ago never to underestimate your opponent. In other words, it's crucial to know who you're up against, and what you're really dealing with.

So, John asked Bill if there was any way he could check this Nick character out for him. John told him that the fella's name was Nick Salerno and he owned two nightclubs in Chicago. He also was able to supply him with Nick's license plate number that Ryan had copied down and brought into John, when he saw Nick drive away after their little confrontation. Bill told John that he actually had a buddy who had ties to Chicago, but was now on the police force in Minneapolis. And then he told John that he would see if he could get anything on this guy. He told him that he sounds like he could be a pretty tough character, but you really never know. If he's got a rap sheet in Chicago, Bill felt certain that he could find out something for him. Just give him a day or two and he'd get right back to them. He'd get the ball rolling with his buddy tomorrow, and get back to him ASAP.

John thanked Bill and asked him how Joni and the kids were. They spent some time catching up and then said their goodbyes, at least until Bill had found out the scoop on this Salerno character.

As John hung up the phone, he felt a bit more relieved; one way or the other he was going to find out about this Nick. How dangerous was he, anyway? If he was truly the gangster he seemed to be, why would he go to all this trouble just because one dancer walked out on him? John knew about the importance of his reputation among fellow gangsters, but this seemed a bit excessive, at least it did to John. But, on the other hand, what did John know about honor among gangsters; that's certainly not something he learned about in seminary? Maybe they ought to teach a class in school on that - Gangster Gospel 101 - How to win a hitman to Christ - Cement shoes, and the plan of salvation - How to be a holy henchman.

John could go on and on, but he was just walking into the door of the parsonage. It was time to have an honest conversation with Wendy; nothing alarming, just enough to keep her apprised of the situation. They would spend time talking about it, and he would try to glean as much information as possible about Nick, and the way he operated. What had she actually seen that would help them both know who they're truly dealing with? If Bill's report came back saying that

Nick had warrants out for his arrest, what's their next step? Should they go to the local authorities, or just let Bill start the process, from his end, in Duluth? And what would they do if Nick turned out *not* to be the gangster he sees himself being? What if he's sleazy and selfish, but not dangerous, in a violent way? What if all of his businesses are protected under law and he's done absolutely nothing wrong or illegal? He may have broken all kinds of moral laws, but what if everything else was on the up and up?

John and Wendy talked about all the possible scenarios, and decided they couldn't really know exactly how to proceed, until they got more information. But they *did* decide on an immediate strategy. They were going to remain vigilant, at all times. They were going to pray protection over their family, while at the same time enlisting close friends to pray with them. And thirdly, they were going to pray for Nick. He may be a hardened criminal, or he may simply be a hardened and selfish businessman, but whatever the case may be, both John and Wendy knew that hard-hearts were God's specialty. Jesus could melt the heart of the most hardened and rebellious person on the face of the earth. Plenty of people in the church could testify of their heart softening under the gospel of love and grace. Why not Nick?

As they chatted for a few minutes, Travis came walking in for lunch. He and some of his new friends from the neighborhood had been fooling around, trying to copy the moves they had seen on Big Time Wrestling. Wendy remembered when wrestling was such a big deal to Travis back in Chicago, with the boys in the neighborhood. That was only about six or seven months ago, but it seemed like a lifetime. So much had changed, but at least one thing remained the same. Little boys still liked tackling other little boys and flipping them over their shoulders. It's something Wendy never really understood, but it seemed to be in their nature. They wanted to compete, they wanted to test each other, they wanted to try their best, they wanted to win, they wanted to protect, they wanted to be the hero. Wendy could go on and on. A mother of a little boy knows these things. She may not understand it all, but she knows.

Wendy found herself putting John into the equation. As they worked side-by-side in the kitchen getting the roast out of the oven, mashing the potatoes, making gravy from the delicious juices, she wondered about John. She knew he was in great shape physically. She knew he could handle himself when he was in the gym; she had watched him hold his own, even with The Tanks. But that was all in fun, and just for a good workout. But how's John feeling about this? This isn't exactly the kind of experience that John's been faced with before. Now, he certainly had confrontations as a pastor, especially back in the days of the painful split at First Baptist, but it was never like this. The church members might have been upset, some even to the point of walking out angrily in the midst of a meeting. But to her knowledge, nobody ever threatened bodily harm to anyone.

But that's exactly what had happened to her; and when it did, she ran. She got away, but John can't do that. He has to stay and face it. She found herself quite conflicted when she thought about it. On the one hand, John is strong and in great shape, and could certainly handle himself if he had to. But on the other hand, he always tries his best to follow Jesus and live by His word. Wendy wasn't too sure how following Jesus, while defending yourself or your loved ones from harm, fit together. Well, Wendy thought, I'm still kind of new to this faith thing, but there are a few things I know for sure. John loves Jesus and will do everything he can to live in such a way as to please Him. And secondly, John loves Travis and me and will do whatever it takes for us to be safe. And thirdly, John loves his congregation and will always do what is best for his flock.

Wendy thought that these three things said it all, and she began to relax in that knowledge. But then, another thought hit her. She also knew that John had given his whole life for the gospel. He knew that Jesus could make a difference in a person's life and that difference is literally between life and death. Wendy knew that everything John did in ministry was so that people would be changed by the gospel. And it was then that she knew, beyond a shadow of a doubt, that John was, even now, praying for Nick's soul. He may hate what Nick has done, especially to me, Wendy thought, but in John's reality, nobody's beyond redemption.

That certain knowledge of her husband, Wendy mused, was more important than anything else. "Lord, please just take John's good heart and righteous motives, and use them for your glory. Protect us Lord, but also answer John's heartfelt prayers. We're in miracle territory, Lord; now it's all up to you.

Chapter 9

"MOM AND DAD, GET UP! I DON'T WANT TO be late for my first day. Come on, where are you guys?" I heard those words in my sleep, but they didn't make any sense in the context of the dream I was having. I was dreaming that I was riding a beautiful, golden Palomino through a field of wildflowers. It was truly one of the most exhilarating dreams I'd ever had. I felt like I was flying, the wind whipping my hair straight back, trailing long and luxurious behind me. The skies were a beautiful blue and seemed to go on and on, so that I could see forever. What a beautiful, marvelous, exhilarating dream. Somehow, when I was riding like the wind, I knew it wasn't real, but I just laid there and enjoyed every moment of it.

But then I heard that voice, that call that dared interrupt this amazing moment of freedom and power I felt on my magical steed, flying along at lightning speed. "Mom and Dad, get up! I don't want to be late for my first day. Come on, where are you guys?" I suddenly lurched and looked at the clock on my nightstand, trying to focus my eyes on the numbers. It took a few seconds to register before I realized what was going on. Travis was in a small panic, a mini-crisis because we weren't in the kitchen starting breakfast, before launching into our day. I just assumed that we'd overslept, and that if we didn't get a move on, Travis would be late and his whole school career would go down the drain. A bit dramatic, yes, but I'm sure that's how Travis felt this morning.

I looked at the clock again and groaned out loud. We weren't even anywhere close to panic time. It was 5:00 AM for heaven sakes; we didn't have to be at school until 8 o'clock. That's three hours, but my son's running around like he's got three minutes, or his whole life will be in ruins. We had set the alarm for 6:00 AM to make sure that we had plenty of time to get ready and give Travis a good breakfast, before walking him the three blocks to Washington Elementary school, for his first day.

Just at that moment, Travis came bounding into our bedroom, aghast at seeing his usually early-rising parents, still in bed. Granted, it was 5:00 AM, and not 7:45, but to Travis it felt like we were going to sleep forever. I looked at him through one eye that wasn't buried in my pillow. As a heavy sleeper I usually only have enough energy to use one functioning eye at any one time, and I used that to stare at my son who was looking quite worried, imagining that something was very wrong with these two unresponsive lumps in his parents' bed.

I told Travis, in a very groggy and sleepy voice, that we were just fine. We weren't late; we had plenty of time. Go downstairs, and we'd be down in a few minutes to start getting breakfast ready. He didn't have to be at school for three hours, and so barring an earthquake, or a volcanic eruption, he'd be to school in plenty of time. That seemed to satisfy him enough that he took my suggestion and turned to go downstairs. Of course, he couldn't just leave quietly, realizing how wise his mother was; he turned around with a big, exaggerated sigh that I can only interpret as a great level of exasperation with his sleepy-head parents. His frustrated sigh made me feel like the oldest, laziest parent in the world. How could I still be in bed at 5:00 AM? Oh, the shame of it.

I lifted up on my elbows and I looked over at John. He was still dead to the world, snoring like a buzz saw. The little exchange between Travis and me hadn't even elicited a slight stirring. He was fast asleep and somehow just escaped the whole exchange. Except, when I turned to look at John, he somehow knew I was giving him a questioning look that asked, "How in the world could you sleep through that?" And then he surprised me by saying, "Is he gone yet?" I took my pillow and smacked him over the head and said, "You weasel, you heard the whole thing." And John answered, "Yeah, I did. But you were handling it so well, I thought I'd just go on pretending to be asleep. I didn't feel like I had anything of significance to add." "Why you big creep," I said, "You let me take all the heat for sleeping in." John replied, "Only because I know you're a strong and powerful woman, and can handle anything." At that moment I launched a surprise attack on John. I reached out and started tickling him in a spot that always reduced him to a blob of jelly, every time. We both started laughing and wrestling around until we were both spent. It felt good to laugh and woke us up completely.

We were both pretty tired from the long night we had spent talking about what had happened at church that morning. The service had been so inspiring and served to encourage our folks to continue on with our dream of opening "Safe Haven" - a place that everyone knew was going to be wonderful for the women and children who would come through the doors. We celebrated not only the money raised at the garage sale on Saturday, but also the special offering we took that morning that put us over the top, by more than $1100. It truly was a morning of inspiration and hope for the future.

But at the very end of the service when I saw Nick, everything that happened in the previous hour seemed to evaporate, and was replaced by a cold chill of what I can only describe as fear. And then, when John urged me to go home out the side door and said that he'd take care of it, I was relieved, to some extent, but still pretty nervous. Running into Max helped me relax some, and yet the butterflies were flitting around in my stomach for those moments I was alone, knowing that a confrontation of some kind was taking place, even as I paced our living room floor.

When John finally came in, after what seemed like an eternity, but, in reality, was only about 30 minutes, I was so relieved. He was able to give me the highlights of what had transpired, but then Travis walked in the door, ready for lunch. We obviously didn't want to discuss all of this with our son, and so we just looked at each other and shook our heads slightly. We both interpreted that as meaning we'll put this discussion on hold for now, and come back to it later.

We spent the afternoon playing croquet and badminton in the backyard, as well as sitting under the huge, shade tree and reading the various novels we were hooked on at the time. Fortunately, the three of us are pretty avid readers and enjoy spending time as a family reading, and then talking about our various books. I realize that some people would find that a bit boring, I suppose, but we love it.

We finally went back into the house about 6:00 PM and began preparing for dinner. The roast and mashed potatoes we had for lunch were going to make a second appearance that day. Pot roast, cooked slowly in a Dutch oven, is probably our family's favorite dinner. I truly believe John would eat that every day of his life if he could, and Travis would be right there with him. But having worked in a diner, I also knew that there were many other dishes they would enjoy, if they gave them a chance. Nevertheless, the leftover roast and mashed potatoes were on the menu for the night, and nobody was complaining, including me.

After dinner and the cleanup, which we all participated in, we sat down to watch "The Wonderful World of Disney", one of our favorite shows. They were actually doing a flashback night where they played portions of shows that John and I had seen as kids. They brought back memories for both John and I, each of us growing up in different states, and in different settings, and yet having the common bond of having watched the same Disney shows. They showed clips from "Spin and Marty," a show about a variety of different guys who spent time on a dude ranch. They showed a five-minute spot on "Corky and White Shadow," a story about a girl and her dog and the adventures they got into. They even showed a few clips from the one called "Applegate's Treasure," about gold doubloons and pirate treasure that was hidden in an old house, just waiting to be discovered.

Travis found it fascinating, and watched the whole show from start to finish, never looking bored or like he wanted to do something else. When it was over, and we asked him what he thought about the shows from our childhood, he said he thought they were okay, but they were a little bland. When we asked him what he meant by that, he commented on the fact that there was no color - they were just black and white - is that all they had back then? Travis stated that color sure added spice to life, didn't it? If everything was just black and white, life could get a little boring. We agreed with his assessment, and then turned off the TV and went into his bedroom to help him prepare for school the next morning. I laid out his clothes while John and Travis double-checked his supplies. After checking everything out, and being confident that all was in order, we kissed Travis good night, told him we loved him and that we'd see him in the morning.

John and I finally had some time to ourselves to process what had transpired that day, and how to continue on from here. By that time, it was about 9 o'clock; too early for bed, and yet we both felt fairly wrung out, probably from the emotion of the day, on several levels. And so, early or not, we decided to hop into bed and just talk about things in the place we felt most intimate, the privacy of our bedroom.

We went over the details of the day, and when we got to the part about the confrontation with Nick, and The Tanks, and himself, John reiterated once again, in more detail, what had taken place. He also told me about contacting Bill, his friend in law enforcement, to see if we could get a clearer picture of Nick, and in turn, see what we were really up against.

After all the details of the day had been laid out and discussed thoroughly, we remained silent for a good period of time. The lights were off and I was wondering if John had fallen asleep, exhausted after his emotionally draining day. But he surprised me a moment later when he asked me what I thought about the whole situation. He wasn't asking me what I thought about any specific detail; he wanted to know what I thought about the whole thing, from the garage sale, to meeting and exceeding the financial goal; from knowing that "Safe Haven will become a reality, to the fact that our financial team was going to make the deal, the very next day. All of those were great things, marvelous dreams that were going to come true. But what about the deal with Nick? Everything was going so well, at least until he showed up. What's that all about, Wendy?

I thought about all that had happened since Saturday, and the only thing my mind kept coming back to was "The Wonderful World of Disney" show we had watched that night. I kept thinking about Travis's assessment that everything being filmed in black-and-white was a little bland, a little too neat, a little too safe. Everything was either black or white; there wasn't any color to spice things up a bit. When you added color, you could begin to distinguish the various shades of color, the depth of a particular scene, or the contours of an object, or even the facial expressions on the actor. Color added so much more than just color - it added depth, and expression, vitality, life, and even meaning. Color made all of life so much more real, something so much more incredible to experience.

And as I talked with John, I proposed that maybe that's how we need to view the situation we're in. We'd like everything to be black-and-white. It's either this, or it's that. And there are no shades of color, not even gray. And yet, if everything was like that, what would life really be like? I mean, if that's what would have been really good for us, if that's what really made life fulfilling for the human race, God could easily have created the world like that - everything black or white. No color, no shades, no vibrancy, no spice – just black and white. It sounds easier in some ways, but is that what we'd really want? God could've done it that way, but look at what we would have missed. Beautiful sunsets, exquisite works of art, the exciting variety of clothes, a myriad of house colors, fancy paint jobs at the car shows, leaves on the trees in the fall, different shades of water in Hawaii, brilliant tropical fish that swim in those waters. Without color, we'd miss out on life itself.

Well, what if color wasn't just about clothes and houses and cars and pieces of art and tropical fish? What if color was also about experiences, some wild and wonderful, and some hard and distressing? What if this situation with Nick is one of those bits of color that God allows in our life because He knows that ultimately, something good and beautiful can come out of it? I'm not saying He caused this whole mess; I'm just asking what if God decided to let this play out? What if He felt that the color it would bring to our lives would eventually be well worth it? I'm not saying that all the stupid choices I made before I became a Christian were part of God's plan for me, heaven forbid, but what I'm saying is that God can take those choices, and the resulting consequences, and eventually add His own color scheme to them. The landscape of our lives can be pretty bleak and barren, but when we invite God into the picture, He can turn that barren landscape into a beautiful field, filled with lush green grass, and gorgeous wildflowers of every shape and color imaginable.

What if the situation with Nick is God's art project? What if He's going to let this piece of color be introduced into our lives because He knows us, and He knows that we'll not only adapt to this color change, we'll actually assimilate it until it becomes a part of who we are, and how we minister to others. The situation with Nick is quite a challenge – we both know that and frankly, we could be shaking in our boots

- but what if God says, "John and Wendy, I know it's hard, but you're up to the challenge. Just trust me." What if that's what God is saying?

And what if it doesn't stop with Nick? I have a feeling that when we launch "Safe Haven" we're going to have experiences that might make this one look fairly tame. I think we're going to hear colorful stories and colorful language and were going to meet a lot of really colorful characters. So, maybe God's preparing us for the future. "Safe Haven" would be a whole lot easier to run if everything was black and white; if all the answers were spelled out with exact lines, and nobody went outside the lines. But you know that's not going to happen. This spirituality thing is messy at times, and just ignoring it or wishing it wasn't so, doesn't change anything. Maybe all the color, both the good and the bad, is what prepares us for the work of ministry.

John took my hand and said, "Wow! I didn't know I had married a philosopher, and a theologian, and an art professor, all rolled into one. That was really quite impressive. I also think that you've hit on something very important. I think we should go to God tonight and actually thank Him for the color that comes into our lives. Because if that color will help change us and shape us and mold us into His character and nature, I'm all for it, Wendy. Let's not be afraid of it, let's embrace it."

I leaned over and hugged John and told him that I loved him, but I wanted to say one more thing. "I'm all for color, but like the announcer says on TV; I want it to be *living* color. So please, just be careful, John, and let's trust God to guide our every move." We assured each other that we'd both be trusting God, but that we'd also be very careful. We are endeavoring to be God's creation, in *living* color.

We kissed good night, realizing that we had talked until past midnight. We were going to be tired tomorrow, but we had a great talk and came to a wonderful understanding. God was moving us away from the black and white "Spin and Marty" scenario, and into the colorful life that is reality in Christ. I wondered if we were ready for that. But, in my heart of hearts, I knew we were.

Chapter 10

AFTER TRAVIS WENT YELLING THROUGH THE house, in a voice that could wake the dead, John and Wendy decided it was best just to forgo the extra hour of sleep they had anticipated, and roll out of bed. Travis was excited about his first day at the new school, but was nervous all the same. He'd met some nice friends in the neighborhood over the summer, but would they pay attention to him once they got to school and saw the familiar faces of kids they had attended with all their lives?

John got up and jumped into the shower, while Wendy went down to start the breakfast. She mixed up batter for the waffles and then set about preparing the various toppings they were going to enjoy. She cut up a couple of fresh peaches and five or six large straw-berries. She also set out a bowl of freshly picked blackberries from the vines that grew in their backyard. They were sweet and delicious and would make a wonderful topping for the waffles. She set the dining room table with the good china and the silverware. And then, to make it extra special, she took out three crystal goblets and poured sparkling cider in each. Her final effort to make this meal special for Travis was to take three cloth napkins that matched the tablecloth, roll them up in a sparkly napkin ring, and then fan them out across the plate.

She sat back and surveyed the table she had set and was quite impressed with her efforts. She went out into the backyard and picked three beautiful hydrangeas, each a gorgeous lavender with a darker purple shade surrounding the edge of each petal. She placed them in a vase and set it in the middle of the dining room table, completing the setting. It looked so nice and she hoped that Travis would feel good about this extra special breakfast she and John had fixed for him. Because the hard reality was that, come tomorrow, it was back to cold cereal and a piece of toast with peanut butter for protein.

As she was admiring her handiwork, John came into the kitchen freshly showered. He smelled like Irish Spring Soap, and his hair was still damp. He saw the table setting and remarked that for a minute he thought he was in a five-star restaurant. A beautiful tablecloth with matching napkins seemed pretty fancy. Fine China with crystal goblets and the special silver; couldn't get much swankier than this. The flow-ers added a beautiful touch to an already lovely table.

While Wendy left to ready herself, John turned to the kitchen counter and saw the three bowls of fresh fruit that had been pre-pared as the toppings for the waffles. He looked in the fridge, and sure enough, saw the can of whipped cream that would top off these delicious breakfast delights. Travis could spray his own whipped cream and could go crazy with it. It's a big day…why not splurge?

John got out the waffle iron from the cupboard underneath the counter and began to heat it up. He placed a good-sized pat of butter in the center of the iron, knowing it would melt when it became hot enough to begin. He waited a few moments, and then began to ladle the waffle batter onto the iron. They would take several minutes to cook and then when he was done, he would place them on a plate and cover them with aluminum foil to keep them warm. And when he finished the first one, he'd start the process all over again for the second.

About 15 minutes later John called out that breakfast was served in the dining room. Wendy came down looking beautiful as always and kissed John, thanking him for being the chief cook this morning. A moment later Travis came in and realized that they were having one of his favorite breakfast meals - waffles with assorted fruit toppings - and best of all, whipped cream he could spray on himself.

They all sat down as a family and John asked Travis to say grace. Travis prayed for the day ahead and that his new friends in the neighborhood would pay attention to him. Wendy got a tear in her eye, remembering how tough it can be sometimes as a kid. No matter how gifted or talented or good-looking you might be, the sense of insecurity was always there, just waiting to raise its ugly head. It certainly had happened to her on many occasions, and she prayed that Travis would be spared.

They finished up breakfast and each went into their respective bathrooms to brush their teeth once again, before starting their day. They met back in the living room; Travis carrying his notebook and bag of supplies, along with his new Superman lunchbox.

John and Wendy had planned to walk Travis to school the first day, but just as they were going to leave there was a knock at the door. They opened it, surprised that someone would come calling this early. But when they opened the door there was a group of five kids from the neighborhood standing on the porch, their bikes parked in the driveway. "We were just wondering if Travis would like to ride with us to school?" John and Wendy were a little disappointed in one way because they thought he might feel more comfortable walking into a new place if they were there to reassure him. But Travis jumped at the chance to go with his friends; the Lord had answered his prayer and let him know that they were definitely not going to ignore him.

John and Wendy quickly assessed the situation and knew that Travis would be just fine. In fact, he'd be more than fine because, evidently, he was already accepted into this new group. Everybody needs people that they can call friends; friends that will stick with them, no matter what. It looked like Travis already had a pretty good head start on that crucial aspect of growing up. So, John and Wendy said it was great and wished him and his friends a wonderful first day at school. Wendy started to bend down to kiss Travis goodbye, but got a slight shake of the head from John. The meaning was pretty clear: Don't kiss him in front of his friends. Kids get embarrassed by that, especially boys. Now, when he's older, he won't care, but right now it's probably best to keep that in the privacy of the home. So, Wendy just gave him a quick hug around the shoulders, and said that they'd see him after school. And with that, Travis went to his bike on the porch, stored his supplies in the saddlebags, and took off with the rest of the kids. They got the distinct impression that Travis was going to have a great year.

John and Wendy went back to the dining room, clearing the dishes and left-over remnants of breakfast from the table. They put the food in the fridge and then started in on the dishes. Once the kitchen was totally clean, and the dishes put away, they sat down to have a cup of coffee together and talk about their day. Wendy reminded John that she was meeting with Barbie at 10 o'clock up at the Pancake House in Leavenworth. He looked puzzled for a minute, and she reminded him that Barbie was the pastor's wife from the Assembly of God church on the outskirts of Wenatchee. They were going to begin meeting on Mondays, so that Wendy could glean from this woman who had decades of experience in the role of pastor's wife. She told John that she really wanted to be the best wife possible for him, but she also wanted to be the best she could for their ministry together. John expressed his appreciation for that and told her that she already was everything he ever hoped her to be. But, if she felt it was important for herself, then he was with her 100%.

She asked about his day and he told her it was shaping up to be a typical Monday. He was going to go into the office, quite a bit later than usual because of the special breakfast, and he would start his day by looking at the registration cards from yesterday's service; who was there in terms of regular attenders and who were the visitors. He would also look for prayer requests that had been written on the back of the cards and, if appropriate, would pass on those requests to his team of deacons and deaconesses who would join him in praying for the various needs. He would also make a list of all the visitors and then place a personal phone call to each one, within the next day or two. He would thank them for attending and then see if they had any questions he could answer. John had discovered several years ago that people appreciated a friendly personal touch, just as long as he didn't come across as a slick salesman for Jesus. That was never John's way of conducting ministry anyway; he just enjoyed the interaction with folks.

After finishing their little coffee-klatch they left to begin their day, reminding each other to be vigilant and careful. As John left, Wendy went into the bedroom and grabbed her purse and car keys and then walked out to her car. She got in, started it up and was soon driving down Main Street and out to the highway that would bring her into Leavenworth. She was going to be about 15 minutes early, but wanted the time to just pray silently, before her meeting with Barbie.

Wendy tried to figure out what she was feeling as she drove to Leavenworth. It was really a combination of things. She was excited about meeting with Barbie. She had really sensed a good connection with this older, and presumably, wiser woman who had years of experience in ministry. She was truly looking forward to getting to know her and her story. But she also experienced the very familiar feelings of nervousness; the same nervousness she felt when she first thought of sharing her past with the congregation at church. It's not easy to bare yourself before people, no matter how nice they seemed. There was always the chance of rejection; on the other hand, there was also the chance of being warmly embraced, not *despite* your story, but *because* of it. That's what happened with the church folks; would that also happen with Barbie?

Wendy pulled into the parking lot of the Pancake House and walked into the restaurant. It was pretty quiet mid-morning on a Monday, and Wendy was thankful that they'd be able to talk without having to contend with a lot of crowd noise. She had just sat down in the booth, looking forward to spending a few moments in prayer for the meeting, when she looked up and saw a smiling Barbie walking toward her. Evidently, she wasn't one to show up at the last minute either, so they had at least one thing in common.

Wendy wasn't too sure how to greet Barbie, but that question became moot when Barbie warmly embraced her and told her how good it was to see her, and that she'd been really looking forward to their meeting. Wendy assured her that she felt the same way and thanked her for her willingness to meet. Barbie laughed and said, "Are you kidding? I love this kind of stuff. There's always a blessing in getting to know a fellow pastor's wife. In case you haven't noticed, there aren't too many of us out there, and so we need to stick together."

Wendy told her that she saw her point and was looking forward to what God was going to do. She was just ready to ask Barbie to tell her story, when she surprised Wendy and asked her to go first. Wendy swallowed hard and said, "Are you sure you're ready to hear this? It's a pretty ugly story, at least until about six months ago. It might be a bit much for you, particularly at 10 o'clock on Monday morning. Do you want the Readers Digest condensed version, or do you want the whole enchilada?" Barbie laughed and said, "I love Mexican food. Lay it on me - give me the whole enchilada."

Wendy did; she told Barbie the same story she had told the congregation gathered in the church all those weeks ago. She didn't leave anything out, including the doubts that still occasionally plagued her concerning her unworthiness to be in such an awesome position. People were going to be looking to her to be some kind of a spiritual giant, and she just wasn't there yet.

Barbie let Wendy talk, and when it seemed that Wendy had said it all, she leaned back in her chair and just said, "Wow!" Wendy wasn't quite sure how to interpret that "Wow!" Did Barbie mean she'd never heard a story like that and was going to have to re-think their relationship? Did her story so shock this mature woman of God that she was left speechless, not knowing how to respond to the ugliness of it?

Did all the details of her past make Barbie think Wendy was indeed out of her element? Wendy didn't know what "Wow!" meant. And so, she did what she'd come to find out was always the best: she just asked her, flat out, with no holds barred. She said, "Barbie, I know what I shared was pretty ugly, and if you don't want to take me on as a friend, I understand completely. I just wanted to know what you meant when you said, 'Wow!' Because that could mean a lot of things, and to be honest, my mind is whirling with possibilities…and none of them are good."

Barbie looked at Wendy and said, "Oh, I'm sorry honey. I didn't mean to upset you. The 'Wow' had nothing to do with being shocked at your story. In fact, as you were telling it, I was just sitting here marveling at the grace of God. I mean, look where you were six months ago and look where you are right now. If that isn't a miracle from God, I don't know what is. No, the 'Wow' didn't have anything to do with you somehow upsetting me or making me re-think our friendship. On the contrary, what you shared just confirms that what we're doing right here is spot on. This is a God thing, through and through."

Wendy looked at her through eyes glistening with tears, reminiscent of when she shared with her own congregation. She looked at her new friend, this precious sister in Christ, and she said, "So what's with the 'Wow?' If you weren't shocked and disgusted by my story, why the 'Wow'? It was an honest question, and even though Barbie had reassured her that it had nothing to do with being shocked, still, she said it for a reason. Barbie looked at her and began to explain.

When Wendy started in on her story, Barbie could tell that it wasn't going to be pretty. The fact is, she had heard this kind of a story all too often; maybe not the exact details, but the basic storyline was the same. A young girl somehow, through abuse by either family or men in her life, gets it drilled into her head that she's nothing; she is worthless and the only thing she's got going for her is her body. Barbie had heard the same version of that story many times. And when Wendy had shared her story, including what happened to her in the last six months, Barbie was elated. And then, as Wendy brought Barbie up to speed by sharing what had happened with the garage sale for "Safe Haven" and the fact that even that very morning the financial team was going to be putting a down payment on the house, God showed her a picture. And it was a picture of a very beautiful home in Pleasant Pastures that was full of women and children. But on the roof of that home a golden ribbon was attached. Barbie saw what she could only describe as a vision, that ribbon stretched out, far into the distance. And as Barbie followed it in her mind's eye, it stretched from the rooftop in Pleasant Pastures, to a rooftop on a lovely home on the outskirts of Wenatchee. The picture was very clear; there was no mistaking it. God was showing her a picture of two homes that were connected for the purpose of helping women find a safe place from which to escape some very desperate situations.

Barbie told Wendy about the home that was run by her church and had been in operation for over a year, completely full from the very beginning. Women coming out of homelessness had found their way to "Mercy House" and had been ministered to by the women who ran it. But recently they've had to turn women away for lack of room. They had gone as far as they could, even putting mattresses on the floor, which wasn't exactly in keeping with the state laws. But social workers were in a bind. The church wasn't taking any state funds, simply wanting to be completely self-supporting, but it was still important to make sure the environment was safe. The social workers, however, knew that Mercy House was the best run house in the state, and provided everything the woman would need and more. The ministry was run with an excellence they had never seen before. As a result, they contacted Mercy House often, whenever a real need arose. They'd look the other way when it was a bit too crowded, because they knew that it was definitely better than a single mom sleeping under a freeway over-pass with her kids.

But lately "Mercy House" had not only become overcrowded, they were also beginning to get more girls that were attempting to escape from prostitution. It was always a dangerous move to try to escape their pimp's control, but many tried and were successful because of places like "Mercy House." And that's where the "Wow!" came in. Barbie saw a distinct picture of two houses, connected by a beautiful gold ribbon. "Mercy House" would remain a ministry specifically for homeless women and children. But "Safe Haven" would be geared specifically for women coming out of prostitution. What God had shown Barbie was that "Safe Haven" would be under the direction of someone who had first-hand knowledge of the sex trade - and that person was Wendy. When she saw the picture God was giving her, and watched it become increasingly clear, the only word she could utter was "Wow!" Look at what God wants to do.

Barbie shared all of this with Wendy; the picture in her mind, the clarification of its meaning, even the results of a ministry of this nature. And sure enough, just like Barbie, the only response Wendy had when she'd heard the whole vision, was "Wow!"

Chapter 11

AS I SAT IN MY OFFICE ON MONDAY MORNING going through the attendance cards from yesterday's service, my mind was partially on the task at hand. The other part was caught up thinking about other things. Travis was already at school and had been in class for about an hour and a half. I wondered how he was doing so far with his new teacher, Ms. Conners. The thing that really made me happy, and quite relieved, was that Travis' new friends had come by to ride with him to school. That's a great feeling for a parent, knowing their kids have friends.

I thought about Wendy and her first meeting with Barbie. I breathed a silent prayer that all would go well, and that a deep and meaningful relationship could develop between these two ladies. I knew that Wendy didn't feel up to the task of being a pastor's wife, but I knew she was. And it wasn't just because she was my wife and I loved her with everything I had. It was more than that. She had some gifts that I recognized in her pretty early on; gifts that would go far in helping her be the person she truly wanted to be. She loved the Lord and desired to serve him with her whole life. That desire, when added to her gifts and abilities, in my estimation, made for a powerful combination. Maybe Barbie could mentor her and help her in some areas, but I knew, beyond a shadow of a doubt, that Wendy was going to be successful in all she did.

I was also once again marveling at what God had done concerning "Safe Haven." I was excited to hear a report from our finance team which, even right now, was in negotiations for the purchase of the property that would soon house women and children from a vast array of desperate situations. We certainly hadn't worked out all the details of the actual program yet, but first things first. Once we got the house secured, we'd kick it into high gear and start putting the finishing touches on the basic plan of ministry.

Of course, as I thought about the service, I also recalled the confrontation with Nick. I really had no idea where all of that was going to lead. I certainly hadn't heard from him since about 12:45 PM yesterday. I hadn't seen his gold Cadillac cruising by our house. The church hadn't been firebombed. The phone hadn't rung at odd hours during the night. So far, everything was peaceful. Maybe Nick just decided it wasn't worth all the fuss and even now was in his car heading back to Chicago. That's what I was hoping. But, I had the feeling that was wishful thinking. Nick didn't seem to be a guy who gave up too easily.

After sorting through the cards, I took out my Bible and several of my favorite commentaries, and began the process of studying for a new sermon. Sermon preparation is crucial for a pastor who preaches every week. You have to study and take notes and write - it's like writing a term paper once a week. And then, after you've written it, either in manuscript form or detailed notes, you have to practice your delivery. If you're a manuscript preacher, you need to go over it often enough that your delivery is smooth, and you don't appear to be simply reading it. On the other hand, if you preach from notes, you want to go over them enough that you know there won't be any obvious gaps in what you're saying. For example, if you make a note reminding yourself to tell the story of the experience you had while in the hospital, three years ago, you have to go over it enough to make sure you're accurate in relaying the story, as well as the story's application. In other words, preparation is the key to effective preaching. I've heard speakers, in my time, who just felt they could kind of get up there and wing it, and, to tell you the truth, it showed. They may have spoken for 40 minutes, but whether they really said anything was another matter entirely.

People come to church expecting to hear the Word of God. Now, sometimes the pressure of that idea can begin to wear on a pastor, especially when the week is so filled with other ministry tasks that sermon preparation seems to take second place. See, here's the thing about preaching every Sunday: it's kind of like delivering a baby on Sunday and then realizing you're pregnant again on Monday. There's seldom a break to even catch your breath. And because of that, I developed a little routine that works for me. It may not work for other preachers, but it does for me.

The basic strategy is to always be three or four sermons ahead. In other words, as a manuscript preacher, I want to have three or four manuscripts in my file drawers, with the dates they'll be preached. I started that early on in my ministry. In the early days, I only preached about once a month, but I'd have the sermon prepared at least two weeks in advance. And now that I'm preaching every Sunday, I'm always three to four sermons ahead. The rationale behind that may not make sense to my fellow preachers, but it does to me. You see, some weeks in ministry are absolutely horrendous, at least in terms of time. It's not impossible to have a major crisis situation arise that needs several hours of counseling and negotiation. Add to that a funeral service in the middle of the week, as well as a wedding rehearsal and dinner and a wedding and reception on Friday and Saturday, and your hours can get eaten up pretty quickly. Add to all of those other special events, your normal weekly duties, such as leadership team meetings, Wednesday night Bible studies, the Pastor's Prayer Fellowship, and a myriad of other worthwhile endeavors, and you can begin to understand the scope of the problem. And, of course, add to that time spent with your family, and you can begin to understand my philosophy of always being three to four sermons ahead. And if all of those elements I just mentioned all come together at once, in the same week - which has been known to happen, by the way - well, you can see the wisdom of my preparation style.

So, I'm sitting at my desk, beginning the study for a sermon that I'll be preaching a month from now. Later on in the day, I'll begin to go over the sermon for this coming Sunday. In fact, I'll go over it and preach it to myself about eight times, before I preach it to the congregation. That's a lot of preparation I know, but it's the only way that works for me.

As I'm sitting there, I look out the window and see Virginia Crupp walking up the sidewalk, obviously heading for the church. I remembered that this was the monthly meeting of the Martha Circle. They always do wonderful service projects for people in need, and I'm thankful for Virginia and her team of faithful ladies.

I'm lost in my thoughts, when suddenly I hear a commotion in the outer office. I hear Kathy, my secretary, speaking rather loudly and forcefully, though her voice is muffled through the walls of my office. I'm just about ready to stand up and go into her office to see what the commotion is all about, when suddenly my door is flung open and I see Nick standing there, in a posture of anger and aggression. The first thing I notice is that he's not armed. He's not pointing a gun my way and, as far as I know, he doesn't have a rocket- launcher behind his back and so I relax just a little bit, but still find myself in an on-guard position.

Kathy, who's been the church secretary for the past 25 years, protests and then tells me that she tried to get him to wait until she buzzed me, but he just stormed in. I told her that it was fine and that we could have our little discussion now and see if we can clear this up, once and for all. Now, Kathy had no idea of what had gone on after church with Nick and The Tanks and me, so she was totally in the dark. I told her not to worry; Nick and I just had a little misunderstanding. But it might be good for her to just remain where she was and watch the moments unfold for a while. This might really be of interest to her and to some others, depending on how the conversation went.

Nick stormed right up to me and reiterated what he said yesterday. He reminded me that Wendy worked for him, and that she owed him. And *I* reminded Nick that we settled that yesterday; she agreed to be a dancer in his club, and he agreed to send Travis to that private school, as an added bonus. She kept her end of the bargain, and he had kept his. That's it - case closed - everybody got what they wanted. So, I told him to let it go and let's just move on.

Well, Nick launched into a loud and demanding tirade, declaring that nobody takes advantage of Nick Salerno. If they try, they'll find themselves in the river, sporting a pair of cement shoes. I thought that was pretty dramatic, even for Nick.

I told him that Wendy was my wife, and that I wasn't going to let anything in her past, stand in the way of what we had right now. And so, I said, "Nick, you need to let this go right now. Wendy's staying right here; you're not dragging her back to Chicago. And not only that, I'm not paying you the $12,000 you somehow insist she owes you. That wasn't the agreement you both made and you know it."

Nick looked at me, turning red in the face. I was standing about 2 feet in front of him and he got up close, until his face was just inches from mine. He gave me his most threatening look, and in a voice filled with mockery and derision he said, "Look here, preacher-man. I'm not letting you, a weak, pretty-boy, pansy-of- a-man, tell me what to do. You're going to fork over my 12,000 bucks, or I'm going to bust your face up so bad, you'll look like a deluxe pizza. I've fought some pretty tough guys in my life and I've never lost - never! So, if you're not into pain and suffering, you'd better do what I say, and do it now, otherwise you and I are going to go at it, and I'm going to clean your clock."

I was just about to speak when Kathy said, "You know, Mr. Nick. I don't think you want to do that. That wouldn't be a good idea." Now, by this time, Virginia Crupp, and her team of ladies, had heard the commotion and had come into the outer office to see what was going on. When they heard what Kathy had said, they chimed in their sentiments also. "Yeah, that just wouldn't end well, mister. You don't want to do that."

Nick looked at the ladies and laughed. "Are you kidding me? What? Are you going to call the police? Do you even have police in this podunk town? What? Is Barney Fife going to come and arrest me? Not too worried about that, sister. And those two goons from yesterday are nowhere to be seen. It's just preacher-man and me and you're telling me that teaching him a lesson wouldn't be a good idea. Well, I got news for you - Nick Salerno isn't scared of anybody, even the Man Upstairs or His flunky."

Nick looked at me, anger coming off him in waves. I watched him closely; watched his eyes and saw the punch coming. He swung at me with his right fist and I side-stepped slightly, turning my head so that his fist barely glanced off my right cheek. Some of the ladies let out a gasp, while Kathy picked up the phone to call the police. I told her not to do that - Nick and I were going to work these things out, between the two of us.

Nick looked at me and said, "Oh, you think so, huh? You think we're just going to talk this thing out?" And then he came at me again, this time throwing a strong left jab at my eye. Once again, I had anticipated the punch, and shifted, turning to the side, allowing his fist to graze the left side of my face. It didn't hurt, and didn't connect well, but I'd probably have a scrape there that I'd have to explain to Wendy.

I looked at Nick and said, "You know, I think that this has gone far enough. You need to back off and get out of my office. I'm not messing with you anymore. Let it go Nick and let's just walk out of here, agreeing to disagree. You go your way and I'll go mine. It's not worth it; just let it go. I don't want to do this."

Nick smirked and said, "I bet you don't preacher-man, but I'm not done." And with that, he swung again. I could see that he put everything behind it and if it would've landed, it could have done some serious damage. However, the operative word here is *if*. *If* the punch would've landed. But it didn't. I threw up my left arm, blocking his fist, while at the same time hitting him on the jaw with a well-placed right cross. Nick fell to the floor in my office and was out cold.

I asked Kathy to get a cold cloth, and within a minute or two, she was back, wiping Nick's brow. His eyes fluttered open as he looked around the room, trying to focus in on the situation. "What happened?" As Nick spoke he stammered, his tongue thick in his mouth. Kathy continued wiping his forehead and simply said, "I told you this wasn't a good idea, but you wouldn't listen to me. These other ladies told you the same thing, but you had to try it your way, didn't you?"

Nick looked at me and mumbled, "What kind of a preacher are you, going around fighting people? What happened to all the peace and love stuff you guys always talk about? Nobody's ever knocked me out - nobody's ever gotten the best of Nick Salerno. Where'd you learn to hit like that anyway?" I looked at Nick and simply said, "Collegiate Boxing Scholarship. And just so you know Nick, I believe in living at peace with people, but sometimes even Christians are called to defend themselves, and the people they love. Besides, it was really quite a biblical reaction." Nick looked at me as he was starting to get up and said, "How do you figure that?" And I said, "Well Nick, the Bible says that when someone smacks us, were supposed to turn the other cheek - and that's what I did. I turned the other cheek. But when you came at me a third time, I just figured that all bets were off and I was free to defend myself. And so here we are."

Nick looked at me for several seconds and rubbed his jaw. It was going to be a beautiful shade of purple, very shortly. He sighed heavily and said, "Well preacher-man, you're not like any other man-of-the-cloth I've ever heard about, but I figure, if you could get the best of Nick Salerno, you're no pansy. And I respect that. I would just appreciate it if you and these ladies here, would keep it to yourselves. It's bad for the rep, you know?" I looked at the ladies, and then at Nick, and said, "Okay, here's the deal: obviously I'm going to have to tell Wendy and The Tanks, since they've been involved in this from the beginning, but what do you think ladies? Can this be our little secret?" They all looked at Nick and assured him that his secret would never leave this office.

He looked at me and said, "Well, preacher-man, I suppose I'll be going for now. But I'm still going to be hanging around for a while; there are just a few things I need to think about and check on. You alright with that?" I told him that was fine, but I just didn't want any more trouble, especially for Wendy. I mentioned that the next time, I might not pull my punch. Nick's eyes got wide and he said, "You pulled that punch?" And I laughed and said, "Nah, I hit you with everything I had. I was just kidding you." Nick smiled slightly, looked me up and down and said, "You know preacher-man, you're all right. You would've done great on the streets of Chicago." I didn't know if I should take that as a compliment or what, but I decided to give Nick the benefit of the doubt and take it.

As Nick turned to walk out, he looked back and said, "I might be seeing you again preacher-man. This whole thing kind of interests me." I looked at him and said, "Come on back anytime - and Nick? Why don't you just call me John?"

He nodded and walked out, still rubbing his sore jaw. I wondered if I would see Nick again, and under what circumstances. Either way was fine with me; I was just glad we had our little come-to-Jesus meeting, and nobody got seriously hurt.

After Nick left, the ladies all crowded into my office, chattering away like magpies. I think they felt that this was the most exciting thing to happen in Pleasant Pastures since the Peterson girls went on that hike and ran into a bear. The girls ran one way and the bear ran the other. But it was the talk of the town for quite some time. But this beat that all to pieces. The only problem was, they had promised not to tell anybody, and I was pretty sure it was killing them. But hey - a promise, is a promise.

Chapter 12

NICK SAT THERE LOUNGING IN THE HOT TUB at the Enzian Hotel in Leavenworth. He'd been staying there since he arrived in town last Thursday. It was a pretty good joint: good food, nice surroundings, located in the heart of a little Bavarian-style town. But right now, the best thing about the place was the hot tub, and the relief it brought him.

Nick's jaw was pretty sore from the blow that preacher-man had successfully landed. Who knew the guy had gone to school on a "Collegiate Boxing Scholarship?" That would've been nice to know ahead of time; maybe his strategy would've been different. Maybe he could've brought Ed and Louie with him, for some added muscle.

The only problem with that was that he was afraid his two henchmen would've gotten carried away and done some serious damage. And if Nick was honest with himself, truly honest, he didn't want that. Nick had found a way to be pretty successful without having to resort to a lot of violence. You get carried away with violence and you're going to wind up behind bars, for a long, long time. Besides, as Nick ruminated on the situation, he realized once again that he didn't really like violence; it made him physically ill. The thing he'd always relied on was his reputation.

And yet, in his heart, buried deep inside, Nick knew that his reputation was pretty much smoke and mirrors. Now to be sure, Nick had won the reputation as a guy you never wanted to mess with when he was just a young street tough in high school. He and his cousin had gotten into several fights and had been victorious every time. These two guys could really fight; that was the word on the street. Stories began to circulate about some of their battles and when Nick would overhear someone relaying the episode, he knew there was a great deal of exaggeration. And that's if there was any truth in it at all. Some of the stories Nick heard about his mean and nasty battles, never even happened. But the key part of the rep thing was that people *thought* they happened. It didn't really matter if they did or not; if people thought they did, that was good enough. And if the police ever came looking for you, trying to gather evidence because they'd heard the same story on the streets, they'd never been able to pin anything on him, because it never happened. There'd be no evidence - there'd be no eye-witnesses. Those stories always seemed to be confirmed by a friend of a friend, or my cousin's best friend's, sister's fiancé.

Nick knew that in terms of violence, other than the fights he got into in high school, he was pretty clean. His reputation may have painted one picture, but in reality, real life was much different. But as long as people kept believing the rep, he was good to go. Besides, Nick had always felt that the whole violence thing, getting even, was greatly overrated. He'd rather spend his time making money, something that would benefit him, and actually, someday, his wife and kids.

Nick hadn't had time for the whole family gig; he was too busy with his businesses, and a family would just get in the way. But he didn't want it to be that way forever. He wanted to find the right girl and settle down and maybe raise a flock of kids - kids who would always look up to him - call him dad - and want to hang out with him, because he was their hero. He had to admit, that sounded pretty good.

It's not like Nick didn't have any women in his life. There'd always been women who had succumbed to his good looks and charm. And the more successful he became, and the bigger his reputation, the more women seemed to throw themselves at him. Lately, he'd been pretty successful at always having a gorgeous babe on his arm, wherever he went. But the thing that bothered Nick was that all of the women were basically one-night stands. They were more of a statement, than anything else. Look at the hot woman Nick Salerno has on his arm. Man, if only I could have his life - he's really got it made in the shade.

Nick sat back and let the waters relax his muscles. He thought back over his life and realized that a lot of it was nothing more than illusion. He presented himself in a certain way, but when it was all stripped off, there really wasn't a lot of substance there. A slew of beautiful women and one-night stands wasn't exactly fulfilling, although he knew that it certainly gave off that impression - at least it did to certain people. But Nick knew the truth. That kind of life is pretty empty. He might even use the word boring. Yeah, that's it. Despite the women, despite all the money he had and would flash around, life just seemed boring. It's like he didn't have a real purpose in life that meant anything. Oh, his clubs provided entertainment for the men who came and nursed their drinks and lusted after his dancers, but at the end of the night, what did it all mean in the great scheme of things?

Nick absentmindedly rubbed his sore jaw that was beginning to turn purple and green. He thought back to just about 12 hours ago when he was in the preacher-man's office and received the surprise of his life. That guy could pack a punch. He should've gone on to be a prizefighter. With his good looks, and his natural strength and ability, he could have really been something. He'd be raking in tons of dough right now and be riding pretty high, instead of living in a little 1200 sq. ft. house, next to the church. Why would this guy settle for something like this? A beautiful, handsome couple like them ought to be able to go a lot further, especially if they had someone coaching them.

He thought about that a bit more and a plan began to come together in his mind. And it was a plan that would benefit them both. It was a natural really, and he could see the possibility of some pretty quick expansion. Now, he would take a modest 30% cut of all the profits, but if the enterprise grew big enough that could wind up being pretty huge. The really good thing about it was the fact that his personal overhead would be almost zip. Very little out of his own pocket, but the dividends could be great.

Nick began to formulate the plan and then went on to fill in the details. He thought back to the last two days as he watched the garage sale and saw the number of people that spent all Saturday working on this project, for free. When you can get people to work for free, you're going to save a ton of money in salary and benefits. However he did it, preacher-man, or John, as he preferred to be called, was able to motivate people to give up their Saturday to come and work at a garage sale.

And then, in church the next day, John and Wendy reported how much the garage sale had netted them - $4000 - and all of that was pure profit. They also took up what was called an offering, and people were putting in checks and cash all over that room. And it's not like anybody was holding a gun to their heads; they gave the money willingly. At least, it looked like that. I don't know, Nick thought, maybe they were somehow being forced to give by some kind of a subtle, but perceived threat. Or, maybe they been given a good incentive - if you give, you wind up getting this - it's amazing what people will do if they think somethings in it for them.

He didn't know how much money came in through the offering, but judging from the crowd there, it had to be several thousand. But it didn't stop there. When they didn't reach their goal, the old guy stood up and recommended that they take another special offering to make up for the shortfall. And the amazing thing about that was the fact that nobody gave it a second thought. They just reached in their purses and their wallets and pulled out their cash and check books and gave. As Nick thought about that he began to do the math. If there was $4000 from the garage sale and $3000 for the special offering and let's say, given the size of the crowd, another $3000 in the regular offering, that's $10,000 in just about a 24-hour period. That's huge, especially when you figure there's very little overhead to speak of.

What if you could take that experience and multiply it many times over? Lots of people low overhead, a great incentive to give, leaders with charisma and the ability to get people to follow them. You couldn't lose. He even began to factor in something he'd remembered from his days in Catholic school. He thought back to the time when the kid with the big nose, asked the sister how the church got their money, and she talked about several different ways that people gave. But one way, the sister said that a lot of people gave, was the idea of a tithe. And a tithe meant 10% of all they made. So, for every $1000 a person made, $100 of it would go to the church. Well, it doesn't take a math genius to know how quickly that would add up.

But what's the overall incentive for people to give? Now he knew that this past weekend the incentive was to give to this house for homeless women. People love to give to causes. It makes them feel good about themselves. As Nick thought that through, he realized what could happen if that became just one incentive for people to give. At the most, the house could support maybe six women and their children. That's not many, but what would happen if you challenged not just the 200 people at Pleasant Pastures to give to the cause? What if you had 5 or 10, or even more churches that would give to keep that house going? So instead of 200 people giving to the house for support, you had 2000 people giving. That's 10 times as much as he saw come in this weekend.

And taking it further, what if those 2000 people in the 10 churches also gave 10% of their income, and yet the overhead at each church remained fairly low? If everybody seems so willing to donate their time, as well as their money, there'd be no need to hire staff, other than the lead guy who kept the wheels turning.

The more Nick considered this, the more excited he got. But he was still trying to figure out what the overall incentive for people to give could be. It can't be just the house for homeless women; there has to be a grander incentive, one that's far reaching and is timeless. Projects come and go all the time. But what incentive would just keep on going with very little energy having to be expended on its propagation? In other words, what would keep people giving on a regular basis, no matter what? All the special projects would be frosting on the cake. But what would the overall incentive be to get people to fork over their money consistently?

And then it hit Nick. He knew what it was. He should've seen it earlier, but it suddenly became clear as a bell. This whole church thing was one big protection racket. Just like in Chicago. Some Italian guy named Luigi opens a restaurant, a family-owned business. And things are going great. But one day a couple of guys come into the restaurant and offer to sell Luigi some insurance on his business. It's a plan that will protect you against all kinds of potential disasters. The price is 5% of your weekly profits. It's a pretty low price to pay for peace of mind. Well, Luigi, not really understanding what these two guys are getting at, says, "No thanks. I think we'll be fine." The guys look at Luigi and say, "Are you sure? This is very important for you and the future success of your business." And Luigi says, "Nah, I'm not worried about it. Now, you guys need to take a hike; I got a lot of work to do." The guys say "Okay" and walk out the door, just as polite as can be. But, later that night, about 2 o'clock in the morning, Luigi's restaurant catches fire, and though it's not a total loss, it does enough damage to hurt him pretty significantly. The next day, the two guys are back, as Luigi's surveying the damage. They mention how important insurance is. It can keep things like this from happening, if he catches their drift. And sure enough, Luigi catches their drift. If he pays for protection, things like this won't happen. If he doesn't, all kinds of bad things can come his way. Luigi finally agrees to the protection plan and he never has another problem. Funny how that works, isn't it?

When you boil it right down to its essence, the whole church racket is a protection plan. You give your money, and we'll keep you out a hell. He remembered back to his days at Catholic school and the times they would talk about that horrible place of torment that as far as Nick could tell, was for people who did more bad things than good things. And who does more good things than bad? Nobody in his crowd, that's for sure. So, Nick supposed escaping hell was a pretty good incentive.

But he still wasn't happy with it. As a kid the idea of hell kind of lost its punch after a while. Even as a kid he began to joke about it saying, "Well, that's where all my friends are going to be; it'll be like one big party." No, hell didn't seem to be a lasting incentive. People kind of gave up on it because they weren't really too sure how to measure if they were bad enough to go, or good enough to miss it. No, there had to be an incentive that was more positive; something that everybody liked to think about. And as Nick continued to chew on that he realized that the positive incentive was there all the time, on the other end of the negative spectrum. He began to turn the possibilities over in his mind.

What if instead of trying to scare people out of hell, what if we try to entice them with heaven? It's the perfect protection racket. You buy into the plan and we'll make sure to keep you safe, and far away from the negative things that can happen when you're not signed up for the deal. And not only are you protected from bad things, we're going to promise you good things, marvelous benefits, for you and your family; benefits that won't just last a lifetime, but way beyond: they'll last forever. Now, Nick realized that the idea of an eternal paradise wasn't a new thing, for crying out loud. People in every culture had some kind of an idea or picture about the afterlife; it was a pretty universal theme.

But what if he could set up an organization of churches that went a step beyond in their message? What if it wasn't just about pie-in-the-sky-by-and-by-when-you-die? What if it was that, yes, but what if in addition, the protection plan promised you benefits now? What if you could somehow convince people that their life could be easier here on earth? What if you could get them to believe that they'd reap all kinds of benefits by investing in their plan: benefits like more money at their disposal, their greatest and most exciting dreams would come true, their health would be better, their influence could be greater, their kids would be happier, the problems that other people have to deal with would be almost nonexistent if you're a part of the plan. And if you did wind up with a problem, you would have hundreds, if not thousands, of other folks just like you, who are in the plan and who would come and help you out? And to top it all off, you were promised, you were assured, beyond a shadow of a doubt, that when you died, after a long and happy life, you'd go someplace even better?

As Nick continued to toss ideas back-and-forth, a master plan began to develop and take shape in his mind's eye. He organized it into steps, just to make sure that he could see it clearly. It was a business model, something he was going to adapt to this whole church scheme. He organized his steps as he lounged in the hot tub. He'd commit them to paper later that evening in his room, but for now, he enjoyed the process of working it out in his mind.

Step one: *Fully develop the incentive package*: what would they get for their money? What could they promise people that would have a lasting draw?

Step two: *Share the idea with the preacher*: Let him see the great possibilities for expansion and growth, taking advantage of the same gifts he's already using, but to a greater effectiveness.

Step three: *Develop a full-proof rationale*: John, you need this; your church needs this; your people need this. This will enhance the quality of their life and give them a hope and a future. And after all, isn't that what you want? You wouldn't want to deny them all of this, would you?

Step four: *Begin to recruit other men with the needed gifts*: Help them to visualize what could happen if they would join his plan.

Step five: *Look for other buildings to hold services in*: Churches, Grange halls, schools. Anyplace would work, as long as the rent is cheap, and it provides people a place to gather.

Step six: *Install one pastor at each location*: Their job will be to gather as many people around them as possible, using the same message of joy and happiness, now and for eternity.

Step seven: *Require a minimum commitment from all members of 10% of their income*: A clearly understood commitment will give them the satisfaction of a personal investment in something bigger than themselves. It may take some time to convince everyone, but the time spent will bring huge dividends in the future.

Step eight: *Establish the goal of 10 new churches in one ye*ar: Each church should bring in a minimum of $20,000 per month, or $240,000 per year. Figuring in the overhead, that should leave a profit of $150,000 per year, or $1.5 million for the group - 30% for Nick, and the rest divided between the 10 pastors, for their salaries. Their tax-exempt, 501-C3 status as a church, will keep their profit even higher.

Step nine: *Train John Larson to be the leader*: He would train the pastors and then keep them on track in terms of the message and the goals. He would also reap further significant financial benefits for him and his family.

Step 10: *Expand outward by 20% per year*: The more churches involved, the greater the profits for everyone: the ultimate pyramid scheme.

Nick was excited about his new idea. It made perfect sense; people were looking for a way to make their lives happier and more meaningful. This would ensure that. You also had all the do-gooders who wanted to "make a difference." So, throw a few projects into the mix. Open up a few houses for homeless moms and kids, or for runaway teens, or those with drug habits. Open a house for overweight cats, for heaven's sake. Who cares, just as long as they keep bringing in donations?

As Nick went to his room to write what he had already pictured in his mind, he knew that his idea was going to generate millions. And 30% of those millions were going to be his. He was the mastermind; he was the one who understood how people thought, and what they felt they needed in life to make them happy. He may not have understood about all this religion stuff, but he was pretty sure they could develop something that would get people to buy in, hook, line and sinker. People are always willing to follow a charismatic leader who gives the impression of really caring about them.

Look at that guy, just about a year ago, who talked his entire church of 900 people into drinking grape Kool-Aid that had been poisoned. This guy used his charisma to lead 900 people to their deaths. What a waste. And what a schmuck he was! If he had any vision at all, he could've turned their fierce loyalty into millions, but he totally blew the opportunity.

But Nick had a better way, one that would actually be good for people, while at the same time fattening his wallet considerably.

Nick was already rich, but in his thinking, you could never have too much money.

The crucial challenge, however, was to somehow convince John, the preacher-man, to buy into the plan. He and Wendy were the key to its success. A good-looking, talented couple like them would attract other leaders who wanted to be just like them. Those leaders would then spend their time attracting ordinary people who wanted to be like *their* leaders and live the successful lifestyle *they* saw modeled. This idea couldn't lose. Protection plans and pyramid schemes have been around a long time. Why not now, in the church?

But John and Wendy were the key. He had to plan his approach very carefully. What would it take to get them to see the beauty of his plan? He was going to have to think on that for a while.

Chapter 13

THEIR HEADS WERE BOWED AND JOHN'S RESO-
nant voice was thanking God for the meal that was set before
them. Wendy had lovingly pulled out the good china that
John's folks had given them for a wedding present. It was a complete
set of Lenox that his mom had received on her wedding day, but hardly
used anymore. It was still lovely and obviously had been well cared
for, but John's folks had several sets of china that they had accumu-
lated over the years. So, they passed the entire 12-piece set on to their
son and daughter-in-law, along with the 12-piece set of sterling silver,
again one of several sets that had come their way over the decades.

They were celebrating Travis's first day at school and were serving one of his favorite meals - Sloppy Joe's. True, it was a little strange to be serving that rather informal meal on good china in the dining room, but they were celebrating today. They didn't know of any etiquette rule that forbade the consuming of Sloppy Joe's in the dining room and on the finest of china. Besides, it was a celebration; the rules could certainly be bent this one time.

As he started eating, Travis began to regale them with a minute by minute description of the events of his day. He was very relieved when the neighborhood kids had showed up at the parsonage to invite Travis to ride with them to school on their bikes. To Travis, that meant he was already accepted as part of the neighborhood gang. Upon arriving, the kids showed him around the school itself and then made sure that he knew where his classroom was. As he walked into the classroom, Ms. Conners was there to greet the incoming students. Travis had met her a few days ago at the "Get Acquainted Orientation" for new students, and he liked her right off the bat. He wouldn't tell anybody this, but he thought that Ms. Conners was a fox. She was very pretty, and in Travis's way of thinking, was going to be easy to look at all year. In fact, he was a little concerned that he had already developed a slight crush on her. Man, that's the first time that's ever happened, Travis thought to himself. All of my other teachers were old and smelled like mothballs. That might've been a slight exaggeration, but not by much.

Ms. Conners had realized at the orientation that Travis was a pretty exceptional kid. She had seen his past test scores and had enjoyed a few minutes of conversation with him. The only way she could describe those few moments of interaction was that it was like talking to an adult who was trapped in a child's body. She, along with some of the other faculty, were concerned about his being so far ahead that he might just tune out from sheer boredom. And so, she devised a little plan that she felt would not only help him get acquainted faster with his schoolmates, but would also challenge him scholastically.

As Travis walked through the door, Ms. Conners realized that he was early and all the other kids were still on the playground waiting for the last bell. They greeted each other and Ms. Conners told him that it was nice to see him again and hoped that he'd had a good summer. He assured her that he did and then asked how hers was. What kid thinks to ask a question like that of an adult? Ms. Conners was once again quite impressed. She reminded Travis of the conversation from a few weeks ago about skipping him a grade but how his folks were concerned about his socialization, particularly since he was the new kid in town. Travis indicated that he was fine with the decision and was positive that it was going to be a great year. Ms. Conners looked at him and said, "Travis, let me lay a little challenge on you. Is that all right?" Travis shrugged and said, "Sure." He tried to come across nonchalant, but inside he was getting a little excited. Ms. Conners made her proposal. "Travis, what would you think of being my right-hand man and spending part of your day tutoring some of your classmates who are struggling in an area of their studies? They're smart kids, but they just need a little help in certain areas. And I've discovered that sometimes a little extra help from one of their classmates can make all the difference in the world. I've got my eye on you, and three others, who I think would be very helpful in this project. What do you think Travis? Would you help me this year?" Travis was absolutely delighted to be asked but in an effort to maintain his recent desire to be cool, he simply said, "Yeah, I could do that for you, no sweat." Ms. Conners, who understood young boys pretty well, said, "That's great Travis. I know it's going to be a wonderful year for all of us." And then Travis headed for his desk which was placed in alphabetical order. That meant that he was going to sit just about in the middle of the classroom. He was close to the front, which provided him with a good view of the blackboard, as well as Ms. Conners. Yep, it was going to be a pretty good year.

He shared all of this with John and Wendy, with the exception of his secret crush. He couldn't bring himself to talk about that and, in all honesty, probably never would. But he was very excited about being a tutor for some of the other kids. He actually felt honored to be asked and hoped that he could genuinely make a difference in some of his classmates' lives. Sometimes it's just a matter of one or two principles suddenly becoming clear that makes the path you're on so much better. He hoped he could help clear the way for others.

John and Wendy listened to Travis talk about his first day and inwardly breathed a sigh of relief. We're going to make it and Travis is going to shine. The year was looking better all the time. It'll be an adventure to see how this tutoring project plays out, but both John and Wendy were convinced that nothing but positive results would come of it.

After dinner, Travis headed off to his room to start his home-work. It wasn't a hard assignment but getting homework the first day was kind of a bummer, at least according to Travis. But John and Wendy knew that Travis would actually enjoy writing the one-page theme on "My Summer of Adventure." Both John and Wendy won-dered how much he'd actually share about the experiences of the last several months. The whole story was indeed very adventuresome and it'll be interesting to hear Travis's take on it.

Wendy cleared the dishes, while John started in washing. Pretty soon Wendy came back and picked up a towel and began to wipe them dry, marveling once again at how much she valued their partnership in both the big and small things. Doing the dishes may not seem like much to somebody else, but being able to do them with her husband was truly a blessing. Others may not see it that way, but Wendy did. She'd been on the other end too long and therefore greatly cherished her new life; every moment of it.

When they were finished they sat down with a cup of coffee and began to share about their respective days. Wendy shared about her meeting with Barbie and how excited she was to see if what Barbie saw was actually going to happen. The idea of two homes for women in need had been eating away at Wendy all day. Could they really do this? Could they really have two homes that were linked together with their two churches in partnership? The task felt overwhelming to Wendy and she found herself second-guessing the vision all day. Where would we get the money to support it? Sure, we had the down payment on the house, but what about the monthly mortgage, not to mention the day-to-day expenses? And if, as Barbie suggested, Wendy would oversee the Safe Haven home for women coming out of prostitution and other forms of the sex trade, how would that work? Would she quit at the diner and take on a job that really wouldn't pay much, if anything, at first? And what about the danger? Women leaving prostitution almost always had a pimp controlling their every move. If they were going to leave the life, an escape plan would certainly have to be put into place. And Wendy knew how scary, and yet necessary, that was if women were going to break the bondage.

Wendy was thankful that she had Mondays off because she didn't really think she'd be much good at the diner. She was processing all she and Barbie had talked about, and though it made her nervous, the fact is, the challenge of it, the excitement of the possibility, overrode any of the qualms Wendy had for the project. She could see God all over this and was very pleased when John expressed excitement also. And true to form, John began to lay out the steps to making that vision become a reality. He was already on the fourth action step, his eyes aglow with the excitement of a new project. But when it seemed that he might go on forever in this frenzied state of determination to get it done, she gently touched his arm and brought him back to reality. Wendy said, "John, could we just take a break for a minute? If this is going to happen, and I pray that it does, and if God wants me to oversee it, and I'm becoming more convinced that this is His plan, if this is from Him and He's going to accomplish this part of it through me, I need to hear from Him myself. I need to hear about His plans and goals, not mine, and not yours, no offense. The counsel of others will come later, but I need Him to solidify His plans to me first, so that I can be absolutely sure. What do you think about just letting the vision cook a little bit? I need to let it ruminate a while and see where God is going to take us. Are you all right with that?"

John looked at Wendy and said, "Of course I'm all right with that. I need to step out of the way and let God speak to you person- ally. He may have something totally different planned and you need to be the one to discern that. I'm going to step back and just pray. But if you need me for anything, I'll be right here and we'll talk it over. But for now, just know I'm praying for you." Wendy thanked John for his willingness to put his "can do/must do" personality aside and just let God and Wendy figure this out together. She leaned over and kissed him on the cheek, knowing how hard it was for John to just let a challenge rest.

And then Wendy asked John to share about his day. How was it being back to work? How was Kathy, his secretary? Did she and her family have a good vacation also? Wendy kept asking for details about all the mundane things that go on daily in any church, and every time John would answer, she'd have a new question right on the tip of her tongue. Finally, John looked at her and smiled and said, "Honey, why are you so nervous? Why don't you just go ahead and ask me what's on your mind? You don't really want to acknowledge it, but we've got a situation, don't we? What you're really wondering about is if anything happened with Nick. Isn't that right? Did I see him? Was there any kind of a confrontation or did he just jump in his Caddie and head back to Chicago? Isn't that what you really want to know?"

Wendy nodded and said, "Oh John, I've been so worried. I was afraid that he'd come by the church and try to start something. Or that he'd see you on the road and try to run you off. I was even worried that maybe he'd come after me, or worse yet, I thought he might try to settle the score using Travis as a bargaining chip. I know I worked for Nick, but I'm not really sure what he's capable of. And it's very scary. I didn't want to alarm Travis, or you for that matter, but after my time with Barbie, and as I began to drive home, my anxiety level just shot up. I've been trying to hold it together so that we could all have a pleasant dinner, but now I think it's time to talk about it. How scared should we be? What if he's really as tough and violent as his reputation says? How much trouble are we really in?"

John looked at his beautiful wife of just over two weeks and he said something that caught her by surprise. He said, "Wendy, let me tell you something that ought to set your mind at ease. Yesterday I called my friend, Bill Parker, who's on the police force in Minneapolis. I told him about the situation with Nick and asked if he could find out a little more about him. How dangerous is he anyway? What should our level of concern be over this? Bill has a buddy on the police force with ties to Chicago, and he assured me that he'd look into it first thing Monday morning. Well, I got a call from Bill this afternoon and he told me to sit down, if I wasn't already, because I wasn't going to believe the news. This Nick Salerno, big-time gangster from Chicago, who threatens to drop people in the river, wearing cement shoes? Well, guess what? He's a fraud. He's a choir boy for heaven's sake. Bill and his friend looked him up and he doesn't even have a rap sheet. He's never been arrested for anything, not even a traffic violation. The only time he was behind bars was for a few hours in Juvie. He'd broken a guys' nose in a fight when he was in high school, but everyone who was interviewed said that Nick was attacked and was just defending himself, and so they let him go and no charges were ever filed. Big, tough Nick Salerno owns a couple of sleazy topless joints, but legally they're both legitimate. He may have tried to ratchet things up a bit with you, but when that failed, he stopped trying. He never did break into the prostitution racket."

The revelation that John had just shared left Wendy stunned. How could this be? Everybody knew how tough Nick Salerno was. His reputation in Chicago was huge and nobody in their right mind would mess with Nick, not if you valued your kneecaps. But this was a real game changer. Wendy's anxiety began to subside almost immediately and she experienced that feeling of safety and security once again, that she'd come to relish with John by her side.

Wendy looked at John with obvious relief on her face and said, "So we dodged a bullet, although probably not literally, given what your friend Bill says? But is that it? Is Nick gone and we're never going to hear from him again? He hasn't tried to make contact with you?" At that, John looked away for just a second. Wendy picked up on it right away and said, "Wait a minute. What aren't you telling me? Come on John, I'm a big girl. Tell me everything that happened today. You saw Nick, didn't you?"

John relayed the story of the early morning confrontation with Nick, with Virginia Crupp and the ladies looking on. In response to Wendy's quest for details he told her that Nick had thrown two punches at him but he'd sidestepped both of them. Both punches had connected, but just barely. He also told her that he had let Nick connect, but had control of the amount of damage they could do. When she asked him why he did that, he reminded her of the passage about turning the other cheek. Wendy was processing this in her mind when suddenly, it all came together and made sense. "You can't be serious? You didn't really do that, did you? You did, didn't you? You let him hit you twice, once on each cheek. I'm a little afraid to ask what you did then. What'd you do John?" John looked a little sheepish and then said, "I hit him once and knocked him on his can!"

"You didn't!"

"Yeah, I did."

"In front of all the ladies?"

"Yep."

"Were they shocked?"

"I don't think so."

"So, you're the punching-preacher now?"

"Evidently."

"You're the Joe Palooka of pastors."

Silence.

"You're the right-hook Reverend."

Silence.

"You're the clobbering-clergy."

"Enough."

Wendy was smiling broadly, absolutely gleeful at this turn of events. She came over to John, kissing the knuckles on both fists, clasped her hands together, and with a flutter of her eyelashes breathed, "My hero." John threw a dishtowel at her and they both started laughing, finally getting control of themselves when Travis yelled, "Hey… what's going on out there?"

They sat back down and Wendy asked for the rest of the details in the Nick Salerno/John Larson battle to the death. John told her the rest of the story, leaving nothing out. Wendy looked at John with questioning eyes and said, "So, is that it then? Is he gone?" John told her that no, Nick wasn't gone yet. In fact, he's intrigued by what he's seen so far and has decided to hang around a while. Wendy asked John what Nick could possibly find so interesting around here, but John had no clue. He just knew that Nick said he'd be here for a while.

John looked at Wendy and asked, "What do you think we ought to do?" Wendy smiled, and with a reflective twinkle in her eye said, "I think we ought to invite Nick over for lunch."

Chapter 14

"**Y**OU'RE NOT SERIOUS ABOUT THAT, ARE you? Honey, after all Nick's put you through, you'd be willing to have him in our home? He was intent on using you to line his own pockets, through dancing and then through prostitution. How can you want to invite him for lunch? Whenever I think about him, it gets me extremely angry all over again at the way he treated you. What's going on with you, Wendy?"

John was genuinely perplexed at his wife's attitude and needed to understand her rationale for the sudden change. He asked her to explain her thinking. Wendy took a few minutes to gather her thoughts, so that it would hopefully become as clear to John, as it was to her.

Wendy began speaking slowly at first, as if she was just processing this new thought herself. She said, "John, I look back over my life and the chaos I was trapped in, and I see very little light. My life was dark and felt very meaningless. There were a few bright spots obviously, Travis being the major one. But even though Travis is the love of my life, his coming on the scene was a result of a very difficult time of despair in my life. It's not like he was born out of a deep love relationship that I had with his father. I don't even know who his father is. But what I've come to understand these many months is that what the enemy meant for evil, God meant for good. God turned it around and brought incredible good out of it. Only God can do something like that and I ought to know that more than anybody. My whole life was a mess until I allowed God to step into the picture. If I hadn't listened to God's voice when I did, we wouldn't be sitting here right now having this conversation. If anybody has a story about redemption and grace, it's me. You know that better than anybody."

John had to agree with his wife. Working for Nick may have been good for her financially, but the cost in terms of her personal self-esteem was extremely high. And to follow through with Nick's grandiose plans for her would have left Wendy a broken shell of a person, in a very short period of time. Given that fact, inviting Nick to their home seemed to John to be self-inflicted torture. Why do that? Why open up the painful memories of the past that John knew Wendy still struggled with at times? Why not just leave Nick alone and let him head back to Chicago and out of their lives forever?

John expressed his misgivings to Wendy and she nodded her head in understanding. "I get it John," Wendy said. "And I don't blame you one bit for feeling like that, but let me tell you where I'm coming from. You see, these past four months of my life have been the best

I've ever had. As far as I'm concerned, if my life ended right now, I'd leave this earth rejoicing over what God has blessed me with in these last months. Coming here and meeting you, falling in love with both you and the church is light-years beyond what I ever thought could happen to me. And I owe my joy, my satisfaction to the Lord. In fact, I owe my life to Him. He took me out of a pretty deep pit of ugliness and brought me into the bright sunshine of a totally new day; a day that I would have never imagined being mine in a million years. And John, I can't adequately express what that feels like. I just can't fully describe what goes on inside of me when I think about the before and after shots of my life. All I can say is that I've been transformed by love. His transforming love is something I'll cherish for the rest of my life and on into eternity."

John looked at Wendy and simply said, "I know what you're saying." She looked into his eyes and responded tentatively, "Yeah, I know you do John, at least to a certain extent. And I don't want to downplay your personal testimony, because I would have given anything to grow up the way you did with a mom and a dad, and a stable home, and a church full of folks who really loved and cared about me. I'd trade my life for yours in a minute. I know you understand grace and redemption, certainly theologically, but also because you, like all believers, have been redeemed from sin. Every Christian has redemption as the basis for their new life in Christ. So, I get that. But when you come out of a life that is so evil and so steeped in sin, the contrast between darkness and light is immense. It's not that I'm more *saved* than you, or redeemed on a higher plane, it's just that the contrast between darkness and light is so very pronounced, that there's not a day that goes by that I don't give thanks for what the Lord has done in my life. I know what it feels like to be hopelessly lost in a pit of despair and then to be rescued and brought into the light of His transforming love. I literally feel it every day."

John put his arm around Wendy and drew her close to himself. He looked into her eyes and said, "I think I'm beginning to understand. I'm so thankful for what God has done in your life and the impact you've so obviously had on me also. You come from a place that I can only understand through the personal testimony of yours, and others from similar situations. That's what makes me think that Barbie was right on in terms of your being God's woman to run Safe Haven. You wouldn't be ministering out of theory. You'd be ministering from raw experience and that's always the most effective."

Wendy agreed with John and reiterated that she was going to continue to pray about God's direction concerning their Safe Haven house for women. But then she brought John back to the topic at hand. She said, "Honey, the thing I've been thinking about over the past 24 hours is just how far that transforming love stretches. The miracle I've seen in my life can't be just for me and a few other fortunate ones in the universe. That's not what redemption's all about, you know that. And so, in the middle of this whole 24 hours of fear and concern over Nick suddenly showing up, I've experienced two major emotions. I mean, there are more obviously, but there are two major areas. The first one, of course, was fear. When I saw Nick sitting in the back row at church, I absolutely panicked. I was instantly transported back to when Nick threatened to kill me. I was so relieved when you told me to walk out the side door, and yet I was worried about you. Fear has been my constant companion these last 24 hours. And yet - this is going to sound very weird - along with that fear came this overlay of what I can only describe as love. And I'm pretty sure it's God's love, because in myself, love wouldn't be a factor. If I'm feeling love, it's got to be a Jesus thing because honestly, what Nick did to me and what he's doing to the other girls now is disgusting and makes me nauseated. But John, I can't get away from this overwhelming sense of love that's invaded my heart. It doesn't make sense, at least not in the natural. But it's there, nevertheless."

As John sat and listened he tried very hard to understand what Wendy was saying. I mean, it's one thing to talk about loving sinners and praying for those who need Christ in their lives. That was easy. Everybody needs the Lord. But what John was finding difficult to accept was the idea that everybody needed the Lord - *even Nick*. All the other folks who needed the Lord were just that - they were other folks. But Nick brings this up close and personal; so personal in fact that John wasn't sure he wanted anything to do with it. If Nick got into his big, fancy, gold Cadillac heading for Chicago and John never saw him again, that would suit him just fine. If the Lord wanted to reach Nick, He could use others to do it. Let God use somebody else who doesn't have a history with him. Why put Wendy through this? And himself, for that matter? But, as he thought through his angry feelings, he realized that he too had been having a battle of emotions the last 24 hours. His wasn't fear. He knew he could handle Nick; he'd already demonstrated that. His major emotion had been anger over the way Mr. Sleazebag had treated his wife. And yet, when Nick had regained consciousness, after John had laid him out, didn't he encourage Nick to drop the preacher-man title and just call him John? What was that all about? John realized, looking back on the experience, that he had actually had a moment of feeling sorry for Nick. Nick wasn't as tough as he pretended to be. In fact, he asked those gathered there who had witnessed his defeat at the hands of the preacher-man, to keep it to themselves. In his line of work, reputation was king. And then to hear from Bill Parker that Nick wasn't the hot-shot, big-time gangster he claimed to be, brought a sense of sadness to John's heart. Not sadness for the fact that Nick wasn't a tough gangster, but sadness over the fact that Nick thought he should be. The idea that being the number one gangster in Chicago was Nick's highest goal for his life, was both pathetic and terribly sad. Two emotions: anger and sadness. The struggle John was having was discerning which emotion was the most appropriate, given the situation.

John and Wendy looked at each other, each processing what the other had said about their emotions. Wendy's were both fear and love. John's were both anger and sadness. As they continued to contemplate the situation it became clear to both of them. They both started to speak at the same time and then laughed when their words collided with each other. "You go first, honey," John said. "You know I'll always get my two cents in." Wendy smiled and acknowledged that John was right. If he had something to say, he'd get it said, one way or the other. Wendy just explained that maybe both of them ought to shift their focus from fear and anger, to love and sadness. Fear and anger, when used selfishly, aren't from God. But love and sadness can very well be used of God to provide motivation to reach out to someone who's in desperate need, whether they realize it or not. Love is the motivating factor for reaching out to the person who's lost and struggling to find their way. And sadness is the motivation to try to understand the person's past experience and current mindset. When you feel sad for what a person's life has been, it gives you both the sympathy and the empathy to help them to get to a better place.

John stared at Wendy, once again marveling at how far she had come in her faith in the last several months. The spiritual insight that she had was truly amazing and he found himself agreeing with everything she said. From now on, they were going to approach the situation with Nick not from the gut-level reactions of fear and anger, but rather from the heart - a heart of love for Nick himself, warts and all, as well as sadness for Nick's self-perception of what he thought he should be.

As they found themselves agreeing together as to their unified feelings, they also began to pray, asking God to give them pure motives and Spirit-led insight. They both instinctively knew that they were getting ready to embark on a new adventure, one they would have never imagined. They both knew, beyond a shadow of a doubt, that God was going to use them to bring redemption to Nick. They didn't know how it was going to happen exactly, but they were positive that someday soon, Nick was going to experience God's transforming love.

Chapter 15

THE TELEPHONE STARTED RINGING JUST AS JOHN and Wendy finished praying for Nick and the change in his life that was awaiting him. Nick didn't know it yet, but he was in the crosshairs. They had targeted him, convinced that God was going to do something miraculous in his life. The details were unknown at this time but one thing was for sure. At some point in time, Nick was going to be a changed man. This should be very interesting John thought. Challenging, but interesting.

As the phone rang, John reached over and grabbed the receiver and said, "Hello." He listened for a couple of seconds and then said, "She's right here; let me put her on." He leaned over to Wendy and said, "It's Barbie. I'm going to tuck Travis into bed while you two gals talk." He gave her the receiver and got up to go to Travis's room.

Wendy said, "Hi Barbie. What's going on? I didn't expect to hear from you this soon. We just spent a couple hours at breakfast this morning. I thought you'd be tired of me after that and would need a few days to recover." Barbie laughed on the other end and told Wendy that she'd been thinking about their conversation for the rest of the afternoon. She'd come up with some ideas that were bugging her and she knew she wasn't going to be able to relax until she shared them. "Wendy, how'd you like to do a repeat of this morning? What's your work schedule like?" Wendy thought for a minute and said, "I'm scheduled to work the lunch shift tomorrow, but don't have to be there until 11:30. We could do an early meeting at 8:30 and that would give us plenty of time to chat. I don't know what you've got cooking in that head of yours, but I'm excited to hear about it. How's tomorrow sound? Same place - The Pancake House in Leavenworth?" Barbie assured Wendy that she'd be there and would look forward to another wonderful meeting. They ended the call, both telling the other to take care.

Wendy joined John in Travis's room and found the guys talking in whispers. "What're you boys talking about? I thought I heard the word girls in there. What's that all about?" John smiled slightly, while Travis just looked the other way, averting his eyes from his mom. Travis looked at John and John looked at Travis. A second later John said, "Hey Trav, this is your thing. If you want to tell your mom, that's up to you, but I'm not going to spill the beans. That's your department." Travis looked at his mom, wondering just what to say. This morning he had decided that he was going to keep his mouth shut and not say anything to anybody, but he was finding that exceedingly difficult. Travis looked uncomfortable, but finally in desperation, he glanced at John and said, "You tell her." John said, "Are you sure? You don't have to, you know." By this time, Wendy is ready to tear her hair out, imagining all kinds of things. "Okay guys. What's going on here? What happened? You didn't get kicked out of school, did you? You didn't accidentally set your desk on fire and they had to evacuate the whole school? You didn't talk some kid into eating paste and now his lips are permanently glued together and his parents are going to sue us for a million dollars? Oh wait, I know. You made a bomb in your chemistry class and accidentally blew up the classroom. Even now, the FBI is walking up to our door." By this time Travis was laughing and denying all of her allegations. "We don't even have a chemistry class, but that would be cool if we did!"

"Okay," Wendy said. "If it's not any of those scenarios, what is it?" Travis took a deep breath and said, "Well, I think I'm in love." Wendy almost choked and said, "You're in love? When did that happen?" "This morning," Travis replied. Wendy thought about this new revelation and wondered why it took her by surprise. Young boys often develop crushes on little girls - nothing unusual about that - it's just that Travis had never given any hint that he had seen girls as anything else but a nuisance. This was going to change things up a bit.

So, Wendy began re-assuring Travis that all the feelings he was having were quite normal, but that even though he felt like it, love was probably too strong of a word. It's perfectly normal for young boys to like someone special but it's a little early to use the word love because after all, that takes time, lots of time. Travis looked puzzled and said, "But dad told you that you were the girl he was going to marry, and that was just after a few minutes of talking." Wendy looked at John, who just shrugged his shoulders as if to say, "What can you do? He's developing the Larson charm."

Rather than argue that point, Wendy decided to take another tack. She told Travis that she knew that whatever little girl had caught his eye, she must really be something. She invited Travis to tell them about this girl who had so captivated his heart. So, Travis proceeded to tell them about this beautiful, dark-haired beauty who was so nice and had a really fun personality. She was thin, not skinny, but seemed to be in good shape. She had brown eyes and a nose that fit her face just right. Travis was sensitive about noses; he felt that his was a little large. He told them that he could tell she took good care of her teeth because she had a wonderful smile; a smile that he could look at all day. As Wendy listened to Travis she thought to herself, how cute. My little boy's growing up and getting interested in girls. That is so sweet. I just hope that he doesn't get his heart broken. She continued to think about the innocence of young love as Travis described his new special friend. She was enjoying the reverie of listening to her son wax eloquently about his first heartthrob, when she was rudely yanked out of her parental bliss by something Travis said that caught her attention. "What did you say, Travis? What was your last statement?" "Gee mom, pay attention. I just said that she was a real fox and she's got a great figure." Wendy gasped in shock hearing those words come out of her little boy's mouth. What does he know about being a *fox*? And what kind of a fourth-grade boy knows about figures? And more concerning, what kind of a fourth-grade girl even *has* a figure?"

Wendy told herself to calm down and let him explain. She said, "Travis, who is this little girl that you're interested in?" Travis replied, "Oh, she's not a little girl, Mom. She's Ms. Conners, my teacher. I think I'm in love and I'm going to marry her someday." Wendy smiled and looked at John for help. They told Travis that it was really good that he liked Ms. Conners. They liked her too. She seemed to be a lovely person and a marvelous teacher. They decided not to burst his bubble. Teacher/student crushes have been going on since time began. They decided that it would run its course in time and that at some point, a little girl his own age was going to appear on the scene, and things would totally change. Let's just let nature run with this one; it's all a part of growing up. But the idea that Travis would use a term like *fox* was a bit concerning. It wasn't a bad word, necessarily. It just meant that he thought Ms. Conners was very pretty. And Wendy still wasn't sure what to think of Travis's assessment of her figure. That seemed a little advanced for a young boy. But then again, Travis had always been intellectually advanced. Who knows what he may have read, or heard on the radio, or watched on television? Wendy wasn't overly concerned, it was just that she wanted her son to grow up respecting women for who they were, not for what they looked like. Physical attraction plays a huge role in love relationships, but other attributes need to be considered as well. She wanted Travis to know that. She wanted him to see women as made in the image of God, and therefore always deserving of love and respect.

After a few moments the conversation seemed to run its course and it was time for bed. Travis was in love with his teacher, and as far as John and Wendy knew, this was his first real crush. They'd just have to let it play out and then be available to soothe any pangs of the heart, should they arise. It's not easy growing up, particularly in a world that's so obsessed with beauty and sexuality. It was becoming more blatant with every passing year and it concerned both John and Wendy immensely.

After tucking Travis in, later than usual because of their revealing conversation, they decided to go to bed and spend the next hour reading until lights out. As they got into bed John asked Wendy what Barbie had wanted? Wendy told him that Barbie had some ideas to share with her, so they were meeting again tomorrow morning, up in Leavenworth. As they talked, both of them expressed interest in the ideas that had so excited Barbie. "I don't know John," Wendy said. "I have a feeling that meeting Barbie was a divine appointment that God orchestrated to bring about some of His plans. I feel like something really good is going to come from our relationship." John expressed his agreement and then went back to his reading.

Wendy tried to go back to her reading also, but found herself unable to concentrate. After realizing that she had read the same passage three times, and still had no idea what it said, she put her book down and closed her eyes. She needed to clear her mind and tap into whatever it was that God was telling her. It's like God was trying to get her attention and kept poking at her, until finally she got it. With the book laying on her lap and her closed eyes removing all other distractions, she was finally free to let God speak to her, not audibly, but rather with impressions, some that were a little fuzzy, but others that were as clear as a bell.

What was God trying to impress upon Wendy about the conversation with Travis tonight? It's just a harmless school boy crush, for heaven's sake. Everybody experiences them; it's a part of growing up and developing into the person you are meant to be. But the references to "fox" and "figure" were disturbing, not because they were bad in themselves, but rather because they were a snapshot of things to come.

Travis was growing up in the decade of the 70s but was basically a product of the so-called sexual revolution coming out of the 60s.

What the hippie generation saw as a new sexual freedom of expression was actually turning out to be bondage. Wendy thought about all those things that were so commonly accepted now, that a decade or two ago would have been shocking. Posters of gorgeous swimsuit models and actresses were everywhere and covered the bedroom walls from college dorms, to the suburban homes of junior and senior high boys. Some images that you could see in movie magazines and gossip papers today, would've been in under-the-counter publications of the 50s. What was passing for entertainment on television nowadays would have been immediately censored years ago. Some of the scenes in popular movies of today would have been available only at little seedy theaters in the shady part of town a decade ago. All of these things were being touted as progressive, bringing freedom to a previously up-tight and repressed society. Freedom was in, but good taste and moral discipline was out.

As Wendy continued to process the impressions she was getting from God, she was suddenly fearful to think about how far this freedom could go and what the consequences would be. What if this so-called freedom kept going, virtually unchecked? In 10 years Travis would be 18. What would his view of women be like then? Would they simply be seen as objects of pleasure for men? Wendy had certainly had her battle with that image since her middle teens. And how would this sexual revolution impact society in terms of marriages? Would easy access to all things sexual have a negative effect on the ability of men to commit to one woman, for life? What would the divorce rate be like in a decade or two? Would illicit affairs run rampant, obviously leading to the breakup of marriages? And what would happen to the kids affected by divorce? Are they as resilient as the so-called experts say they are?

Or, are we going to find ourselves in a quagmire of cynicism concerning the stabilizing impact of healthy marriages in our society?

As Wendy caught a glimpse of a frightening future, she also realized that there was still hope. There's always hope for those who want to change. She and John would just have to work hard to model for Travis what it means to be people of the cross. He needs to see strong morals and godly principles lived out in his parents' lives, as well is in the lives of other folks at church. It doesn't mean he won't struggle and maybe even get off track at times, but at least a solid foundation would be there. Wendy realized that this wasn't just for Travis alone. It was also for all the other kids that God had entrusted to their care at church. Hopefully, the kids in their church would grow up knowing the difference between walking in light as opposed to walking in darkness. We're going to have to really put our time and attention on this one, Wendy thought. We have a whole generation of kids growing up in a "freedom," that would more accurately be termed bondage.

But what happens to those who get fully enmeshed into this so-called freedom? So enmeshed in fact, that it goes from simply being unhealthy, to being truly deadly. Those caught up in addictions to alcohol and street drugs, for example, are vastly increasing in numbers. The popular phrase of a few years ago that expressed "blowing your mind on drugs" wasn't just a funny way of saying that a person was a little high. This didn't refer to being a little tipsy. This kind of experience had a real impact on a person's ability to function, participating in the normal activities of life in our society. Couple drugs with the sexual revolution, and you have a recipe for disaster.

Wendy realized where this was going. She understood what God was trying to tell her. She and Barbie's conversation and mutual vision for Mercy House and Safe Haven was exciting and challenging. But at that moment she knew that was just the tip of the iceberg. Those two homes would be just the first of many such homes. They were going to have to provide homes of this nature to minister to the broken people who would come to their doors in the decades to come. It didn't take a prophetic genius to see the results of a society throwing off all moral restraint. And who better, but the Church, to pick up the pieces of shattered lives? And it wasn't just a matter of providing food, shelter and a warm bed, although that was certainly important. It also had to involve dramatic change; not only a change of lifestyle, but more importantly, a change of headship. Who's heading up your life? You? Or the God who made you?

Wendy fell asleep and didn't wake up when John reached over and switched off the light. Her dreams were of warfare and competition; of good versus evil. In her dreams, she was required to fight long and hard, but in the end, good always won over evil; light always drove out the darkness - every time!

Wendy woke up Tuesday morning excited about what God had shared with her. She knew, beyond a shadow of a doubt, that if they continued on the right path concerning the two homes for women, victory would be theirs. She also knew that somehow, as impossible as it seemed, the vision was going to climb to higher levels. Women were going to be snatched from the jaws of hell and given a second chance at real life.

At 7:45 AM she said goodbye to John and Travis and headed off for Leavenworth to meet Barbie. They both drove in at exactly 8:15 and laughed at their mutual compulsion to be early. They went in and found a secluded table at the rear of the restaurant. They talked about how things had been going the 24 hours since they had met and Wendy filled her in on the details. She told her about John's encounter with Nick or, more precisely, Nick's encounter with John's fist. "You're kidding," Barbie exclaimed. "I would have loved to witness that!" Wendy said, "Yeah, but we think God wants to hit him with something more powerful than John's fist. We think God wants to hit Nick with His love." Barbie laughed and said, "Oh yeah, I'd like to see that even more!"

Wendy then told her about their conversation with Travis and the resulting night of impressions, thoughts and dreams. And then she shared that she felt that God was telling her that this is just the beginning; that Mercy House and Safe Haven were going to be the models for many more homes in the future. Barbee's eyes shone with excitement and she shared that God had been showing her the exact same thing. Wendy expressed her amazement that they both had the same visions, but admitted that she had no idea how God was going to pull this off. Barbie smiled at Wendy and said, "I do! I think I know how! Listen to this and tell me what you think."

Chapter 16

A S THEY CONTINUED TO ENJOY THEIR BREAK-
fast, both Wendy and Barbie experienced a growing excitement about the possibilities of watching God do something
truly amazing. Barbie explained that the idea she had was a very simple concept really and had certainly been effective for other ministries
down through the years. It wasn't new, but it was powerful nevertheless. Of course, Wendy being a newcomer to the whole church gig
didn't have experience in these kinds of situations, so almost everything was fresh and innovative to her.

Barbie talked about how effective a personal testimony can be in
terms of helping to get people on board with a specific project. "For

example," she said, "Look what happened when you told your story to the congregation at Pleasant Pastures. You had no idea how they were going to respond. They could've heard about your past life as a dancer and rejected you right on the spot. They could have done that, but they didn't, did they? You know why they didn't do that? Because you're the perfect example of the power of redemption. For crying out loud, if we Christians get fearful and judgmental over a story of one person's journey from the dark side, why are we even in church in the first place? It's those stories of triumph over what the world dishes out that help to prove what we've been preaching all along. You talked about it yesterday, when you were telling me about Nick. Someday, you said, Nick's going to be a changed man. He's going to be changed by God's transforming love. Well, Wendy, there are a lot of Nicks out there and when they're transformed, people need to hear about it. It's a boost to their faith and encourages them to keep going in the fight against everything that traps us in a life of chaos and pain and hopelessness. Do you see?"

Of course, Wendy understood what Barbie was saying because she had experienced it firsthand, in dramatic fashion. She asked Barbie to go on, anxious to see how this was going to play out exactly. Barbie looked at Wendy and said, "Well, it's simple really. We want to have homes available for women coming out of all kinds of difficult situations, don't we?" Wendy nodded in agreement. "And those homes," Barbie continued, "are going to come, one at a time. It's not like we can snap our fingers and get 10 houses up and going. We have to build a solid foundation and grow from there. Mercy House is the first one. It's been operating for a few years now. And during that time, the church was able to work out some of the kinks, so that when we took over as pastors, it was already running pretty smoothly. That's the first one. Safe Haven is the second one and it's already got a good start. The down payment was made yesterday, right? So, now the task is getting the money and the volunteers on board. That's the next step. So, what do you think about adding a little shot in the arm to your Safe Haven campaign that starts this Sunday? What would you and John think about having one of the ladies from Mercy House come to your service this Sunday and share her testimony? Let her share what God has done in her life through the ministry of Mercy House. Wendy, I've heard her story, and believe me, it's powerful. What do you think?"

Wendy knew she'd have to check with John, but was positive that he'd give the thumbs up. As they continued to chat, Wendy realized that Barbie was seeing the bigger picture. She had no doubt in her mind that Safe Haven was going to be up and going fairly soon. And then, when they felt led to do so, they'd go after a third, and then a fourth, and so on. Wendy marveled at Barbie's vision and wondered if she'd ever get to that place in her faith. It all seemed a little overwhelming and, evidently, it was showing on Wendy's face. Barbie looked at Wendy's knitted brows and said, "Hey honey, don't worry about this. Enjoy the run. Don't concern yourself over the vision of the 10 homes, for heaven's sakes. That's a very distant goal that both of us would love to see. But that goal will be reached, one step at a time. You have to break the vision down into bite-sized chunks, so it doesn't become overwhelming. The goal in front of us right now is very manageable. We need to inspire your folks this Sunday to commit their time and financial support to Safe Haven. And if John agrees to it, I'll come up and bring a gal named Jackie with me. I'll tell a little bit how the home is run and then turn it over to Jackie to give her testimony. She's very good in front of an audience. I've heard her give her testimony before and it's extremely powerful. This girl is a poster child for changed lives.

When people hear what's happened to her and how Mercy House changed her life, they'll jump at the chance to be involved, in whatever way they can. And in the future, you and I could go to other churches all over Eastern Washington, laying out the challenge to do the same thing. A project of this nature can breathe new life into a church and we could help them see the possibilities. Who knows? Someday we might even be in a position to offer a little financial assistance to those churches – maybe a few thousand dollars of seed money. But whatever the case, don't worry about that now. Just keep your eyes on Safe Haven and watch God do His thing. You're going to be amazed at how powerful He really is."

Wendy looked at this woman of God she had known for what – all of two weeks? But once again she marveled at her faith. Barbie got it. She saw the big picture and had no doubt that God would bring it to pass. And the thing that really amazed Wendy about Barbie and her passion for changed lives? It had nothing to do with her. She wasn't going to somehow get rich over this. Her church wasn't suddenly going to be the focal point of this ministry, thereby bringing all kinds of growth and fame and fortune. That wasn't Barbie's motivation at all. She just wanted to live out her faith in Christ. She sincerely wanted to do what Jesus did, and this was one way to do that. Jesus brought healing everywhere He'd go and Barbie wanted to do the same thing. Wendy heard herself breathe an inward prayer. "Oh Lord, I want to do that too. I really do. Please use me in whatever way pleases you."

They finished their breakfast, alternately talking about plans for Safe Haven, as well as life in general. Wendy had learned so much from Barbie in the few hours they spent together, yesterday and this morning. She remembered how she'd asked the Lord to bring another pastor's wife her way, one that might be willing to mentor her. And within a matter of days, Barbie walked into her diner and into her life. Wendy didn't really know what she was asking for exactly in a mentor, but figured that maybe there would be written lessons of some kind, or intense Bible studies. That might've been good, but Wendy began to see how God was orchestrating this. Being mentored wasn't going to involve lessons from a book, but rather lessons from a *life*. Listening to Barbie talk and dream, praying with passion, weeping from genuine concern for others, declaring God's faithfulness, presenting herself in humility, all of that together had taught Wendy so much more than she could have ever imagined. The thing that really blew her away is that they'd only spent a few hours together in conversation, and yet she had learned so much. What a gift this woman was in Wendy's life.

Wendy finished her French toast and realized that it was time to go. She had an hour to drive home, jump into her uniform and make it to the diner for the noon shift. Wendy told Barbie that she'd call her later that day and confirm about her and Jackie coming to share on Sunday, but she was confident that John would be all over that one. It was going to be another wonderful service this Sunday, and Wendy could hardly wait to see the people's response.

As she drove home, Wendy kept getting pictures in her mind of women whose lives had been changed. She saw their *before* and *after* shots in her spirit. She visualized chains dropping off each one of them and a circle of light enveloping their very being. Safe Haven was going to live up to its name, but it was going to go further than that. Women coming to the home were going to find shelter and safety from all the evil that had come their way. But it wasn't going to stop there. She also saw women leaving the shelter of Safe Haven, venturing out into the world to face the same forces that formerly had been their tormentors. But this time, they faced those forces from a position of power and authority - the scent of victory flooding from every pore. They had gone from tragedy to triumph, but their journey had only begun.

Chapter 17

WENDY DROVE INTO THE DRIVEWAY OF THE parsonage and jumped out of the car, making a beeline toward the back door. She walked into the house and called out, "Anybody home?" She didn't expect to hear a response and sure enough not a sound greeted her. Travis was in school and John was either in his office at church or out on calls.

Wendy went to her closet and grabbed her freshly laundered uniform and laid it on the bed. She hung up her pants and blouse and slipped the uniform over her head and buttoned up. She exchanged her calf-high leather boots for her ugly, but comfortable work shoes. She tied the laces and headed out the door for the short walk to Maggie's Country Diner.

As she glanced at her watch she saw that she was early and so decided to stop in and see if John was available. She walked into the church office and greeted Kathy, who was sitting behind her desk typing. She asked if John was available and Kathy gave her a thumbs up. And so, Wendy knocked once and then opened the door and went into John's office. The first thing she saw was John's desk, which was covered with books. He had four commentaries spread out and was obviously in the middle of sermon preparation.

He looked up as the door opened and when he saw Wendy he broke out into a smile. "Hi honey. I didn't expect to see you. But this is a nice midmorning treat." He got up and put his arms around her, kissing her rather passionately for a Tuesday morning in the church office. Wow, thought Wendy, I wonder what tonight's going to be like!

Wendy then went on to tell John about Barbie's idea of bringing Jackie to the service and having her share her testimony. John thought the idea was wonderful and would kick off their Safe Haven campaign very effectively. He asked Wendy what she thought about giving Barbie and Jackie the entire 30-minute sermon time, so that they didn't have to feel rushed. Sometimes a personal, real-life testimony can speak more powerfully than a finely crafted sermon. Wendy thought about that for a minute and then agreed with John's idea. She told him that she'd give Barbie a call and line it up.

With that settled, she was just about to leave when she remembered their agreement about Nick. "Have you seen Nick, by any chance?" "No, I haven't. He told me he was going to hang around a while, but maybe he changed his mind and headed back to Chicago. But the deal still stands. Whichever one of us sees him first, provided he's still in the area, will invite him to lunch on Friday. Are we still good with that, Wendy? I don't want to do it, if it would make you uncomfortable." "No, I'm fine," said Wendy, "it was my idea in the first place. I just hope it works out. This could be the beginning of something totally new for Nick. On the other hand, he could think this God thing is a bunch of baloney and split for Chicago the first chance he gets. He could do that, but that's not the impression I'm getting. I guess we'll just have to wait and see."

John agreed and then drew Wendy close and kissed her a second time. "Let me guess," he said, "French toast?" She swatted him on the arm and said, "I was going to brush my teeth at the diner, just before my shift. Don't be a wise guy." John smiled and said, "You don't have to brush your teeth on my account. You know French toast is always one of my favorite breakfasts." Wendy laughed and said, "Well, maybe it would be a good bedtime snack too" She hugged him again and said, "As much as I would love to stay here and kiss you in this sacred office, I've got to get going or I'm going to be late." She smiled, seductively raising one eyebrow, and said, "Catch you later," and then left the office, leaving John with an enticing hint of things to come.

John glanced at his watch and realized that he had to be in Wenatchee for his monthly meeting with the pastors from the surrounding area. This month they were meeting in the back room of the Brad's Restaurant, which featured a lunch buffet with way too much food offered. John reminded himself that he didn't have to eat it all; he could be moderate. And that usually worked pretty well, except with desserts. Those were harder to resist, but he determined to be disciplined. Yeah right, he thought, we'll see how that works out.

He got into his car and realized his gas gauge with just a hair above empty. He drove down Main Street and pulled into "Floyd's

Service Station and Mini-Mart." He jumped out and began filling up. Just as the nozzle clicked off, he heard, "Hey preacher-man, how's it going?" Johns first thought was, "Oh boy, I hope Nick didn't bring a gun this time." But then he remembered Bill Parker's words about Nick's lack of any real trouble with the law; he was awfully law-abiding for a gangster.

John turned and saw Nick standing beside his big, gold Cadillac. John looked at Nick, smiling, and said, "Hey Nick, whatcha doing? Driving around seeing the sights of our thriving metropolis?" Nick laughed and said no, that he had actually come into town from Leavenworth, where he was staying, to see John. "You see preacher-man, I've got something I want to talk to you about." John looked at Nick and said, "Nick, I'm just heading out of town for the afternoon. Is it an emergency or can it wait a bit?" Nick told John that it wasn't an emergency, but he'd like to talk to him and Wendy both, in the next couple of days. Nick looked kind of sheepish and said, "That's if Wendy's willing to see me." John assured Nick that Wendy was just fine and, in fact, wanted to ask Nick over for lunch. Nick's eyes opened wide with surprise and he said, "You gotta be kidding me. Why would she do that?" "I don't know, I guess we both want to get to know you better Nick and let the past go. We've all got a past and we've all got to move on." Nick looked at John, processing what he just said. "I guess you're right, I've just never been very good at that. But hey, let's see what happens – can't hurt, right?"

John agreed and then asked Nick about coming over on Friday, which was their day off. Nick thought that would be great and said, "I'll see you at 12 o'clock preacher-man." John looked at Nick and said, "Just call me John...my friends all call me John." Nick said quietly, "You got it ...John. I'll see you Friday."

As John got back on the road towards Wenatchee, he replayed the encounter in his mind, wondering why Nick wanted to see them. Maybe he was still angry over all that had gone down since Wendy ran out on him, but was going to try a more rational approach to get the money he felt they owed him. Well, John concluded, if that's the case, he's going to be disappointed. Wendy didn't owe him anything, that's for sure. By Nick's own accounting, he figured he was owed $12,000. First of all, that was hogwash. Secondly, they didn't have that kind of money anyway. So, all in all, it was a moot point; Nick wasn't getting a dime.

But as John thought more about it, he realized that Nick didn't seem mad, in fact, it was more the opposite. He seemed to be in pretty good spirits. I wonder what's going on with him, John questioned. Maybe he's just acting like everything's fine, but just when we begin to trust him, he'll drop the hammer on us. Just because he's never really been in trouble with the law, doesn't mean he won't start now. I just don't know what he's thinking. I don't know what his endgame is, John mused, but come Friday, I guess we'll find out.

John arrived at Brad's Restaurant in Wenatchee and once again steeled himself for the food frenzy at the buffet table. Okay John, he said to himself. One dessert - two at the most - maybe three, if they're really good, but no more than that. He was proud of his discipline at holding to three desserts, although he wasn't sure if Wendy would see it quite the same way. It was a good thing he didn't drink, John thought, he'd be dangerous on the road. He'd heard a health expert say, one time, that too much sugar was just as bad for you, as too much alcohol. Well, that may be, John thought, so I'll have to do better. But when it comes to comparing alcohol and sugar, he just figured that when he was driving, he'd rather meet a fat man coming down the road, then a drunk man. That was his rationale and he was sticking to it.

Chapter 18

JOHN AND WENDY SAT IN THEIR LIVING ROOM relaxing after the busy day. Travis was already in bed and snoring like a buzz saw. Wendy was on the couch, with her feet tucked underneath her, and a cup of tea in her hand. John was in his easy chair, reclined slightly. He loved that chair, but it had its drawbacks. In some ways, it was almost too comfortable and he often found himself nodding off, especially when he was tired from the day's activities.

But tonight, John was fully awake and alert. He and Wendy had been discussing what the next several days were going to hold, on many fronts. Safe Haven, for example. This coming Sunday was the perfect day to kick off the fund-raising campaign. People were excited because the old Sinclair home was now the property of the church. The down payment was made yesterday and all the papers were signed and delivered. As exciting as that was, now the real work was just beginning.

John had been thinking about that on his drive home from Wenatchee this afternoon. When he started thinking through details, it wasn't long before his head was spinning. *Now that we've secured the house, where do we go from here? The steps to making Safe Haven a reality have just begun. Now there's the fund-raising. We got to have money for the monthly mortgage.* Then there's the task and expense of fixing the long-neglected place up - fresh paint and carpeting - new appliances designed to accommodate a bustling household of several women and their children - plumbing and lighting issues - repairing the fence that surrounds the property - outfitting the home with new furniture, including two beds, and in some cases, bunk beds in every room - finishing up with beautiful decor that would send a message to the women who lived in the home. The extra touches would let them know that they're special and the people who ran the home wanted them to enjoy living in an atmosphere of warmth and caring. Adding those special touches could go a long way in helping these often abused and neglected women, begin to feel better about themselves and more hopeful for the future.

But all of these changes to the house, as well as the furnishings themselves, would cost money. The preliminary estimate for labor and furnishings was in the $25,000 range. Add that to the price of the home and we're now at somewhere around $100,000. While the average home in this uncertain decade of the 70s had shot up to $36,000, Safe Haven would be almost 3 times that. And that's not taking into consideration the monthly expenses of housing the women with food and clothing, toiletries and so on. When John began to add it all up, he found himself getting a little bit nervous.

And yet, he also was able to relax in the fact that God had led them to take this step. Safe Haven was on the Lord's heart; John had no doubt about that. Maybe John's thinking was a little simplistic, but he just figured that if this was God's idea, He wasn't going to have any problem bringing it all together. Still, it did feel rather daunting. And it wasn't just about the finances; it was also the overall management of the project. It was difficult for John to see himself in that role because he had so much going on, every day, in terms of pastoring the church in general. There were all the usual tasks of sermon and Bible study prep, various ministry teams that needed his input, planning the weekly worship service, and helping people in crisis navigate those very difficult seasons of life, as well as the hundred and one other things that always took his time, leaving him worn out by the end of the day.

He noticed that both he and Wendy had grown silent, obviously lost in their own thoughts. How did I ever make it through without Wendy, John thought? He found himself breathing a prayer of thanksgiving to the Lord for bringing Wendy into his life. "Apart from Jesus, Lord, she's the greatest treasure you've ever given me. Thank you for your marvelous gift," John prayed silently.

Just as John looked up from his thoughts and prayers, he saw Wendy glance his way with a look of either concern, or perhaps intense concentration. Whatever it was, her facial expression indicated that something was obviously on her mind. John looked at her and smiled. He'd seen that look before. Wendy's face always looked like that when she was thinking something through, usually something that was new and different, or very important. "Okay honey," John said. "What's going on in that pretty little head of yours? You look like you're just on the verge of discovering something that's going to change the world. What's going on with you?"

Wendy looked at John and said, "Oh, it's not quite as dramatic as that, but I was just thinking about Safe Haven. We're going to be bringing Barbie and Jackie in Sunday to share their testimonies. People are going to be excited about the Home and anxious to get going on it. But I feel like we're kind of behind on this. I mean, we don't really have a plan. We've never told them how much the entire project is going to cost, or exactly how we're going to fund it. We're not sure how all the work is going to be done, or how long it's going to take to actually get Safe Haven up and running. I think there are just a lot of details that we haven't figured out yet, but we're going to need those answers fairly quickly. For example, John. This Sunday, we want to kick off the giving campaign, right?" John nodded, wondering where she was going with this. Wendy said, "That's great! We need to strike while the iron is hot. And those testimonies are going to heat up that iron pretty quickly. But the problem is that we have no plan for raising the funds. We can't just take an offering, like we did last week, and expect to raise all that's needed. I think we need to have a plan that makes sense to everyone. But it needs to go further than that. It should be a plan that invites participation from everyone. Our kids in the lowest grades should be able to participate in this and know that they can play a part in it too." John saw the wisdom of that, but was curious about what Wendy had in mind.

Wendy looked at her husband and said, "I have an idea." "I figured you did," replied John. "I'm just anxious to hear it; so, lay it on me and let's see what you've got." Wendy grew very excited and reiterated the fact that the entire project, from actually purchasing the house and repairing it, would be about $100,000. They wanted to pay

the mortgage off in five years or less, if that was possible. They'd obviously like to pay it off sooner in order to save the interest, but that
could be tough, not impossible exactly, but tough. This wasn't going
to be a little walk in the park or leisurely Sunday afternoon stroll. No,
this wasn't a stroll, this was a journey. In fact, Wendy proposed that
they call the campaign "Journey to Safe Haven." She explained that
each step in the journey brought them closer to their goal. So, what if
they challenged their congregation to join in and fund steps along that
journey? That means that everybody could participate in some way.
Each step would be $10. Even a little kid could be challenged to save
$10 from his allowance. Or, a fourth grade Sunday school class could
be challenged to fund five steps over the next year. And others might
want to fund 100 or 200 or 300 or more steps, again several times over
that five-year journey. They could even design a graphic that indicated
where they were on the journey. The graph would get updated along
the way so that people could celebrate the progress that had been made
and be encouraged to go on. And, in addition to the occasional plea for
funding of the steps, they could also challenge the congregation to buy
meals along the journey. John looked a little puzzled at this idea and so
Wendy said, "John listen. It's just like when a family takes a road trip,
they have to stop and eat along the way. Well, what about challenging
the congregation to provide meals for the journey. If it costs $50 a day
to provide meals for the residents, that comes to approximately $1500
per month. If 300 people, from both the church and our community,
committed $5 a month to purchase meals, we'd have it. And again, kids
could do this. Their Sunday school offerings could provide meals. The
"Journey to Safe Haven" allows everybody an opportunity to give, at
whatever level they can. Everybody gets the chance to go on the journey. We're taking a big family road trip together. And that road trip

will not only make Safe Haven possible, it'll also build our faith and tighten our relationships. It's a win all around, honey."

John looked at Wendy and admired his wife's vision for the bigger picture. But he was also impressed with her ability to break that vision down, in such a way, as to make it accessible to everyone. He knew the importance of the church and community coming together around a common goal. There was simply no substitute for the benefits of a group of folks working together for the greater good. That's what being a member of the Body of Christ was all about anyway. Every person had gifts and talents that could be used in service to others. And John had discovered, years before, that using those gifts was a source of great joy. Sacrificing yourself is extremely rewarding when it's for a heavenly cause. And he couldn't think of a cause that was more heavenly than Safe Haven.

John and Wendy continued to talk and dream of the future. The "Journey to Safe Haven" funding campaign was just the beginning. They would also have to plan and oversee the refurbishing of the house and grounds. They'd have to plan the decor and secure the necessary furnishings, as well as the little extras - those specialty items that can turn a functional house, into a real home, with warmth and charm. There were tons of details that needed to be addressed and Wendy had no doubt they would all be accomplished. But, how that would happen, was still a mystery to her. They needed an overall project manager, but who had the time for that, let alone the energy? She supposed that they could just form a team of folks to handle the myriad of details and decisions that would come up, but she remembered what John had told her, many times. You can have a team, but there still has to be somebody with whom the buck stops. Otherwise, a lot of time and energy can be expended, but much of that energy is lost in wheel spinning. "Oh God," Wendy prayed, "Please don't let us be a bunch of wheel spinners. There's just too much at stake with Safe Haven. The sooner we get it up and running, the sooner we can get women off the streets and into the shelter of a home that can potentially change their lives. Please Lord, we need your guidance here, every step of the way. I know you're in this Lord; just let us tap into what you're doing. Because if we do that, I know we'll be successful."

John eyed Wendy carefully and then observed, "You were in a different place for a minute there, honey. Where'd you go and what'd you find out?" Wendy told John about her concern over the details, as well as the need to find a project manager who could oversee the whole thing. That person's out there, yes, but God was going to have to reveal him. Whoever he is, we need him soon.

John went over to the couch where Wendy was seated, feet still tucked under her, and lightly kissed her on the cheek. "Wendy," he said, "what makes you so sure that the project manager God has for us is a *him* and not a *her*? I could be wrong on this, but I don't think so. The first requirement to be a project manager of something like this is to have the vision, to be able to visualize the dream coming to pass. The second requirement is to see what needs to be done and then have the ability to delegate each aspect to the best person, or team of people, in order to accomplish it. The third requirement is to have the ability to troubleshoot, because things don't always go smoothly, as planned. And the fourth requirement is to be able to keep it all straight and on schedule, so that the project is completed on time. That's what it takes to be a project manager. But I ask you again, what makes you so sure that the person God has for the job is a *him* and not a *her*?"

Wendy stared into her husband's eyes, looking for a bit of clarification. "Are you saying, what I think you're saying? Are you suggesting that I should be the project manager? John, that's crazy, on so many levels. Look at the business world. There may be more women working now, but I doubt very many are heading up major projects for their company. Besides, even if it wasn't an outlandish idea, what makes you think I'm the person for it? I've never been in a position to handle all those details."

John let out a laugh and said, "You've got to be kidding me. I watch you almost every day at the diner. You handle multiple situations throughout the day. I've seen you take an eight-top table of fussy people, all who have special requests for everything, and yet you never miss an order, including their personal preferences. You handle multiple details throughout your entire day. I've also seen you with the new wait-staff Maggie's hired over the past months. The diner's grown in business and therefore the number of staff has grown. And you, my beautiful wife, have not only trained them, but you manage them expertly. You are a natural at making people feel appreciated and valued for what they do. You know what that does? It just makes them want to work harder and do an even better job. Don't tell me you can't manage projects, or people, Wendy, because I see you do it every day."

"You really think so, John?"

"Yeah, I do."

"Well, what should we do?"

"I think you should pray about this and if the Lord confirms it to you, you need to get with Maggie and tell her what you're thinking. I can almost assure you, that it won't be that much of a surprise. Maggie is pretty perceptive, in case you haven't noticed."

"Oh, I've noticed all right."

They both laughed at their shared knowledge of their good friend. Maggie truly was a very insightful person and John was positive that when she heard Wendy's proposal, she'd be in full support. Of course, it would mean that Wendy would quit her position at the diner, but as John said, she had trained the staff wonderfully. Besides, all the waitresses could use the extra hours. Money was tight, especially for a couple of the gals who had kids.

The excitement that Wendy felt inside was palpable. As she thought more about it, she could really see it happening. She could do this. With the Lord's help and with the support of the good people at church, she could do this. But then a thought struck her. She asked John about the finances. She was going to quit her job and work for free. Could they handle that at this time? John assured her that they'd be fine. The salary the church paid him was more than adequate. The question though, was how did Wendy feel about doing this for free? It was going to be a lot of work and a lot of time, with no financial reward. Wendy smiled at John and said, "Honey, being able to work full-time on this dream is reward enough. Nothing would make me happier." John encouraged her to keep praying and they'd address it again in the morning, just to see if anything had changed. If not, she'd be taking her own first step on the Journey to Save Haven.

Wendy was very excited, but decided to let her mind switch gears for the next hour or two. She remembered her fairly blatant hint to her husband this morning, as he kissed her passionately in his office. His gentle, yet passionate nature, made Wendy long for physical intimacy with John quite often. And tonight was no exception. Finishing what they started this morning would be the perfect way to end the evening. She took John by the hand and slowly, seductively led him to their bedroom. As she lay there, enjoying the embrace of his strong arms, Wendy responded as she knew she would. She relaxed and let herself go...enjoying the bliss of wedded love.

Chapter 19

JOHN AND WENDY WOKE UP EARLY THE NEXT morning and lay entwined in each other's arms for several minutes, savoring the memory of their lovemaking, a few hours before. The joy of physical intimacy with the one they loved was one of God's most precious gifts. They never ceased being grateful for that holy bond known as marriage.

As they lay there, they begin to talk about their conversation from the early evening. Safe Haven was very much on their minds and the decision to have Wendy take on the role of project manager still seemed right to them. No red flags had appeared through the night. No stop sign had suddenly popped up, issuing its familiar message.

Once again, this morning everything appeared to be a go - greenlight, all the way.

So, with that in mind, they both got up to face the new day. It was decided that the best course of action would be to get the ball rolling as soon as possible. That meant that Wendy needed to have a conversation with Maggie about her employment situation. Wendy recalled, with great fondness, her initial meeting with Maggie those months ago. The love and acceptance Maggie had offered her was, perhaps, the single most important event leading to Wendy's healing of her heart and soul. The love of Jesus was so strong, as it flowed effortlessly from Maggie, that Wendy had been impacted by it almost from the moment she walked into the diner. Everything that Maggie had done for Wendy since day one just made the conversation they were going to have that much more difficult. And yet, it had to be done. As nervous as she was, Wendy had no doubt that the direction she and John were heading was from God Himself. She was pretty sure that Maggie would recognize it also.

Wendy jumped into the shower, while John went to get some breakfast on the table for Travis. Tom, Travis' school chum, would be coming by in about 30 minutes so that they could ride to school together on their bikes. If this morning was like the past couple of mornings, there'd actually be a group of four or five that would ride together. John and Wendy were both so grateful that Travis had established himself with a group of good kids. They, like all good parents, just wanted their son to be liked and accepted by a positive group of friends, a group that he may very well be with all the way throughout high school. It'll be interesting to see what the future holds for Travis and his gang of friends, mused John.

Wendy finished her morning preparations, kissed John and Travis goodbye and started walking the few blocks to the diner. She purposely planned to arrive 45 minutes early, in order to have the conversation with Maggie. As she walked, she rehearsed what she was going to say. She kept going back-and-forth in her mind, concerned about the best way to approach the fact that she was quitting. After mulling it over from several different angles, she finally began to relax, deciding that the best course of action was honesty. She'd just tell Maggie what she and John had discerned in their discussions and prayers over the last several hours. She also felt quite confident that this wouldn't be that big of a shock to Maggie. She must have realized that, at some point in time, being the pastor's wife might mean a change would be forth-coming. And besides, Wendy thought, smiling to herself, Maggie's the one responsible for getting John and I together anyway. So, this is actually all her fault. Wendy chuckled to herself, yet once again, breathed a silent prayer of thanks for Maggie's not-too-subtle conspiracy to get the two of them together. Thank God for Maggie's no-nonsense approach to romance.

She walked across the parking lot and through the back door of the diner. And sure enough, just like every morning, there was Maggie sitting in the kitchen, drinking a cup of coffee and reading the newspaper. She always started her day in this fashion, giving herself an opportunity to prepare herself mentally, for the rush of the day. Wendy wasn't too sure how reading the headlines could relax a person, but different strokes for different folks. If it works for Maggie, who was she to argue?

Maggie looked up, noticing the clock on the wall and said, "Oh boy, here it comes." Wendy looked at her and said, "What do you mean, here it comes? I'm just a little early." "You're always early - that's one of the things I appreciate about you - but not 45 minutes early. Something's up and I betcha I know what it is. You're pregnant!" Wendy looked at Maggie and exclaimed, "What? Pregnant? We've only been married a little over two weeks. Why would you think I'm pregnant? We couldn't know this soon anyway." Maggie smiled at Wendy and said, "Oh honey, I'm just joshing you. I'm just having a little fun, at your expense. Sorry about that. Please forgive me for messing with you." "Oh, that's all right," Wendy said. "Maybe I needed to be shocked. Maybe it'll help me get my head on straight."

Maggie smiled at Wendy and said, "Come on, sit down and tell me what's going on. I think I can probably guess, but tell me the whole story. Don't leave out any details. You know I can't stand to be in the dark." Wendy laughed and said, "Boy, that's for sure. One of the first things I discovered about you, Maggie, is that you were more up on the news than the paper you read. People ought to come to the diner and save the price of their paper subscription. You could fill them in and they'd get a good meal, and a piece of pie to boot. That's quite a deal."

Maggie laughed, agreeing with her, and then looked lovingly at Wendy and said, "Okay, tell me what's on your heart." Wendy was taken aback with what Maggie said and how she worded it. Most people would say "Tell me what's on your mind." But Maggie had changed that familiar phrase and said, "Tell me what's on your heart." That struck Wendy as being rather insightful. What she was about to share with Maggie wasn't the result of thinking something through with her mind. It was more about dreaming and praying it through, with her heart. It was her heart that was on the line this morning, not her mind. And so, Wendy decided, right then and there, to put aside all the imaginary conversations and scenarios that she'd come up with on her walk to the diner and simply share her heart.

She walked Maggie through the whole scenario, from her initial conversation with Barbie, through the subsequent hours of prayer, as she drove or worked. She understood what the Apostle Paul meant when he encouraged believers to "pray without ceasing." She'd been carrying on an almost constant conversation with God since her Monday morning breakfast with Barbie - a breakfast that turned out to be quite revelatory. She had the vision of Safe Haven and how it could be funded in a way that would ensure that the ministry would continue on, perhaps for decades to come. And when John heard her ideas, and how the Lord seemed to be leading and guiding, he suggested that she would make an excellent project manager. But, in addition to that, she and Barbie could also team up and take their vision "on the road" so to speak, encouraging other churches to pray about establishing their own homes for women. And, in helping them on their way, Barbie and Wendy could offer valuable experience, as well as seed money to get started. It was a dream that was very much on Wendy's heart. And so, as Maggie had requested, Wendy shared the reason for this early-morning conversation.

After Wendy was through, her eyes fairly shining with excitement, Maggie got a rather wistful look in her eyes and admitted she knew this day would come. She didn't know when and how, and she certainly didn't know all the details, she just knew that God would lead Wendy to use her time and talent for special ministry. And not only her time and talent, but, perhaps more importantly, her experience. Maggie confirmed what John had said about Wendy being the perfect person to manage the project and get Safe Haven up and running, in as little time as possible.

With that discussion out of the way, and both agreeing that God was certainly leading, the next issue was timing. Obviously, managing a project of this nature was a full-time job and would mean that Wendy would have to quit waitressing at the diner. Wendy looked at Maggie and felt a sadness wash over her. Maggie had been her savior, when she wasn't sure God even existed. Maggie was indeed her savior, but only because, ultimately, she led Wendy to *the* Savior. Maggie portrayed the best picture of Jesus that Wendy could have ever seen, in that dark season of her life.

Maggie looked lovingly at Wendy and said, "Honey, let's make this easy on both of us. Why don't we let tomorrow be your last day? You've trained the other gals so well; they're going to step up to the plate and never miss a step. And that's all on you. The continued success of the diner is due, in large part, to you and your work ethic, not to mention your ability to recruit and train the other staff. So, Wendy, even though I'll miss seeing you every day, I know we'll see each other regularly. I have to have Travis Time. I can't do without that. I'm going to turn him into a first-rate chef, if it's the last thing I do. He's got a pretty good start already, don't you think?" Wendy nodded in agreement, her eyes misting over. She was going to miss working at the diner, all the hustle and bustle of getting orders out on time and with accuracy, all the customers and their individual quirks, even the challenge of winning cranky customers over to the good side. She was going to miss it all. But she also knew that this was what God wanted.

Maggie saw the look on her face and the tears in her eyes and said, "Don't you dare do that, or I'm going to start flooding too." They both laughed and hugged each other, recognizing they weren't saying goodbye, for heaven's sakes; they were going to see each other all the time. It's just that the circumstances for seeing each other would change. Maggie followed that insight up with an idea that excited Wendy, on several levels. She said, "What if I come in once a week and hold cooking classes for the ladies? Coming out of the chaos of homelessness and abuse, it's a good chance they may have never learned how to cook, beyond micro-waving a burrito or frying an egg. We could do that together sometimes and I could have Travis, right alongside of me, for slicing and dicing. It'd go a long way in helping him feel included in the ministry also. What do you think? It's something to consider anyway."

Wendy agreed and actually found herself intrigued by the idea, picturing it in her mind as they continued to talk. But as for the imme-diate issue at hand, Wendy thought that tomorrow would probably be best in terms of it being her last day. She'd have to be sure to thank her loyal customers, but also let them know that they'd run into each other often around town. If they asked why she was leaving that would give her a chance to talk about her heart for Safe Haven and invite them to come to church on Sunday to hear the initial plans, as well as the testi-monies of Barbie and Jackie. She didn't know how many would take her up on it, but interest in Safe Haven among the few thousand residents of Pleasant Pastures was high, particularly since the garage sale had been such a success. Wendy hoped that interest in the project would remain high, because that could be greatly beneficial on so many levels.

Maggie and Wendy both heard the little bell above the door and realized that the 45 minutes had gone by very quickly. They hopped up, and from that point on, hardly had a minute to rest. People were in and out all day and Wendy loved every minute of it. She wondered what it would be like to manage a different kind of operation, one that didn't just feed the body, but fed the soul as well. Well, she was going to find out the answer to that question, starting in a few days. And truth be told? She could hardly wait.

Chapter 20

WENDY WENT HOME THAT AFTERNOON, having worked the breakfast and lunch shifts. Travis had just returned home, still excited about his first few days of school. That was truly a blessing to hear, and Wendy prayed that he'd always have that positive feeling about school and friends. His groups of friends seemed to be pretty good kids and as far as she knew they all came from stable homes. That could go a long way in helping the future be a little more secure for Travis and the others. There was so much out there in the world that wanted to grab their attention and lead them down a dark path. A stable home life would have a huge effect on counter-acting potentially harmful situations.

She hugged Travis as he was going to his room to do his home-work for the evening. He didn't have much, but what little he did have each day, he wanted to finish before dinner so that he'd have time to meet up with Tom afterwards. The weather was still warm and they enjoyed riding bikes or just "kickin around," as they referred to it. Wendy wasn't too sure what "kickin around" entailed, but assumed it just meant hanging out with each other.

They had dinner that night and, as usual, talked about their days. Travis went first and then John. Both had days that were pretty normal, nothing exceptional or out of the ordinary, just good days of accomplishing whatever challenges and tasks came their way.

Wendy shared last and reported on her conversation with Maggie. Travis immediately voiced concern over the idea of Wendy quitting at the diner. When John asked him what he was so concerned about, Travis blurted out his fear that he'd never see Maggie or Terry again. Both John and Wendy assured Travis that he'd still see them on a regular basis. And, in fact, according to Maggie, she had to have her Travis Time; that was part of the deal. Travis was delighted and felt much better after that. He enjoyed spending time at the diner and Maggie had let it be known that he could always come around for another cooking lesson, or just for a chance to greet some of the customers who had grown to enjoy conversations with this young boy who talked like an adult at times.

After Travis' fear about the diner had subsided, Wendy told them how excited she was to start as the project manager for Safe Haven. She really felt that God had tapped her on the shoulder for this season of life and that Safe Haven may very well be just the beginning. But as much as she was envisioning years down the road, and the opening of several new homes for women in the area, she also knew that she had a lot to learn and that launching Safe Haven would give her the experience she needed for the future. She asked them to pray for her in the days to come, so that she'd be able to tackle this new endeavor with wisdom and ability, outside of herself. This wasn't a Wendy project. This was a God project, and she wanted the whole process, from start to finish, to honor Him.

After assuring his mom that he'd pray for her and that she was going to do great, Travis asked to be excused from the table and, when given permission, he ran out the back door to meet up with his friend Tom. John and Wendy sat at the kitchen table enjoying the quiet sanctuary of their home. John asked Wendy what her immediate plans were. Wendy told him that she was beginning to formulate the plan in her mind and felt she'd have a pretty good grasp on it in a few days. But her first step was to stop in and see Kathy, the church secretary, tomorrow morning before she went to the diner for her last shift, beginning at 11:30. She wanted to talk with Kathy about designing a bulletin insert that would highlight the launching of the Safe Haven project. She wanted it to contain enough information to keep people excited and informed, while at the same time, helping them to plan as to what their part might be in the project. The major message she wanted to challenge them with was one of commitment. It was going to take all of them to get this project up and running; each one had a part to play, and only they and God could determine what that part would be.

Wendy had already designed the insert in her mind and now it was just a matter of sharing it with Kathy. Thursday was a little late to be printing up an insert for the bulletin on Sunday, but Kathy assured her it would be no problem. She also saw the importance of having the initial kick-off this Sunday when people were still excited about the Garage Sale, as well as the acquisition of the old Sinclair mansion just a few days ago. We've got to present the challenge while the momentum's still going full speed ahead. There's nothing more deadly for a project, than to let it stall for weeks or months on end. So, this Sunday was going to be the official kick-off. Kathy was going to work her magic and produce an insert that grabbed people's attention. Between a bold, colorful insert and Barbie and Jackie's testimonies, along with encouraging words from both John and Wendy, it should be a marvelous launch.

Tomorrow was Thursday and was already jam-packed. Between meeting with Kathy and working a double shift on her last day, Wendy was going to be very busy for the next 24 hours. She wondered how she was going to do, saying goodbye to her regular customers. True, she wasn't really going anywhere, at least not in terms of the big picture. She wasn't leaving Pleasant Pastures; she was just leaving her position at the diner. But it was certainly a bittersweet decision. As excited as she was to work on Safe Haven, Wendy really was going to miss the interaction and personal conversations with her customers, many of whom she'd come to see as friends. Some of her customers never really went too deep, in terms of the level of conversations, and that was all right too. But she'd at least miss the friendly banter that went on back-and-forth, certainly nothing profound, but pleasant and enjoyable nevertheless. She was going to miss it all. On the other hand, Wendy realized that she had the best of two worlds. She would still see her customers around town. For heaven's sakes, it's not like Pleasant Pastures was Seattle. This was small-town USA, where everybody knew everybody else. Wendy took comfort in that fact because, in all honesty, she realized that the church and the town had become the extended family she had always longed for, and yet had never experienced. So, Wendy took comfort in the fact that she'd still see the people she'd really grown to love and appreciate.

But as for part two, of the best of two worlds, she was going to have the privilege of seeing something truly great come together. And, in the decades to come, this home was going to take scores of women out of the messiness of their life, and help them get a firm foothold on both the present and the future. Many women were going to enter the Kingdom over the next few years as they encountered the Lord Jesus through the loving ministry of Safe Haven. Wendy marveled at the privilege she had to be an integral part of that dream.

The next day was a whirlwind of activity. Wendy met Kathy at 8:00 AM and shared her vision for the insert that would run for three weeks in a row, in an effort to reach everyone. Being very good at lay-out, as well as having the eye of an artist, Kathy was able to add her own personal touch. The way Kathy closed her eyes, processing all the information about the vision, the need, and the ways to help, and then shared with Wendy what she saw that would make the concepts come alive, was truly astounding. And Wendy knew, that what Kathy was seeing in her mind, would be an attention-grabbing piece of work that would be the foundation for sharing the vision with anyone who was interested. It was going to be a valuable promotional tool and Wendy was excited to see the finished product.

After meeting with Kathy, Wendy had a few hours before her shift, so she decided to work on a to-do list. She was going to put together a preliminary action plan that included everything from fundraising campaigns, renovation schedules, yard projects, decorating, furnishings, as well as the actual program itself. Much of her list included recruiting others who could either help with the task at hand or, at the very least, could give her insightful advice as to the best way to accomplish it. She also included regular meetings with Barbie that would allow her to pick the brain of one who's had years of experience in these kinds of endeavors.

As Wendy's list grew larger, so did her level of excitement. With that excitement coursing through her very being, Wendy looked at her watch and realized that she was due at the diner in 45 minutes. She reluctantly put her list aside, went into the bedroom, donning her uniform for the last time, and then started walking toward the diner. It was hard to believe that this was her last day. She was going to miss it - no doubt about that - but she was replacing it with something that truly was of eternal value.

She was excited about what lay ahead for their family, for the church, and for Safe Haven. The only thing that clouded the sunshine of this glorious day of new beginnings, was the fact that she and John were scheduled to meet with Nick, tomorrow at 12 o'clock noon. Her first day on the job as project manager and she had to meet with her former boss - a boss, who by the way, had threatened to kill her. How's that for a fun way to spend a lunch hour? Well, Wendy thought, we've been praying for Nick. Maybe we'll see some real breakthrough here and Nick will have realized the error of his ways, and as they say, turned over a new leaf. I believe in miracles, Wendy thought, but that one would be a challenge - even for God.

Chapter 21

WENDY'S LAST SHIFT AT THE DINER HAD gone better than she'd hoped. There had been tears, of course. She was going to be missed and she, in turn, was going to miss her co-workers and customers. But, as she kept reminding herself, she was leaving her job, not Pleasant Pastures.

The day went by very quickly until it was time to serve her final customer, close the door, and begin to help clean up in preparation for the early shift tomorrow morning. Her beloved co-workers would do just fine without her. It was a good crew and Wendy walked out that night knowing that she had done a good job in the few months she'd been there.

Wendy expected that she would have shed even more tears on her walk home, but surprisingly, her eyes remained dry the entire way. She was thinking about the bittersweet feelings she'd been experiencing for the last 48 hours, but she realized that now she was centering in on the sweet, and not so much the bitter. Wendy was truly excited about the adventure that was ahead. What was it going to be like to get up tomorrow morning, knowing that she had the whole day to work on the Safe Haven project? A shudder of delight ran through her as she thought about the adventure on which she was about to embark.

Wendy walked in the door and was greeted with cheers, by her two favorite guys in the whole world. They had the table set for a party, with balloons and little paper hats, and even a cake. John and Travis had gone up to the Safeway store in Leavenworth and had thrown themselves on the mercy of the cake decorator. Could she please write "congratulations on your retirement" on the chocolate cake they had found in the display case? She informed them that they usually needed at least 48 hours' notice, but she'd do what she could. And sure enough, she broke the 48-hour rule and a few minutes later they were heading home, the cake securely tucked away in the trunk. It was fortunate indeed to have happened upon a pastry chef with a rebellious streak. Rules or no rules, they were going to get their cake.

They had a marvelous celebration and Wendy was truly grateful for her two boys, as she called them. Retirement didn't seem like quite the appropriate word, given her age, but it was the best they could come up with and served the purpose just fine. They ate a light dinner of leftovers and then enjoyed a piece of the cake. Their conversation centered on Wendy's last day and the customers she saw.

Finally, it was time to hit the sack. It'd been a long, tiring day, with Wendy choosing to work a double shift in an effort to say thanks to as many customers as possible. She and John soon fell asleep after discussing plans for Friday's lunch with Nick. Both were a little nervous, and yet they knew they were doing the right thing.

The next morning dawned with clear blue skies and the promise of a beautiful, sunny day. John left for the office and promised to be home at 11:00 AM, to help Wendy prepare the lunch. Wendy told him she had it all under control, but she'd enjoy his company. She was planning on a simple lunch of French dip sandwiches, with a green salad on the side. They'd have their choice of ranch, blue cheese or Green Goddess dressings. Dessert would be left-over retirement cake. The meal was simple; the lunch with Nick wasn't really about the food. It was about letting go of the past and getting a fresh start for everyone, including Nick. Neither John nor Wendy could predict how this was going to go, or whether Nick would have any kind of heart change, but they were excited, though a bit nervous, to be part of the entire process.

John came home at precisely 11 AM, as promised, and promptly began to help Wendy with the preparations. At 11:55 there was a knock on the door and when John went to answer it, there was Nick. John invited him in and told him it was good to see him again. Nick said that it was nice to be invited. Awkward silence. Neither knew quite what to say. Fortunately, Wendy came in and saved the day. She walked up to Nick, looking at him with a hint of a smile playing at the corner of her mouth. It wasn't a smile that bespoke humor or joy; it was more of an expression of wonder. It was a look that said: Huh… who would've thought this scene would have ever played out? Wendy Baker and Nick Salerno in the same room? Not in a million years!

And yet, here they were. And at that exact moment in time, Wendy knew that something had changed within her. She wasn't angry and disgusted with him. She wasn't afraid for her life. She didn't have second thoughts and demand that he leave. Though it surprised her, the first feeling she encountered was forgiveness. He had threatened to kill her, and it scared her enough that she ran. But she had also come to realize that was just that: a threat. There was nothing in Nick's background that gave any indication that he would have been capable of following through with it. He wasn't the tough-guy gangster he always tried to portray himself as being. The second thing that struck her was how much she would love to see his life turned around, just as hers had. She wasn't the same person she was six months ago. And if God could do that for her, He could certainly do that for Nick.

Much to her surprise, Wendy walked up to Nick and gave him a slight hug, saying that it was nice that he could come. Nick was taken aback by her kind gesture and stammered something about it being good to see her too. Awkward silence again, nobody quite knowing what to say. Finally, Wendy said, "Okay, let's not ignore the elephant in the room. It's not going to go away, so let's just admit it's there and get on with things. Nick, the last time we were together, you threatened to kill me. Isn't that right?" Nick looked at Wendy, rather sheepishly, and nodded his head. Wendy acknowledged his answer and said, "Okay then. I have only one question. Would you have done it, Nick? Would you have killed me?" Nick looked at Wendy and said, "Nah, I wouldn't have done it for two very good reasons. Number one: I always liked you and the kid. I didn't always show it, but I did. And number two: I can't stand violence; it makes me nauseated. I'm kind of a wimp when it comes to that stuff."

Wendy started to chuckle and then broke out into a wide grin, leading to outright laughter. It wasn't an unkind gesture; it just broke the ice and brought a measure of calm into the formerly tense situation.

Nick found himself smiling and chuckling also and shaking his head, saying, "I can't believe I just admitted to that. Don't ever let that out or I'll be ruined, and every goon in Chicago will come gunning for me. My rep is everything." John and Wendy smiled again and promised absolute discretion. The agreement being made, Wendy looked at Nick and said, "Okay Mr. Tough Guy…let's go have some lunch." Nick smiled and agreed that lunch sounded like a great idea.

They talked about life in Chicago and how different it was from life in Pleasant Pastures. Wendy related her story of her trip out West, after hearing the voice telling her to run. She talked about taking precautions against being followed and how, after 2 ½ days on the road, she accidentally found herself in this quaint little town. But, of course, she now realized that it wasn't an accident at all. She firmly believed that God was leading her every step of the way; she just didn't know it. Nick looked at John and Wendy both, and haltingly said something that was obviously very difficult for him. He looked at them and said, "You know, I don't usually do this, but I'm going to make an exception for you. Wendy, I want to apologize for the way I treated you towards the end there. I asked you to do something that I thought was the next step in growing the business, and when you ran, it surprised me. I couldn't figure it out. You would have made a ton of money for you and the kid. I thought it would have been great for both of us. Now, I gotta tell you, I'm pretty rich. Those clubs have made me a lot of money; so much, in fact, I could retire now and do pretty good for the rest of my life, especially if I lived someplace other than Chicago, where the price of everything is nuts. But you know me. Being a success in life has always been about the money. For a guy like me, what else is there? Money's the great motivator in life. There's never enough, no matter how much you got."

Both John and Wendy were saddened, but not surprised to hear Nick's definition of a successful life. A lot of people felt that money was the surefire road to happiness, and Nick was no exception. It's what Nick said next, that shocked them, and got their immediate attention. Nick looked at Wendy and said, very matter-of-factly, "That's why, when I found you here, and saw what a sweet deal you had landed, I had a new admiration for you. You weren't just a dancer who was going to be working for someone else the rest of your life. No, you had fire. You had guts. You had the power to call your own shots, make your own way into the business with no help from me. What I saw last Saturday and Sunday, and the amount of money that came in those two days, showed me that you two really know how to run a deal. And you know what? All of that could be just the beginning, if you wanted it too. You've got a sweet operation going here, but I could show you how to really clean up in this religious scam. You haven't even begun to tap the potential yet. You're sitting on a gold mine, and I'm not sure you even realize just how lucrative this thing you've got going could really be. And guys, I'm willing to help you for a small percentage of the cut, say 30%?"

John and Wendy were dumbfounded. They literally were at a loss for words. It was John who first found his voice and said, "Nick, you've kind of lost me here. What scam are you talking about? I'm a little confused." And Nick, having no idea that John's look of innocence was genuine said, "Come on guys, you know what I'm talking about. You've got a protection racket going on here, pure and simple. You convince people to do the Jesus thing and they'll be protected, after they kick the bucket. They'll have an iron-clad guarantee of escaping the fires of hell. But you don't stop there. They're not just promised an escape from hell, they're also promised a one-way ticket to heaven

- harps, angels, pearly gates - the whole lasagna. And then, you add one more thing that really cinches the deal. When they make their commitment to this whole Jesus thing, you promise that God Himself will walk them through life and get them the best of everything. What do you preachers call it? Oh yeah, the abundant life. Well, think about it. Who doesn't want a surefire guarantee of escaping hell and walking through the pearly gates? But not only that, on their way to pie-in-the-sky-by and by, they get to live the good life - pretty much getting whatever they want. Now *that's* a sweet deal. Who could walk away from that? You've taken the old protection racket and kicked it up several notches. I gotta tell you, I admire you for that. It's pure genius. But I could show you how to really bring home the big bucks. We could be partners in this and both make more money than you could ever dream of. I could get guys who could charm the socks off snakes. I've got guys who are so slick, they could sell sunlamps in Arizona. All you got to do John is teach them what to say, and how to act, and we could open up a slew of these churches over the entire eastern Washington area. I saw the money that came in last weekend. It had to be at least $10,000. Well, imagine doing that every week with, what, 10 different churches? That's 100 grand a week. I could get the guys, and you could teach them. We'd have more money than God. And this home for women? Fantastic idea! People will give to that kind of thing constantly and never even question it. Multiply that out by 10 and it's just more money in our pockets. I'm telling you guys, you're sitting on Fort Knox here, but you haven't even begun to tap the potential. I can do that for you. We could be partners and make more money than you ever dreamed of."

John and Wendy sat back absolutely amazed at how far Nick had missed it. He had no concept of what they were doing and why they were doing it. Is that how all non-believers saw church and the work of the Lord? Did they all see it as a scam, or was Nick the exception? What had they done that gave Nick that impression? And even more importantly, what could they do to convince him that the Lord's work that was being done at Pleasant Pastures was legitimate? They did, indeed, present the gospel as a way of escaping an eternity without God, and, at the same time, promised them the joy of heaven when they died. But that wasn't a protection racket. That was the gospel of Christ that saves and sets people free. And the abundant life? That was a promise from Jesus Himself. It wasn't a way to get people to open their pocketbooks. It was just simply Jesus' way of saying that walking with Him brought true joy and peace to life. It had nothing to do with money and possessions, but it had everything to do with meaning and purpose. Nick had this wrong on so many levels, and they were going to have to set him straight. He may not believe it, but they couldn't let him walk out of their house without understanding what was really going on.

Wendy looked at Nick and spoke first. She said, "Nick, that's an interesting take you have on what we're doing here. And your idea about multiplying the number of churches and bringing in 100 grand a week is really something. I could really see, given the right circumstances, and the right cast of characters, how that kind of charade would work. There's only one thing wrong with your idea. It misses the point of what we do, entirely. It's so completely opposite of what we're trying to do, I'm not even sure where to begin in trying to change your mind." Now Nick was the one who looked confused. "What do you mean?" He asked. John replied, "Nick, believe it or not, this scam, as you put it, isn't all about money. In fact, it's not a scam at all. We've dedicated our lives to presenting the gospel message that changes people." Just then, Wendy spoke up and said, "It changed my life, Nick and He gave me everything I ever wanted." Nick retorted, "Well, I don't want to be crass here, but you're living in a 1200 square foot cottage, in a little podunk town, in the middle of nowhere. Not exactly a vacation at the Ritz!" Wendy looked at him and said, "But we're happy, Nick, and we thank God for our little house and family. It's really not about money, either for us, or for our church."

Nick looked at them both, with a hint of fire in his eyes, and challenged, "You mean to tell me, that if I offered you $100,000 as a gift to your church, you'd turn it down? You're telling me that money doesn't mean anything to you? I'd offer you $100,000 and you'd say no thanks?"

"Well, it depends, Nick," Wendy replied.

"Okay, now we're getting honest here. It depends on what?"

"It would depend on your motivation."

"Okay, so the motivation is the same as anyone else. The $100,000 would buy me some brownie points with the Big Guy upstairs."

"If that was your motivation Nick, we'd turn the money down."

"Why would you turn it down? That's everybody's motivation. Give money to get God to look the other way. So, I've done a few bad things in my life? $100,000 ought to take care of some of that."

"But that's just it, Nick. You can't by God's silence, or somehow make Him temporarily blind. And you can't buy your way into heaven, I don't care how much money you give. You can't buy your salvation."

"Hey listen you two. In my world, you got enough money, you can buy anything."

"That's just it, Nick. This isn't your world…it's God's. And it's not for sale. You can't buy your way into heaven."

"Then how can you get there, for crying out loud? That was always going to be my ace in the hole. When it looks like I'm getting ready to buy the farm, I'll go see my priest, cough up a bunch of dough, and go waltzing through the pearly gates and down the streets of gold."

"If that's your plan Nick, I have to tell you, it isn't going to work and you're going to be lost."

Nick stared at John and Wendy, a look of disappointment, and perhaps anger in his eyes, and said, "Okay, if that's the way you want to play it, fine. I just wanted to offer you something that could expand your business and get that lady's house opened up - maybe several of them over the next year - but if you don't want in on it, that's your loss, not mine. I got all kinds of ways to make money. There are suckers born every minute and I know how to tap into them. Keep doing your own thing folks, but if you ever get smart and change your mind, you know where to find me."

With that, Nick stood up indicating that he felt it was time for him to go. As he stood up, Wendy came over and put her hand on his arm and said, "I know you're upset Nick. I just hope that in the days to come, you'll understand what we're saying. No matter what this looks like to you, we're not running a game here, this isn't a scam. It's a ministry. And it's a ministry we believe in sincerely."

Nick looked from Wendy to John and back again and then said, "Okay. I don't get it, but it's your call. Thanks for lunch. It was nice of you to invite me over. I guess I'll be heading back to Chicago." "When are you planning to leave, Nick?" John asked. "Oh, probably tomorrow." Wendy spoke up and said, "Hey Nick, would you do us a favor? Would you come to church on Sunday? Just don't sit behind Melverna and her big hat this time; we'd actually like to see you." Nick chuckled and said, "Okay, I'll see you in church, then I'll head out. By the way where does she get those hats anyway? She could hide a family of monkeys in there."

Chapter 22

JOHN AND WENDY STOOD AT THE DOOR WATCH-
ing Nick get into his car and drive away. They shut the door
and then turned to each other and hugged, silently processing all
that had gone on during their lunch with Nick. Neither of them could
quite come to grips with what Nick had said. The idea of their ministry being a protection racket, a scam, if you will, was shocking and
disturbing. The idea that he could actually *think* that was the shocking
part. How could he ever come to that conclusion, just by observing
the activities of this past weekend? Yes, they took in about $10,000,
Nick was right on about that one, but nobody had been forced to
give. People from all over the community took part in the garage sale,

buying items they were happy to find. And yes, the offering had been taken and was indeed around $3000 - not huge, but certainly adequate to cover the bills. And yes, the extra offering was over $3000 also and made the down payment on the house a reality the next day. They took in over $10,000 that weekend. John and Wendy saw it as a tremendous blessing from the Lord, and in many ways, the seal of His approval. But Nick looked at it in an entirely different way. He saw the sacrificial giving as a game, a scam designed to fleece their congregation for as much money as possible. That was shocking.

The other thing that disturbed them greatly was the idea that Nick's probably not alone in his view of their ministry, or any ministry for that matter. What if a lot of people, who had no understanding of the things of Christ, had the same philosophy? What if many of them felt that the only thing churches wanted was your money? They don't really care about you as a person; they only cared about your wallet. That was deeply disturbing and caused both John and Wendy to sink into each other's arms with heavy sighs. The thought that someone could so misread their motives, wasn't an easy pill to swallow. And so, they simply clung to each other for several minutes, each of them processing what they'd heard.

Of course, allegations of churches being after your money certainly weren't new. John remembered talking to a guy he'd met at the post office, back when he was on staff at First Baptist. They somehow got talking, while standing in line, and the conversation continued in the parking lot outside. John discovered that Tony grew up in Minneapolis and had lived in the general vicinity his entire life. But Tony got around. He had traveled the country as a long-haul truck driver and had driven in every state, except Alaska and Hawaii. The hours were long and being away from his wife and kids was tough, but that's what he did for a living and he didn't really see a way to change that, at least not for now. When John asked him if he and his family had a church home that could give them some emotional support while he was on the road, he looked at John as if he was crazy. "Are you kidding me? We stay away from churches. All they want is my money and I don't have any extra to give. And besides, if I had extra money, why would I give it to them? The last time I was in church was probably 15 years ago. A friend had invited me to go with him and so I thought, why not, maybe I'll really like it. Well John, you know what happened? Things were going along fine for a while. And then they started to pass the plates for the offering. And I thought, that's cool. Every organization needs money to run itself, right? So anyway, I'm sitting on the end of the bench and the guy next to me passes me the plate, and I put in five dollars. I was just about ready to take out four ones for change, when the usher snatches the plate out of my hand and passes it on to the next row. I didn't want to make a big scene and so I just shut up. But I've never been back since. Money is not easy to come by and that five dollars could have paid for a number of things I needed, more than sitting in a church service. Anyway, all that to say, I don't trust churches or preachers. They just seem too slick and have their hand out all the time."

John had ended the conversation shortly after, before Tony asked him what he did for a living. It wasn't that John felt bad about being in the ministry; he just knew that it would embarrass Tony, after all he had said. But looking back on it, if he had the chance to do it all over again, John had felt that perhaps he'd missed an opportunity to help Tony see a different view of the church, as a whole. And again, just like the lunch conversation with Nick, it bothered John to think that there might be many folks out there with the same opinion of churches and ministers.

Another example Tony had given made John squirm a little bit, at least inside. A few years earlier a traveling evangelist had made headlines when he revealed that he was a phony. The guy was billed as the world's youngest minister: the boy-preacher. He was preaching sermons and praying for people while he was just four years old. And people would come from miles around to witness this phenomenon. But when he got to be about 15, and started growing up and looking more like a grown man, his popularity waned. He wasn't quite the sensation that he had been before, as a little boy. Several years later, when he and his wife hit a snag, and really needed to find a good source of income, he came up with the idea to go back on the road as an evangelist. So, he bought himself some fancy duds and sent letters to the various contacts he had from years before, telling them he was back. The boy-preacher had grown up and was coming to their area to preach the gospel and heal the sick. He began getting invitations to preach and hold revival and healing meetings. And sure enough, pretty soon the money was pouring in from the offerings. People were more than willing to part with their hard-earned money in order to help support this "man of God" who was doing so much for the Lord. He was pulling out huge crowds as he crisscrossed the country, preaching the gospel.

But then one day a shocking thing happened. He went on a late-night television show and revealed that he was a phony. He admitted that he didn't believe the gospel he'd been preaching. He told how as a young boy, his father would hold his head underwater in the sink, until he learned his sermon by heart. When people asked him where he got his messages, he'd always claim that they came from the Holy

Spirit, sometimes in dreams. But in reality, his father wrote them and forced his son to memorize the short, but impressive sermons - at least impressive when delivered by a four-year-old boy.

But when he got back on the "Gospel Road" as an adult, he simply took the basic messages he'd learned as a boy, and lengthened them out. They still included all the elements of the gospel: the cross, the blood, escape from hell, a promise of heaven. All the typical themes any evangelist might preach. But in his case, though he preached it, he didn't believe it. He just knew from past experience what people expected to hear, what they wanted to hear. And so, he delivered the message in a very theatrical presentation that was built on the Word of God, and the truth of the gospel. The only drawback to his ministry was the fact that he didn't believe a word of what he was preaching.

When he revealed himself as a phony, the admission made news headlines around the country. He became even more well-known than he'd ever been as an evangelist. He even began to get bit parts in a few movies, but that petered out after a while. And sure enough, this phony evangelist faded into obscurity over the coming years. And other than the occasional role in films, or maybe an interview for a "Where are they now?" article, not much was out there concerning him.

It was a sad day for the cause of the gospel when he finally came clean. Although, on the one hand, it was good that he wasn't living a lie anymore, it also had the effect of giving people an excuse to live their lives with no thought as to the God who created them. After all, look at Reverend Moneybags, people would say. He preached the gospel and yet didn't believe it himself. He was in it for the money. "Religion's all about the money," they'd say, "I don't want anything to do with it." End of story.

John and Wendy spent the next hour talking about people's perception of preachers and churches. They agreed that, over the years, the occasional revelation that a particular evangelist was as phony as a three-dollar bill, had taken its toll, but they personally had never run into it, that is until today. Their lunch conversation with Nick had shaken both of them up quite a bit. The idea that Nick thought they had a "sweet deal" going here, really bothered them. But it also started a conversation between them that was very crucial, not only for the present, but also for the future. They were forced to deal with the questions that Nick had, inadvertently, brought to the surface.

Why were they doing all of this anyway? Was it just a way to make a living? Was it simply a job, like any other job? Did they crave the recognition it brought them as pastor and wife? Did they need the respect their positions held, in order to feel fulfilled? Did they like the sense of power that might be felt when people would open up their wallets and give their hard-earned money for the church, or special project such as Safe Haven? It all boiled down to one basic question: What was their motivation for being in the ministry?

As John and Wendy continued to talk, hitting each question with honesty and forthrightness, the answer became crystal clear. This ministry gig wasn't a "sweet deal." It wasn't a scam. It wasn't a protection racket. It was all about the gospel that saved people and set them free, from the things that bound them up. That was it, pure and simple. Even though they were paid to do the work, it wasn't about the money; it was about the calling. This is what God had called them to do. And even though John and Wendy knew they'd run into more "Nicks" in the years to come, that wouldn't deter them from fulfilling their calling. Cynics would come and go, but the gospel was forever.

But they also determined to make something else a priority in their lives. Not only were they determined to live out their calling as ministers of the gospel, they also made the commitment to do that in such a way as to never bring reproach on the name of Jesus. In other words, though there would always be those who tarnished the name of the Lord, through their unwise choices and less then righteous behavior, John and Wendy committed to walking in purity of lifestyle. They determined to ask for the Spirit's guidance daily, in order to keep them from temptation, and to give them discernment to know what was of God, and what wasn't. They made a commitment to each other, and to God, to never purposely behave in such a way as to give people an excuse to walk away from God and their faith. They further determined together that if that should ever happen, no matter what the circumstances, they would walk away from ministry in an effort to limit the damage to the faith of others.

The conversation with Nick had indeed left them shaken. And yet, at the same time, it had made them stronger and more resolved to live like Jesus. After all, that's what the word Christian meant anyway. It meant "little Christ." That said it all.

Now, how they were going to be "little Christ's" to Nick, remained unclear. It appeared that Nick was going to be taking off for Chicago again tomorrow, and they would be separated by thousands of miles. It's pretty hard to have an impact on a person's life when you're not in touch with them. But John and Wendy had a secret. They knew something that Nick didn't know. And that secret was prayer. They were going to continue to pray for Nick. In fact, they were going to set their prayers on warp speed and maximum power. They knew that their prayers would release the Holy Spirit to work in Nick's life, in such a way, that he'd never know what hit him. It may take a while, but they were convinced that Nick was going to see his need of the Lord.

It was actually kind of funny. Nick was so worried about his reputation. As he said before, if word got out that he was going soft, every goon in Chicago was going to come gunning for him. John and Wendy shared a chuckle over that one, because they knew the truth. It's not the goons that are coming after Nick: it's God. And when God's after you, you better watch out, because you're in for the ride of your life. God has His sights set on Nick. And it was only a matter of time before God pulled the trigger.

Chapter 23

THROUGHOUT THE REST OF THE DAY FRIDAY, AS well as much of Saturday, both John and Wendy replayed the lunch with Nick in their minds. There didn't seem to be much hope that they were going to change his mind anytime soon, so whenever they thought about it, they simply sent up a short, silent arrow prayer targeting Nick's attitude. Maybe, if he'd actually show up at church on Sunday, something would change. It was a longshot, but you never knew, something might get through to him.

Saturday evening Wendy called Barbie, just to make sure that everything was still a go for her and Jackie the next day. Barbie assured her that everything was going as planned, and that Jackie was excited to share her story. Barbie also expressed thanks that John was willing to give up his pulpit time for them. It's much more liberating not to feel rushed. Barbie planned to take 10 minutes to share the ministry of Mercy House, while Jackie would spend about 25 minutes telling how her life had been changed since coming to stay at the home.

Wendy assured Barbie of their prayers and said that they'd be there to greet them when they arrived the next morning. She also suggested that, if possible, Barbie and Jackie arrive about 10:30 AM, so that they could have a short sound check and then go back to John's office for a time of prayer.

Wendy hung up the phone and then joined John and Travis in the living room. They were watching Big-Time Wrestling again. Evidently, this was one way that John and Travis were building their father/son relationship. Wendy wasn't particularly interested in the whole idea of pro-wrestling, but if her two guys liked to watch it together, who was she to argue with that. They were both whooping and hollering when something exciting took place, and so Wendy sat there and tried to join in. As she continued to watch, she was puzzled about why there were so many wrestlers in the ring. She finally asked the question and Travis answered her immediately. "Mom, this is a "10 man over-the-top-rope battle royal." There are 10 men in the ring and the point is to toss everybody out. But you can't get them out any other way but by throwing them over the top rope. The last man in the ring is the winner and takes home the grand prize. Wendy continued to watch, wondering how any of them could ever walk away from a match like that. They looked like they were killing each other.

Finally, when the show was over, Travis headed for bed and John and Wendy went to their room to read. Wendy asked John why the wrestlers could be thrown down to the mat, stomped on, hit full in the face with fists or forearms, get violently tossed out of the ring, and yet still walk away. How could anybody take that kind of punishment? John smiled at Wendy and said, "Honey, let me share one of the secrets of professional wrestling. It's fake. Now, don't get me wrong. Fake doesn't mean they're not great athletes. These guys are incredible and if they didn't know what they were doing, you're right; they'd never be able to get up and walk out of there. And sometimes, one of them might land wrong, or a particular move goes bad and then an injury can result. But, for the most part, it's safe and the outcome is always decided ahead of time. And they're trained to throw punches and execute moves, in such a way, as to never really do serious damage." "Yeah, but John, I saw one of the guys with blood on his forehead. That didn't look fake to me." "No, that was real blood," John replied, "but it still wasn't as bad as it appeared. Some guys have the ability to bleed, fairly easily. The open cut on the forehead begins to bleed and, when it's mixed with the wrestlers sweat, it looks like they're bleeding profusely. There's a saying in pro wrestling - red is green. In other words, if you're a bleeder, that's going to translate into more money. Red is green." Wendy shook her head and said, "Why do you watch this stuff? Is it good for Travis to see all of that?" John chuckled and said, "Oh, it's fine. It's just a way for Travis and I to spend a little time together, watching something he's pretty excited about. We've talked about it before. He knows the score, but it's still fun to watch together."

Wendy shook her head and said, "Well, I guess that makes sense to some extent. But I'm not sure I'm ever going to totally get it. It's fake, and yet you and Travis want to watch it together, cheering for your favorite wrestler, even though the winner has already been decided ahead of time. How does that make any sense? Why would you want to waste your time with something that's not real? It might give the appearance of being real, but it's not. Why would you even want to watch it, let alone pay money to go see it in person? I don't get it." John just shrugged his shoulders and said, "I don't know, honey. It's guys being guys. Don't worry about it with Travis. He'll grow out of it." "Well, you haven't grown out of it, so far." exclaimed Wendy. "You're as bad as he is!" "True," John replied, "but you love me anyway." John gave his pouty face and Wendy had to laugh. For a big guy, he could scrunch up his face and look like a little kid. She may not understand everything about him, but she knew one thing. She sure loved this man. And she especially loved the fact that he wanted to spend time with Travis, even if it was watching giant men toss each other out of the ring.

That night, Wendy's sleep was filled with schizophrenic dreams, darting back-and-forth in her unconscious mind. They all seemed to center around a ring full of wrestlers, vying for the top position. In her dream, she saw 10 men in a battle royal, fighting to be the last one standing - the winner in this match, destined to take the top prize. They looked hard and sinister - perhaps evil. But one wrestler stood out from the rest because he was so different. The other wrestlers were evil, but this one personified purity and goodness. Though he was engaged in the battle and fought with great ability, as did the other wrestlers, his attitude and countenance were vastly different than the rest. His was an attitude of confidence. Not arrogance, but confidence, based on an inner foundation of strength and authority. Wendy saw him in her dream and was actually positive that, in spite of all the evil that surrounded him, he was going to come out on top. As she continued to watch the match, as if from a distance, she saw writing appear on the foreheads of each wrestler. As she strained to read the message, each being one word, she realized that what she was seeing was actually the name of each contender. She saw names such as anger, hate, lust, greed, prejudice, violence, lying, cheating and more. But standing out among this den of sin was the one she'd noticed right away. On his forehead, in contrast to the others, was written one word: Love. Each wrestler was engaging in the battle and appeared to be motivated by the character of his name. It was obvious to Wendy, even in her dream, who was going to win. Love always conquered all and this match would be no different.

Except, that's not what happened. The expected winner was love, but someone behind the scenes, decided to change the outcome. And in the end, hate wound up winning. Even in her dream Wendy knew how wrong this was. Love always won, but not this time. She cried out in her dream, asking how this could have ever happened. How could hate ever defeat love? Wendy's mind spoke back to her in her unconscious dream state, and what it said shocked her. Her thoughts were running rampant. What you saw wasn't love at all - it was fake - it was all part of his act. They all had a character they played, and he was no exception. His very purpose was to play the part of the good guy - to look and act like love - but, deep inside, he was no different than the rest. Nobody was really who they claimed to be, because the whole setup was fake. It was a show. It was a scam. It was designed to fool people. The grunts and groans, the violence, the pain, even the blood, was nothing but show. Pay your money, buy your tickets, suckers, and we'll give you what you came to see.

Wendy cried out in her dream, "But that can't be. It can't all be fake - it just can't!" And just then, "Love" stepped out of the ring and came and stood before Wendy, his face just inches from hers. And with an evil smile, his putrid breath assaulting her nostrils, he hissed, "And how are you any different?"

Wendy woke up from her nightmare in a cold sweat. Words like fake, scam, lying, cheating, racing back and forth in her mind, with lightning speed. A familiar sense of evil began to creep up her body, beginning in the very tips of her toes and making its way up slowly, until she could feel it in her head. She hadn't felt this level of evil since she ran from her former life. But there it was again, accusing her, making her question all she had come to know and experience, in the past several months. There it was, throwing the old familiar questions in her face: "Who do you think you are? Why do you think you can escape me? Why would I ever let you go free? You're mine, and you'll be mine forever. You don't really believe all that stuff anyway. You're just pretending. This is your own battle royal. It's fake - it's a scam - the outcomes already been decided. And guess what, slut - you're going to lose. It's a done deal!"

Wendy shook from fear, as the verbal assaults kept coming into her mind. But...deep within, she knew that what she was hearing was absolutely *not* true. She knew, beyond a shadow of a doubt, that the love and grace of God had absolutely brought total change to her life. She knew she wasn't the same person she was before. She knew that the enemy was trying to mess with her head and get her to turn back from her new life. But deep inside, a seed of faith was beginning to grow, and it was growing at warp speed. It might have suffered a blow from the nightmare and the assault of accusations against her, but that seed wouldn't die. In fact, it shook off the assault and began to expand, doubling in size every second. And when it felt as if Wendy couldn't contain it any longer, she sat up in bed and addressed the enemy of her soul, with the strength and authority of a heavenly warrior, because that's what she was, and she knew it. With every ounce of her being, she knew it! And in a calm voice, the fear completely gone, she declared, "Satan, you're a liar and a thief. You are *not* going to steal what's mine. You're not going to steal what Jesus purchased for me. It's mine and you can't have it, ever. So, Satan, I'm telling you now: you leave me, this instant! And don't ever think about coming back. In the name of Jesus Christ, take a hike!"

And with that declaration of faith, Wendy sensed the darkness and dread leave her body. At the same time, a wonderful feeling of peace and serenity filled her soul. She knew that she'd been involved in a major battle with the enemy of heaven. But, whereas before, she didn't know how to fight him, now she not only knew how to fight, she had the authority to do so.

During this entire battle John never woke up. She knew that if she called out to him, he'd be there at her side in an instant, praying and doing warfare with her. He was a strong prayer warrior and she knew that he'd faced some pretty major battles himself, particularly from the depression that attacked him during the church split last year. But during the attack, she felt that this was her battle to face. She sensed that this was a pivotal moment in her quest to be a strong woman of God. And sure enough, armed with the power and authority that was hers in the name of Jesus, she fought back and won. She knew there'd be other battles, but she also knew that with every victory, her faith would be strengthened.

Wendy lay back down and checked the clock. It was 3 AM and she'd have to be up in just three hours to get her family ready for church. She wondered about the timing of this attack. She didn't think it was a coincidence that it came just before they launched the drive for Safe Haven. She also recognized the obvious elements that were a combination of the conversation with Nick and the wrestling match, from a few hours before. This battle was over and she'd experienced the victory, but she wasn't naïve. There would be more. In fact, as she lay there, just on the verge of drifting off, she sensed in her spirit that another challenge was coming soon. She knew it wasn't going to be the same kind of in-your-face assault, as this one had been. It was going to be different. It was going to be hard, yet hard in a different way. But rather than that thought driving her down into an abyss of fear, she experienced exactly the opposite. A feeling of total peace washed over her and Wendy fell into a deep, dreamless sleep.

Chapter 24

THE ALARM WENT OFF AT 6:00 AM AND WENDY reached over and shut it off. In spite of her battle of just three hours before, she felt fully awake. But more than that, she felt alive - energized - full of the Spirit. It wasn't a new sensation exactly; she had felt the Spirit's power in her life several times over the last months. But this was different. The intensity of it, coming off the battle in the early hours of the morning, magnified it greatly. It's as if she saw her life in a whole new way. We are in a war, she thought. And that war is for the souls of people. That was made very clear to her last night. And although Wendy had certainly known that since coming to faith in Christ, she realized that she had never had it demonstrated quite so clearly. Last night was up close and very personal. Wendy knew she'd never be the same again.

She hopped out of bed and jumped into the shower, eager to start the day. She was genuinely excited for the church service. She knew, beyond a shadow of a doubt, that God was going to use Barbie and Jackie in a big way this morning. As the water cascaded over her body, she found herself praying that the service would be powerful, the intensity of the topic palpable, the result life-changing for everyone in attendance. Oh God, Wendy prayed silently, please use this to accomplish your perfect will.

The next couple of hours were spent getting herself and her family ready for church. They walked into church by 9:30 AM, greeting people along the way. Travis went to his Sunday school class, while John and Wendy slipped into the adult study, sitting in the back row, in order to slip out early and meet Barbie and Jackie. They left at 10:20, planning to wait in the narthex for the two ladies to show up. But when they got there, they found that the women had already arrived, looking energized and alive also. Yeah, it's going to be a wonderful day, Wendy mused. I'm looking forward to watching God do His thing!

They went into the sanctuary to do a mic check, as well as run over last-minute details of the service. After they were all satisfied that any technical glitches had been worked out, they left for John's office, while the instrumentalists did a final check for themselves. John and Wendy ushered the ladies into the office where they spent 15 minutes praying for God to use the service for His honor and glory. Jackie was the last one to pray and Wendy could tell just how much sharing her testimony, with complete strangers, meant to her. She knew that when people heard what she'd been through, and how the Lord had led her through the valley of despair, their lives would be changed also. They may not have been through the same kind of trauma, but they would certainly hear enough to at least begin to understand why Jackie was so joyful, over what amounted to a fresh start. No, that didn't begin to describe it adequately. It wasn't just a fresh start; hers was a brand-new life. The old had passed away and everything was new.

The service began promptly at 11 AM. Wendy noticed that people were streaming in from the foyer during the five verses of the hymn. She also noticed that there were quite a few more people in the pews than was normal. She recognized many of them from the previous Sunday and realized they had come back again, because of their interest in Safe Haven. She was also thankful for Kathy's suggestion to send out postcards to all of the folks on their mailing list, including the visitors from last week. Wendy sensed, once again, how powerfully God was going to use this service.

After the congregational singing and the offering, Wendy stood up to speak to the congregation. She reiterated the purpose of the morning and then quipped, "So you won't be hearing my husband preach this morning. Can I get an amen?" The people shouted amen and then began laughing. John stood up and said, "Gee, thanks folks. You really know how to make a guy feel special." At that everybody laughed again and Virginia cried out loudly, "We love you, pastor." More friendly laughter. John said, "I know you do and I love you too. Now, can we stop all this mushy stuff and get on with things?" The congregation nodded in agreement and then listened as Wendy introduced their two guests.

She asked Barbie to come to the front. As she was stepping up to the platform, Wendy told about meeting Barbie at the diner a couple weeks back. She let them know that Barbie and her husband Ken - yeah, that's right, Ken and Barbie - pastored the New Life Assembly of

God church just on the outskirts of Wenatchee. They brought her here specifically to give a few words about the ministry of Mercy House, which is a home for women coming from any number of difficult situations. Wendy assured the congregation that Barbie had some things to say that would be of great interest to all of them, particularly as they were launching Safe Haven.

With those few words of introduction, Wendy sat down and Barbie took over. Wendy was amazed at how relaxed and in command of the situation Barbie was. She was an excellent communicator and chose her words very well. She only spoke for about six or seven minutes, but she challenged the congregation to fully grasp the opportunity that was before them. She assured them that running a home on the order of Safe Haven would not be a Sunday afternoon walk-in-the park. There'd be some challenges, and even some defeats along the way. This kind of ministry is messy at times, totally heartbreaking. "However," Barbie repeated the word three times, "however, the victories always make the challenges worth it!" People broke out in applause, inspired by Barbie's honest, but encouraging word. Barbie then introduced Jackie as one of the residents of Mercy House. She also made it clear that, although there was no time limit as to how long a woman could stay, Jackie was just getting ready to graduate from the program and begin a new phase of her life in Christ. And with that, Jackie walked up to the stage, took the microphone, holding it close to her mouth and began to share her testimony.

"It's such an honor and a joy for me to be with you this morning, sharing in your service. Pastor John and Wendy... thank you for taking a chance on someone you've never met or heard before. I hope you'll be inspired by what the Lord shares through me this morning also.

You know, life can be tough sometimes, can't it? If we had our way, most of us would want life to be smooth and easy, beautiful and lovely, fun and exciting. That's what we want, isn't it? And yet, how many of you know that life isn't always like that? In fact, to be honest, life is actually seldom like that. There are always challenges; challenges that manifest themselves in so many different ways, so many random scenarios. We expect those things to happen and so, because those challenges are unpleasant and hard, we do whatever we can to limit them; to limit the number and limit the nature of those challenges. And as an adult, we have the ability to do that, at least to a certain extent.

But a child doesn't. He or she doesn't have the resources available that lets them at least *help* control the circumstances. Children are vulnerable. They have no resources on which to call. That's why loving parents are an absolute necessity in helping that child grow up to be a strong, healthy, well-adjusted adult. That's how God designed life to work; that's how it's supposed to be.

But what if that's not the case? What if a child doesn't grow up having parents who are watching out for them? What if a child grows up with parents who are doing more harm than good? Well then, the outcome is naturally going to be significantly different than the one God originally intended. And the only reason I'm standing here before you this morning is because I'm one of those kids. I'm one who grew up without the guidance and protection and nurturing of loving parents.

My mom and dad had problems from the very beginning. They were like two ships that were heavily loaded with toxic gas, as well as high impact explosives. That's a deadly combination, but that describes my parents to a tee. Along about their late teen years, those two ships collided. And out of that collision, I was born. Their lives were toxic and explosive. By the time they got married at age 18, they were both well on their way to becoming alcoholics. They both were raised in alcoholic homes and actually knew no other lifestyle. You drank alcohol to celebrate, when times were good. And you drank alcohol when times were bad and you needed to wipe away some of the misery. I remember as a little girl, maybe four or five years of age, my father had been drinking all day and was drunk. In fact, there are very few days I can ever remember him being sober. But anyway, that particular day, I remember him telling me that he wanted to introduce me to his best friend - a friend who had always stuck by him, through the ups and downs. He put a bottle of beer in my hands and said, 'This is my good friend Bud. Now drink it.' I was very afraid of my dad because he could be so volatile, and so I did. I gagged the whole bottle down. You may drink a beer and not feel too many effects, but when you're four years old, it really does something to you. I remember feeling woozy, and very queasy, and I don't remember much after that. But I do remember, later on, not ever wanting to drink that stuff again. And I didn't. With all that's happened to me over the years, I'm thankful that at least I stayed away from alcohol. I only tell this story to give you an idea of my home life and the lack of stability.

I grew up, obviously, in an extremely unstable environment. And please believe me when I tell you this: I never felt safe. I never felt secure. I never felt cozy and warm. I never felt loved. And you might say, how's that possible? You must've known, that as broken as your parents may have been, at least they still loved you. Well, if they did, they never showed it. They were so caught up in the mess of their lives, I think I could have run away and I'm not sure they would've even noticed. In fact, it got to the point as I got older, and by older I mean eight or nine, it got to the point that I was the one trying to get the supper on the table, even if it was just cold cereal, or a can of soup. By the time I was 12, I was already writing out checks for the light and water bills, and signing my dad's name. The utilities had been shut off several times for lack of payment, and I figured that if I didn't want that to happen again, I'd better do something about it. So, I learned how to write checks and pay the bills. I just hoped that there was enough money in there to cover those checks.

Believe it or not, my dad held down a full-time job driving a forklift at a warehouse. You would think that the job required complete sobriety, but no, my dad could go to work buzzed and still do his job. And then, after quitting time, he and his fellow workers would go to the corner tavern and get sloshed. How he got home every night, without killing somebody, was always a mystery to me...but he did.

All the way up to my first year in high school, I had to take on more and more responsibility for running the household. And finally, my father got to the point where he couldn't work anymore at his job. The functioning alcoholic ceased functioning, and we went on welfare. And at the age of 15, it was up to me to somehow keep things going but for less money. I often considered just running away and starting a whole new life. I figured I could probably do better on my own. But I still had this little seed of hope that maybe someday our life would turn around and we'd become a real family.

One day, when I was 15, my mom was over across town visiting her sister, and my dad had a bunch of his scum-bag friends in the house, drinking beer and talking about the good old days, when they were all part of a motorcycle gang. Some of them still were, but most had to sell their bikes because they couldn't afford them. I remember feeling very uncomfortable with the way a few of the guys had been looking at me. My dad told me that it was my job to keep bringing the beer and chips, so I'd walk in and serve everything, and then walk out to the kitchen. Every time I'd come in and go out, they'd make rude comments about my body and my dad would just sneer and laugh right along with them. At one point when I walked in, I caught part of a conversation concerning the idea that maybe it was time I learned about real life. I wasn't sure what that meant exactly, but one of the men took me into my parents' bedroom and raped me. And all the while my dad was sitting out in front, in a drunken stupor. And when he was finished, another guy came in. It went on like this until every guy there had his way with me. The only one who didn't was my dad, and sometimes I think that was because he was too drunk. I had been gang raped by six guys - supposedly friends of my dad's. From that point on, my little naïve dream of ever having a happy home was gone forever. I was hurt and embarrassed and very confused. But most of all, I was angry. And I decided, right then and there, that nothing like that would ever happen to me again. Not ever! I went into my dad's drawer, where I knew he kept a switchblade knife, with a long 10-inch blade, and I stole it. I hid it in a secure, but easily accessible place in my room, and from that point on I was never without it. I took it with me wherever I went, because it gave me a sense of power and control.

I hated my dad so much for what he allowed his friends to do to me, that I seriously thought about killing him. But I never got a chance to follow through on my plan. A few days later, after the rape, I heard my parents fighting and the yelling was escalating. When I listened at the door, it was obvious that my mom had heard about the gang rape and she was confronting my dad. But the thing that really shocked me was her argument with him. She yelled, "How could you do this to me?" I froze when I heard her say that. At first, I thought she was fighting for me…that she was hurting for me, every bit as much as I was hurting for myself. But I only had to listen for a few seconds, before I realized that she was making this all about her. How could he do this to *her*? If I had any tiny glimmer of hope that she'd be my advocate, it flew right out the window.

I was so angry that I opened the door of my bedroom, planning to storm in there and tell them what I really thought. But just as I opened the door, I heard a gunshot. I walked down the hall and into the living room, just in time to see my mom standing over my dad, the smoking gun still in her hand. She slowly turned and looked at me, with tears streaming down her face, and she mouthed the words, "I'm so sorry." Then she put the gun in her mouth and pulled the trigger.

My head felt like it was going to explode, but I knew enough to call the police. I thought about just running away and never looking back, but I figured that the police would think I did it, so I called them. As they were examining the scene, they took me into my bedroom and asked me to tell them the whole story. Fortunately, they had also asked a female social worker to come to the scene when they found out I was just 15. It really helped to have her there as I shared the disaster of my life. To make a long story short, it was ruled a murder/suicide. I was then sent to live in a variety of foster homes, which weren't much better than the one I grew up in. But at least I wasn't raped.

When I was almost 16, I figured I'd had enough of this and could definitely do better on my own. I got a few bucks from my folks' estate, which, as you can imagine, wasn't much, but I used it to run away from Oregon to Washington. I didn't have a car. In fact, I didn't have a driver's license and so I took a Greyhound bus and got off in Seattle. I hadn't been off the bus for more than five minutes, before I met this really good-looking guy who was friendly and joked around with me. He asked me some questions about where I was from and what kind of job I was looking for. I told him I didn't know, but I had to find something quick. He asked me where I was staying and I told him I didn't know that either. And so he said, 'Look, I know we've just met, but I kind of like you.' Now, nobody in my whole life had ever said, 'I kind of like you.' My mind began to whirl with thoughts of a fairy-tale romance. Maybe this was going to be my chance at a real life. He looked kind of embarrassed, but then said, 'You could stay at my place tonight. And then tomorrow we could see if they have any apartments available in my building, and if not, I can help you find one someplace else. I've got two bedrooms - you could stay with me tonight.' Obviously, I was concerned, but he seemed so nice, and besides, I had my switchblade with me and so felt that I could take care of myself if I needed too.

Well, I went to stay with him that night and never left. But you can guess what happened. I thought we had become boyfriend and girlfriend, but by the time I found out differently, I was already totally dependent on him. My money was gone and so he was footing the bill for everything. We had begun sleeping together, almost immediately, and that made me feel a sense of connection with him, as well as feeling wanted for the first time in my life. But then I found out that he had lots of girlfriends and they all worked for him. Each one was under the impression that *they* were the special one in his life. All the others were just business associates. *They* were the special one. That's what they thought. That's what we all thought.

Well, I'm not going to go into all the gory details, but obviously I wound up being a prostitute and my boyfriend was my pimp. He kept all of us in nice clothes and small, but clean apartments. He also supplied us with decent food and enough grass to keep us mellow. I prostituted myself for five years, turning several tricks every night, including

Thanksgiving and Christmas. I could really turn on the charm with the men, but inside I hated every one of them, especially when I was still 15. What kind of a guy would take advantage of a 15-year-old girl? Oh, that's right. I grew up with that kind of guy, didn't I?

Anyway, when I turned 20, I knew I was going to have to have a change, or I wouldn't live to see 30. Prostitution is a hard life and really takes its toll on women. You're full of hate, anger and, in all likelihood, drugs. It's the pot and the drugs, interestingly enough, that help keep you sane to do what you have to do. But at age 20, I knew I had to escape.

One night I was talking with a friend and she told me that she was leaving the business. In fact, that was going to be her last night. She made me promise not to tell anybody, but she was going to go east of the mountains, to a women's home she'd heard about, called Mercy House. She already had her bus ticket and was going to sneak away after meeting up with her last john. She had saved some money and was hoping there'd be a place for her. She asked me to come and I said I'd think about it. Well, the upshot is, Destiny never got to go. Her john that night turned out to be a serial killer who preyed on prostitutes. And when I heard that she'd been killed, I knew I had to make a choice. Either stay here in this lifestyle and never see 30, or get away and try to find some semblance of normalcy.

That night I packed a small bag with just my essentials, including some cash and my switchblade. I went to the Greyhound bus station and took an early morning bus to Wenatchee, eventually finding my way to Mercy House. I've been at the house for just under two years now and to try to adequately express all that they, and the Lord, have done for me would take forever. But let me just say this. Mercy House welcomed me with open arms of love and compassion. During these almost 2 years, I've come to know Jesus as my Lord and Savior. I've come to accept that He's forgiven me for my lifestyle of prostitution, as well as all the other sin in my life. And equally important I think, He showed me the necessity of releasing forgiveness to people who've hurt me through the years. I've truly forgiven my mom and dad. Their lives were a mess. I'm not even sure why their lives took that route, but I can almost bet it started in childhood. But regardless, I've forgiven them. I also forgave my dad's buddies, who I hope will someday repent of their sin towards me when I was just 15. I wouldn't even mind seeing one or two of them in heaven someday, by the grace of God. I've also forgiven my customers, the john's, who would search out the broken girls who served them as prostitutes. I even forgave those men who searched for young girls - the younger the better. I've forgiven them all, just as Jesus has forgiven me.

And as I close, let me say one more thing. There are thousands of girls out there who are just like I was…hurt, lonely, messed up, and longing for love. They're selling their bodies as dancers in clubs, or workers in massage parlors, or actresses in porn films, or prostitutes on the street. Whatever their particular niche, they're suffering and need to be rescued. Thank you for taking on the project of Safe Haven. You're going to have a tremendous impact on girls' lives in the coming years. In fact, you won't even know the full extent of your impact, until you get to heaven.

Saving these women is perhaps one of the most important things you could ever do in your life. Bringing girls out of that lifestyle will literally save lives. I know this for a fact, because I was one of those girls."

By the time Jackie was finished, there wasn't a dry eye anywhere. People were so very touched. But sitting in the back row, behind Melverna the hat lady, was Nick. If you would've looked over at him, you would've seen a frown, a scowl perhaps. And if you had been listening closely, as Pastor John gave the closing prayer, you would've heard the screech of tires, as a big, gold Cadillac burned a patch of rubber down Main Street.

Chapter 25

PASTOR JOHN CLOSED THE SERVICE, AND THEN HE and Wendy ushered Barbie and Jackie into the fellowship hall for a special coffee hour in their honor. As they sat at the tables, people would come up and share how much the service had meant to them. The fact that Mercy House had been very successful and had paved the way for other homes, was a good indication that Safe Haven would be successful also. It was wonderful hearing from Barbie, as she shared the nuts and bolts of running a home for women. And although while listening to Jackie, you could come away with the idea that every woman had a great success story, in reality, that certainly wasn't the case.

Sadly, there were those few who, for whatever reason, just couldn't break free from what had been a lifelong pattern of self-destructive behavior. They refused to conform to the house rules of no alcohol and drugs and, when it was exposed, they were informed in no uncertain terms that the next time it happened, they'd be gone. But as strong of a warning as that was, some women just couldn't, or wouldn't, come under house authority - an authority that was set up to protect everybody in the house. Wrangling against authority was something that contributed to some of the women being in need of the Home in the first place.

For others, it wasn't so much about refusing to come under authority, as it was about being victims of those who abused their authority. For example: husbands who had a warped view of what the Bible meant when it talked about the husband being the head of the household. John and Wendy had established a pattern, very early on, of mutual submission. In other words, they recognized that both of them had gifts and talents that they brought to the relationship. So, there were certain things that John could take the lead on and other things where Wendy called the shots. It's like John used to always tell people, when asked how he and Wendy were going to set up their household in terms of authority. They had discovered that people had all kinds of ways of interpreting certain passages of Scripture that spoke to that issue and, depending on their past experience, as well as their own personality, they could be very flexible or very rigid. John, in an effort to help people have a full and happy marriage relationship, would talk about the very biblical concept of submitting to one another, out of love for Christ and love for their spouse. John would tell people that, in their household, he was the one who paid the bills. It wasn't because he was the man and men were always supposed to handle the money.

It was just because Wendy had her hands full with other responsibilities. It would be a great help to her if she didn't have to worry about the finances. John would also point out, however, that Wendy had a wonderful artistic flair. So, it only stood to reason, that when it came to making their home look nice and inviting, Wendy always took the lead. "You don't want me decorating," he'd say. "It would be a disaster."

There were some women who came to the Home who were victims of abusive husbands; husbands who latched onto a few verses of Scripture, always taking them out of the context of the broader meaning, and used those verses in an effort to control their wife, sometimes to the point of abuse. They'd usually tell them that it was for their own good and it was the way God had commanded. It sounded very spiritual, very pious, but it totally missed the heart of what God was saying. Both John and Wendy recognized that some Christians were like the Pharisees, the religious leaders of the New Testament that always seemed to be butting heads with Jesus. The Pharisees' main problem was that they would center in on the *letter* of the law, but miss the *spirit* of the law by a country mile. Even in those few short months of building their relationship, John and Wendy had discovered the joy of mutual submission, that was grounded in a foundation of love and trust; always desiring the highest good and happiness of their spouse above their own. That key to life went a long way in building marriages that were pleasing to God.

But a lot of women never experienced that in their marriage, or any relationship for that matter. They were victims of abuse, both physically and emotionally. Their marriages had been plagued with episodes of infidelity, or angry and hateful arguments, or financial insecurity due to addictions to gambling or alcohol or drugs. Any number of things contributed to the breakdown of the marriage. And when the pressure became just too much to bear, the woman would plan her escape. And, if she was fortunate, she would find her way to a place like Mercy House, where she could begin to put her life back together. But this time, hopefully, her view of life would change and she'd begin to see what God had wanted for her all along.

There were all kinds of reasons women wound up in places like Mercy House. All kinds of reasons, but one desired outcome. The purpose of Mercy House was to help women become all that God wanted them to be. The way that would come about was as varied as the situations that each woman came out of - situations that were unique to her. All kinds of situations, with all kinds of roads leading to healing. But the goal was always the same: empower each resident to become a strong and healthy woman of God.

When the folks at Pleasant Pastures heard Jackie share her story, they knew that she had, indeed, become that woman. Not that there still wasn't room for growth. Who doesn't need to grow, for heaven's sake? Growing in the Lord is a lifelong process. It's really more about the journey, than it is about the destination. It's a rather odd trip, actually, because the destination isn't really reached until we go to be with the Lord. Our whole life as a Christian is a journey; we're always on the road, encountering the new and different experiences that come, simply because we're alive. How we handle those varied experiences will determine the actual course of our journey. Although life can seem like a series of random experiences, people who've walked with the Lord for any length of time can look back and say, "Aha...now I get it; now it makes sense."

Both Barbie and Jackie helped people see the way God was working through Mercy House. As a result, everyone was very excited to see that very same thing happen with Safe Haven. The idea of being part of something that could be so powerful really spoke to the people who were in attendance that day.

In fact, it spoke so powerfully, that something took place that actually was rather unexpected. The insert that Wendy and Kathy had designed not only gave information about Safe Haven itself, it also suggested ways in which they could donate towards the project. The original idea was to keep the inserts in the bulletin for three weeks and then, on the third Sunday, have people bring their pledge cards to the front. On that Sunday, they'd be able to see how much they'd have in one-time gifts that would help with the immediate costs of renovation. They'd also see if they'd have enough to sustain the program monthly. Both one-time gifts and long-term monthly pledges were needed. So, that was the plan. Bring the cards in on the third Sunday and lay them on the altar, as an offering. Great plan - dramatic effect - wonderful results. The only problem was, people didn't want to wait. Many of the members, and visitors, for that matter, brought their cards to John and Wendy at the coffee hour, already filled out. The excitement, after hearing the two ladies speak was so high that lots of people wanted to respond immediately. And as the cards kept coming in, John and Wendy knew they'd have to change their plans. They certainly weren't going to say, "Oh no, you can't turn your card in yet, that's not according to our plan. You have to wait three Sundays." People were excited *now*. People wanted to give *now*. And so, John and Wendy took the pledge cards and simply determined to total them up in the coming week and then add them to the pile on that third Sunday. The totals would then be announced at the end of the service. They knew, without any question, that the third Sunday was going to be spectacular. A joyful expectation was running high among the people and would, no doubt, continue to grow throughout the next few weeks.

What a marvelous day it had been in church. As Barbie and Jackie sat having lunch at John and Wendy's, after the coffee hour, the sense of anticipation continued to grow. They talked about the ups and downs of this kind of ministry and yet, how even though there were definitely challenges, it was well worth it. There had never been a challenge so great that they felt like giving up. Whatever the challenge, God always helped them meet it, head on. And He'll do the same for Safe Haven. No challenge is too great for God.

By the time lunch was over, and the conversation was pretty much exhausted, it was 3:30 PM. They all gasped when they looked at their watches and saw how much time had elapsed, but they all agreed it was time well spent. They got up from the table, said their goodbyes, promising to stay in close communication. Barbie and Jackie headed out to their car, got in, and drove off. John and Wendy talked about the day, while they did the dishes and cleaned up. Travis was out with his Sunday school class, having gone for Burgers and bowling up in Leavenworth. Their teacher always tried to do one special event each month, in an effort to get to know the kids better. With Travis gone, John and Wendy were able to spend those hours talking about the incredible response of the people and how excited everyone seemed to be.

Travis came home at 4:30 PM, wondering what was for dinner. They suggested he have a snack to hold him over, because they wouldn't be eating until about 6:00 PM. Travis grabbed an apple and went out to read on the hammock in the backyard. The weather was still beautiful and quite warm. Nevertheless, you could feel a nip of fall in the air. Wendy was excited to experience the change of seasons in Eastern Washington, as compared to those in Chicago.

Wendy was so happy that God had led her out here. The future looked bright and promising. Safe Haven was becoming a reality and she was going to have the privilege of playing a major role in that.

She and John went to bed that night, exhausted from all the emotion of the day. They kissed each other good night and both fell into a deep sleep. They'd gone to bed about 9:00 PM, knowing that 5:00 AM would come quickly and they would need to be well rested, for what was going to be a very busy week.

Wendy was dreaming that she was cleaning the house on her day off. She was in the middle of scrubbing the kitchen floor on her hands and knees, when she heard the cat meowing and putting up quite a fuss, out in the living room. Something must've been really bothering that stupid cat, because he wouldn't shut up. His crying was incessant and becoming increasingly louder. Wendy tried to get up off her knees to go into the other room to see what was causing the cat such intense and prolonged distress. But her legs wouldn't move. Trying to get up and reach the cat was like slogging through thick mud. As hard as she was trying to get to the living room to stop the cats loud, annoying wail, she just couldn't get to him. But then, in her dream, she thought, "Wait a minute. We don't have a cat. Where's all that wailing and crying coming from? This is crazy. What's happening?" Just then, John and Wendy were jolted awake by the ringing of the phone located on the nightstand. John reached over and grabbed the receiver, offering a sleepy, "Hello." He suddenly sat up straight, listened for 10 seconds, and said, "I'll be right down." Wendy looked at him and asked, "What's wrong, honey?" John looked at her gravely and said, "Safe Haven's on fire!"

Chapter 26

MAX SHERMAN HAD MADE THE CALL THAT woke John and Wendy up out of a sound sleep. He had been unable to sleep himself and was just lying in bed, tossing and turning. He finally got up around midnight, thinking that maybe a little hot chocolate would settle him down a bit. He heated up the milk and poured in a good amount of Nestlé's Quik. He then went out onto the front porch and sat in the old rocking chair. The hot chocolate was beginning to work its magic and Max could feel the tightness in his muscles beginning to evaporate. He was just ready to go inside and try getting to sleep again, when he noticed something down towards the end of the block. He stared at the shimmering glow and then realized what he was seeing. He put his cup on the little table by the rocking chair and began to run toward the dancing orange light in the distance. As he got closer, he realized that it was as he had suspected. It was a house fire that had gained in intensity, in just the short time since he first spotted it.

As he got closer, he realized that it was the old Sinclair mansion. Safe Haven was going up in smoke and there was nothing he could do to stop it. He ran to the house next door and banged on the door. The sleepy gentleman who was making his way to the door was yelling, "Hold your horses! What's all this yelling about?" When he opened his door, in an effort to silence the crazy guy who came calling at midnight, he saw the flames from the house next door and was immediately awake.

Max demanded to use his phone and the man let him in. He then went to wake up his wife and kids in order to move them to a safe place, in case the fire jumped the property and onto his. Fortunately, the Sinclair mansion was located on a double sized parcel of land and so was fairly isolated. The fire didn't present much danger to the surrounding neighbors, but the man was taking no chances. He roused his family and moved them out onto the front porch.

Max, in the meantime, had called the fire department and, even now, could hear the sirens off in the distance. They would be here in 3 to 4 minutes, but judging from the intensity of the heat, as well as the rapid spread of the flame, he wondered if they'd be able to save any of it.

The next call Max made was to John and Wendy. They, in turn, called Maggie to see if she could come over and stay with Travis, while they went to the site of the fire. Maggie jumped in her car, wearing nothing but her bathrobe and curlers, and was there in less than five minutes. John and Wendy arrived at the fire two minutes later. What they saw shocked them.

It had only been about seven minutes since the call from Max had come in, but in that time, the house was completely engulfed in flame. The house had stood there for nearly a century; its strong wooden frame supporting the stately mansion. But though the frame was strong, it was also extremely dry. Enduring the hot Eastern Washington weather had taken its toll on the old house and once started, the fire raced as though the house was made of kindling. By the time John and Wendy arrived, the fire trucks were shooting massive amounts of water on the house, in an effort to douse the flames. But those standing by watching, knew it was of no use. There was no stopping the path of the flames and within a relatively short period of time, the house was gone. A structure that had stood there for longer than any of them had been alive, was now gone. An important piece of Pleasant Pastures' history had gone up in smoke and it left those watching the blaze with a great sadness. It was like watching the family matriarch, breathe her last.

The loss of this fine old home was devastating for the town, but for John and Wendy, and the members of Pleasant Pastures Community Church, it brought a particularly painful feeling of grief and loss. This was going to be the house that would change lives. This wasn't just the old Sinclair mansion; this was Safe Haven. This was going to be the home that would take women off the streets and provide shelter in a safe, protective environment. This was going to be the means of rescuing desperate women from their bondage to prostitution and other related occupations. This was going to be a crucial step on the road to recovery, for so many. But now...those dreams had been shattered.

As John and Wendy looked at the blaze, they remembered something that very few others knew. The house was insured, yes. But according to the lawyer who handled the acquisition a few days ago, the insurance was inadequate. It was based on what the house had been worth decades ago. But the insurance money wouldn't even begin to cover the cost of rebuilding. The pledges that were going to be coming in for renovation would help some, but again, it wouldn't be enough. The financial team from the church was scheduled to meet with an insurance broker this coming Tuesday, in order to bring it up to date and to determine a more realistic replacement value. But now…

It was devastating and for the first time since Kevin's death, Wendy found herself questioning God. Why? With all the good we wanted to do, with all the excitement surrounding the project, with all the lives that were going to be changed, why this? It wasn't a matter, so much, of being angry at God; it was more about being puzzled; perplexed at this unexpected turn of events. It just didn't make sense and how this was ever going to be anything but devastating was a mystery to Wendy. She wasn't sure how anything good could ever come out of a disaster of this nature. And yet, deep inside, Wendy's faith flared up, not as bright or as intense as the fire she was witnessing, but the flare-up was there nevertheless. Deep inside she felt that, contrary to what her eyes were telling her, all was not lost. The building may be gone, but the dream was still alive and well. That was it. She didn't have any great revelation or vision. She actually had no idea of the details that would make the dream become reality. She had nothing. Nothing, except the slightest flare-up in her spirit; not much more than a spark, really. But it was there, nevertheless.

John and Wendy talked to the Fire Chief, as the blaze died down. Stu Nagel was a member of the church and obviously felt awful about not being able to save the house. He had been in the service that morning, cheering on the project and wiping away tears after

Jackie's testimony. He'd also been one of the first ones to turn a pledge card in to John at the coffee hour. But Stu was wrestling inside with questions also. What good would his $500 pledge serve, now that the price tag had jumped so significantly? What was the cost to build a six bedroom home nowadays anyway? And how would a new house even fit in with a neighborhood of turn-of-the-century homes? Would the Historical Society try to block construction, insisting that the property be turned into a park that would enhance the neighborhood, instead of a new house that stuck out like a sore thumb? Stu knew how these little political wranglings could go, even in a small town like Pleasant Pastures. Even if a new home could eventually be built, it could take years to get the permits, if the Historical Society was fighting it. He supposed that Safe Haven could look for another house, but truthfully, there wasn't another house like it in all of Pleasant Pastures. It was large and centrally located - two crucial elements to the success of Safe Haven. And it was beautiful. Sure, it had fallen into disrepair to some extent, but the architecture, the graceful lines, the myriad of details in the overall design of the exterior, were stunning. Living in a newly refurbished mansion of this quality, would have been like a dream come true to those ladies, some of whom were more used to seedy motels and run down, rat-infested apartments. That's one of the things that was so exciting about Safe Haven. A lot of shelters were operating on a shoestring budget and were barely a step above what the women had been used too, for much of their adult lives. But Safe Haven was going to be a very beautiful oasis, in a dry, thirsty desert. But now, the oasis had burned to the ground, only ash and soot remaining.

As Stu talked with John and Wendy, they asked him the question that he knew would come up at some point. At some point along a journey of this nature, the victims would ask how the fire started.

And, sure enough, John asked the question, certainly not expecting a definitive answer at this time, but simply wanting to get the ball rolling for some tough conversations in the future. Stu looked at John and Wendy and gave the only answer he had. He told them that they were going to investigate it, but it shouldn't take too long to come up with an answer. But until then, they'd all just have to be patient.

Stu mentioned that it could be any number of things, but the first cause he wanted to rule out was arson. Could they think of anyone who would want to stop Safe Haven? Did they know of any enemies, or folks that were unhappy with the decision? Had anybody from the neighborhood been strongly against having a home of this nature in such close proximity? Did they know of pimps from the Seattle area, for example, who had lost girls to Mercy House? Maybe they decided to do a preemptive strike on the new house that was designed specifically for women coming out of prostitution, as well as other such careers? As Stu continued to ask questions, John and Wendy felt totally helpless; they had no answers that would help to explain the cause of the fire, if it was arson, in the first place.

Stu thanked them for their time and then left to talk with his crew about the next steps in the process. Some of the crew would be there for several more hours, making sure that hotspots were totally out, to avoid dangerous, unexpected flare-ups. The actual investigators would be out at first light, to begin the arduous process of sifting through the ruins for clues as to the origin of this fire.

The Tanks came up to John and Wendy, after seeing Stu head off to join the rest of his crew. Ryan spoke up and said, "We heard Stu asking you questions about a possible arson. We couldn't hear your answers and just wondered if you had any ideas." Wendy looked at Ryan and said, "Boy, I've been racking my brain trying to think of somebody, but I'm coming up blank. What about you guys?" The brothers looked at each other, concern etched on their faces, and said, "Well, we're not sure if it really means much, but we're wondering about Nick. What's been going on with him, anyway? He's been hanging around the whole week and we're not sure why, especially since you decked him, John. It just seems that after that, he would've gone back to Chicago. What's he been doing?"

John and Wendy reiterated their contacts with Nick over the last several days. Even though it had started out on shaky ground, with the skirmish in the office, they felt that it ended on a decent note. It's true that Nick seemed upset that they didn't want to join him in his scheme to cash in on the supposed scam they had going, but he didn't seem particularly angry. He just seemed perplexed that they wouldn't jump at the chance to increase their income greatly. Turning a deal of this nature down was beyond Nick's comprehension. He thought they were being small-minded and foolish, but he didn't seem angry, necessarily.

As The Tanks continued to talk, Max let John and Wendy know something of which they were unaware. They had invited Nick to the service, but because they didn't see him afterwards, they just assumed that he didn't make it, choosing instead to get an early start back to Chicago. To be honest, everything had been a little hectic that morning and their minds had been on Barbie's and Jackie's presentation. When they talked later in the day, after lunch with the gals, neither could remember seeing Nick there. That was a disappointment, but it was certainly understandable.

John asked Max if he'd seen Nick at the service and he nodded in the affirmative. "Where was he sitting?" Wendy asked. "Behind Melverna," Ryan answered. Well, Wendy thought, that explains it. Hidden once again by that tent she calls a hat. "But where was he after the service? We didn't see him at the coffee hour," Wendy said. The brothers once again looked at each other and Max said, "Okay, that's just it. Ryan and I got up to go out and get in position to stand at the door as people were leaving; just like we do every Sunday. But before you had finished your closing prayer, and just a second or two after we got into position, Nick came walking toward the door and left without saying a word. But he didn't look good. He had a frown on his face and he wasn't happy…at all. We called out goodbye to him, but he didn't even acknowledge it. He headed right toward his Caddie, started it up and gunned the engine. Then he tore out of there, burning rubber for 20 feet. Whatever he was upset about, I got the feeling it was eating away at him, big time. Then people started coming out to either go to their cars, or into the fellowship hall. We started greeting and just forgot about Nick… until now. Maybe Nick was upset because you refused his offer. And remember, that's the fourth time he hasn't been able to control the situation. The first time was with Wendy ditching out in Chicago. The second time was in church a week ago when we came in to back you up, when Nick was confronting you. The third time was when you cleaned his clock on Monday morning. And the fourth time was when you turned down his offer to help make all of you a lot of money by expanding your so-called protection racket. Maybe all of this sent him over the edge, and finally, it was just too much. Nick is used to controlling his environment and the people in it. But he couldn't do that here. Maybe Nick just figured that there was at least one thing he could control and nobody could stop him. Maybe he torched the place as a way of sending a message that he was still in control of the situation. And there's nothing you can do to stop him.

John and Wendy looked at each other, wondering if Max's theory could be true. Nick seemed fine when he left their house on

Friday. He wasn't exactly thrilled that they turned down his offer, but he seemed to take it in stride, even if it didn't make sense to him. But maybe he spent the hours between the lunch on Friday, and the service Sunday morning, stewing about it. And maybe it got to the point, that when he heard they were going through with Safe Haven as planned, instead of his scheme to fleece the congregation for the big bucks, he just snapped. John and Wendy weren't really sure what an angry and disappointed Nick could do, but they both figured he could do some real damage if he wanted too. They also knew that Nick was smart enough to discern what would cause the most pain and heartache for them. Safe Haven was a dream that they were really looking forward to becoming a reality. If Nick wanted to wound them, taking Safe Haven out before it actually got off the ground was the most effective way to do it. Was Nick the arsonist? Only time would tell.

Chapter 27

THE STEADY HUM OF THE TIRES ON THE HIGH-way was finally giving Nick a chance to relax a bit. He stretched each muscle in his body taut, while at the same time maintaining control of his car. The last several hours on the road had been tense. His mind was racing back-and-forth as he kept thinking back to the way he left Pleasant Pastures. As far as Nick was concerned, he couldn't get away from that podunk town fast enough. The whole trip out here had been a waste. He should've just stayed in Chicago and not been concerned over what had happened to Wendy. She may have been special, but hey, girls are a dime a dozen and if there's one thing

Nick Salerno knew, it was how to get girls to do his bidding. Coming out here had been a big mistake and he was glad it was over.

Nick had to get out of town fast. Let's just say that it would have been highly "uncomfortable" to stick around and try to chitchat. He didn't want to talk to John and Wendy, that's for sure. In fact, he didn't want talk to anybody at the church. He had made a stupid choice going to the service; he should have just gotten an early start and hit the road, as he originally had planned. But after the lunch on Friday, Nick felt that he owed John and Wendy and decided to accept their invitation to go to church before he left. At the time, he figured why not? It would just put him on the road a little later and it's not like he was on a tight schedule to get back. He'd get there, when he got there - no big deal.

So, he was heading back home to Chicago. He had a full tank of gas and a wallet full of money. He was planning to stop along the way and enjoy some good meals, see a few sights and just soak in the solitude of the next couple of days. Soon enough, he'd be back to the constant challenge of running his two clubs. There was always some crisis to attend to, some problem that needed fixing, some employee that needed straightening out. But as much hassle as it was, and as hectic as his life could be, he'd always thrived on it. Living in a big city where there's constant noise and movement was just part of the game. That's all that Nick had known the last several years of his life and he'd always loved every minute of it. There was just something about being in that environment that made Nick feel that he was a part of something big and powerful, something that would allow him to leave his mark on the world - a legacy of sorts, that would set his name apart from all the others. Nick had always wanted to make a name for himself. That, and making a ton of money, had been his goals for as long as he could remember. And he was well on his way to making those goals become reality. He already had made a name for himself. A lot of people certainly knew the name Nick Salerno and they accorded him the respect he was due. And as for money, he had more than he'd ever be able to spend in his lifetime. He'd done well - really well. And that wasn't going to stop anytime soon. Nick Salerno was riding high, that's for sure.

But as Nick was piloting his Caddie along I-90, his mind began to wander. He was successful, well-known, wealthy - he had it all and it was only going to get bigger and better. And yet, in these hours of solitude, since walking out of the church and tearing out of Pleasant Pastures, something kept nagging at him. Every time he considered his name and his money, his success in Chicago, his plans to go further, Nick would have second thoughts. He wasn't sure what was happening and every time these other thoughts would cross his mind, he'd do everything he could to bury them. The thoughts that had been bugging him were causing Nick to feel something that, up until this point, had never been a part of his adult life as a businessman. He was having doubts for the first time. A little question would pop up in his mind as he drove and he'd force it back under, instead thinking about things he really knew about. But the questions, the thoughts, the concerns kept coming and were making it very difficult to concentrate and enjoy the ride home.

After several hours of being on the road and forcing random, foreign thoughts and ideas from his mind, Nick finally gave up and just decided to deal with them, once and for all. He determined to let the reoccurring thoughts and ideas play out, so that when he finally reached Chicago in a few days, all of this nonsense would be gone, and he'd be in top shape to get back into the race. A race he'd always loved and found energizing.

Nick began to process the past 10 days he'd spent in Pleasant Pastures. The outcome certainly hadn't been what he was expecting. He found that after a pretty rocky start, he was actually happy for Wendy. He originally had come out to make her pay up what he felt she owed him for ditching out on his latest business venture, but it hadn't ended that way. She and John seemed genuinely happy doing their ministry gig in that little town. What he thought was a scam evidently wasn't at all. They had a good thing going there and his promises of expanding and making them richer every year meant nothing to them. He'd never met people who couldn't be swayed by the promise of more money, but not John and Wendy. They were the real deal and as much as he wanted to dismiss them as lacking drive and vision, he realized in his moments of solitude, that he actually admired them. They truly believed that they were doing good and were serving the Lord with their lives.

The idea of serving the Lord wasn't a totally foreign concept to Nick, although he hadn't thought about it in years. The sisters at his Catholic school used to talk about the same thing. They'd talk about how God could use every one of us, if we simply gave everything to Him. It didn't really ring true to Nick back then. But recalling what the sisters had said, as well as seeing it lived out in John and Wendy's life, it suddenly began to make sense. The thought that kept coming to Nick, as the miles ticked off, was that he had truly seen that in action. And although he didn't understand it completely, he had to admit that he admired it.

The other thing that Nick was trying to understand were the people he'd met at the church. Yeah, he was only there a short time, and maybe if he had spent more time there he would've discovered something different, but from what he'd seen on the surface, those folks at the church were like a family. They all seemed to care for each other and have each other's backs. He thought back a couple of Sundays ago when he was trying to intimidate John, and those two giant brothers came up, in a not-so-subtle way, and provided backup for their pastor. Nick smiled to himself, rubbing his jaw where John had hit him with a strong right cross. John didn't really need the backup, but it was impressive nevertheless. Nick had to admit that the sense of commitment to each other was both strange and wonderful at the same time. It was strange, because in Nick's world, that sense of caring for one another was absent. It didn't mean that you didn't have buddies, or business associates that stood by you. There were always people that were around and would lend a hand, when you needed something. But the difference was like night and day. In his line of work, people would help you out if there was something in it for them. I'll do this favor for you and when the time comes, you'll do me a favor. It's all very cordial, but it's motivated by selfishness and a desire to get ahead. But what these church folks had was so completely different than that. And the only word Nick could come up with was wonderful. He'd never used that word in his business; maybe because he didn't run into anything he considered to be in that category. But it was a good word, and he wondered when he got back to Chicago and to the business, if he looked hard enough, would he find anything that fit that definition. In all honesty, he didn't think so.

How is it that you can be a success in your business and not find something you considered to be wonderful? As Nick contemplated that question, it drove him back to the real reason he had left the church in such a hurry. He should've stayed for the coffee hour and, at least, said goodbye to John and Wendy. They were good people, doing important work for all the right reasons. And that was part of the problem. When Nick compared himself with John and Wendy, he realized he was coming up short - real short. If you were to place John and Wendy alongside of Nick and ask the question who was the most successful, in terms of power and money Nick would win every time. He had it all over John and Wendy on that one. But Nick couldn't help but feel, that the conclusion that most people would come to, would be wrong. For the first time in his life, Nick was considering the possibility that his definition of success was misguided and that the very foundation of the premise was wrong. Maybe success was demonstrated in a whole other way. Truth be told, the thoughts that Nick was having were shaking the core of his very being.

But finally, Nick couldn't ignore it any longer. As much as he tried to dismiss it as being simply emotional foolishness, he couldn't escape the feelings he had when he was sitting in church listening to the two ladies speak. As much as Nick wanted to insist that all these thoughts were about seeing John and Wendy in action, or observing the close-knit community of the church, or maybe having to look at different definitions of success, to be perfectly honest, Nick knew that these things weren't the heart of the issue. They were important, yes. They obviously had impacted him, more than he ever thought possible. He had done more in-depth thinking about life itself in the last few hours, than he had probably done in his entire life. So, all these things that had been nagging at him, mile after mile, were indeed important. He absolutely needed to think about those things and come to grips with how they were impacting him.

But they still didn't get to the heart of the issue. They still didn't explain why several hours ago, while sitting in church, he knew he had to get out of there fast. He just couldn't stay. He was angry and he was getting angrier by the minute. And when John began to close the service with prayer, Nick knew that he needed to leave and not look back. He couldn't go to the coffee hour with this anger seething inside of him. And so, he stepped out of the pew and walked out of the church, as fast as he could. He didn't even say goodbye to the two giants at the door - he just knew he needed to get out of there fast. He knew that he had laid a patch of rubber when he took off, but that wasn't intentional. He just realized how very angry he was and it was coming out in his behavior behind the wheel. He forced himself to calm down as he left Pleasant Pastures and started out for Chicago.

Why had he been so angry? Why was he getting angry even now, hours later, just thinking about it? Nick once again decided that he'd better use the time to think some of these things through, because once he hit Chicago, there'd be no time for solitude or reflection. The busyness of life would be all-consuming. He'd jump back on the merry-go-round and the ride would be endless.

Why had he been so angry? The answer was right there, staring him in the face. He was angry because of Jackie's story. He was angry because she was describing the hell her life had been as a prostitute. She explained how sick she felt when she saw herself simply as an instrument for men's pleasure. She talked about feeling worthless as a human being and that nothing in life really mattered. This was her life, and for whatever reason, she was stuck with it. That's all she had known - from the gang rape, to the prostitution, and everything in between - that's all she had ever known. Nick found himself getting angry at the story of the gang rape. How could a father ever let anything like that happen? Why would he allow those scumbags to take advantage of his daughter like that? Every one of them should be shot dead for what they did to that young woman. And he'd be the first one to pick up the gun. But then, as he sat there fuming, a single question forced its way to the surface of his being: "How are you any different?"

Nick pounded on the steering wheel and yelled, "I'm not like that!" He was furious. His breathing grew labored and he wondered if he was having a heart attack. He began to purposely and methodically slow his breathing down, until he once again felt like he had control. He whispered, "I'm not like that." Whether he was trying to convince himself, or convince the God he had abandoned a long time ago in the halls of his Catholic school - whoever he was talking to, it was imperative that the message was crystal clear. He wasn't like Jackie's father and his gang.

But as Nick continued driving, it slowly dawned on him, that even though he found the gang rape to be absolutely abhorrent, how many men in his clubs had fantasized about doing the same thing to his dancers? If he went back and coaxed and bribed his dancers to meet men on the side, wasn't he basically giving them the same message? You're here expressly for the pleasure of men. That's the sum total of your existence. Wendy ran from his offer and now she's living a life that's a 180° change from what he had wanted her to do. And she's happy, truly happy, for the first time in her life. And that's great for her. But his other dancers weren't like Wendy. They were college students and single moms. They needed money to pay tuition and raise their families. He could understand how his plan to have the dancers spend a little extra time with his most valued customers could make them nervous - it was a huge step - but it was a lucrative step for everyone concerned. Everybody wins, Nick said to himself. Nobody loses, everybody comes out with something. He was actually doing the gals a favor. They'd have more money than ever before. And money could buy a lot of really cool toys for their kids. Money could pay the tuition for their college degrees. Money could take care of a sick parent who didn't have long to live. Money could do all of that and more. Nick could provide them with a bankroll that anyone would be ecstatic to have. That's what money can do - nobody can argue with that.

As he drove along, thinking through the organizational steps in his potential venture into prostitution, Jackie's words kept coming back to him. She said that prostitution was a very hard life; a life that was full of hate and anger, both for herself and her customers. But one day she realized that if she didn't get out soon, she'd never live to see 30. Sobering. The second thing she said that really ate away at Nick was about the turnaround she had made after finding Mercy House. She had found Jesus there and that made all the difference in the world. She wasn't controlled by hate and anger any longer - now she was controlled by God's love. True?

Nick thought long and hard about these things…in fact, he wrestled with those same questions and thoughts for the next couple of days. When he was just 100 miles outside of Chicago, he whispered once again, "I'm not like him. I'm not like Jackie's father. I care about these girls and want them to have a chance at success, whatever the cost." He'd made up his mind to implement his new plan. Nick had no doubt that this would be best for everyone concerned. And with those words anchored firmly in his mind, he entered the Chicago city limits.

Chapter 28

THE NEXT THREE DAYS WERE NOTHING BUT A blur for John and Wendy. They continued to do all the expected chores and duties of the ministry, but they felt as if they were slogging through mud. Sometimes it seemed as if life had suddenly been set on permanent slow motion. Things were getting done, but it took all the energy they had to get even the most basic tasks accomplished.

They were stuck in no man's land. They didn't have the answers they needed to move forward. The plans they had from just a few days ago now, quite literally, had gone up in smoke. What was their new plan now? How were they supposed to move on, when everything was up in the air? They needed to have several questions answered before they could make definitive plans for the immediate future. Was this an arson? If so, who was the culprit? What would stop the same person from sabotaging it again if they rebuilt? If somebody was that upset with the idea of a home for women in the neighborhood, whoever they were, they could make recovery very difficult for them.

There was also the major question of rebuilding, in the first place. Could they build again in this economy? Did they have the money or would it be cost prohibitive? They had already discovered that what they'd suspected was indeed true; the insurance on the house covered what the value had been decades ago, but had never been updated. They'd be fortunate to get $50,000, and according to the initial estimates, it would cost at least three times that to rebuild.

And sure enough, just as they thought, the Historical Society had contacted them immediately and had made it known, in no uncertain terms, that to build a house in the style of the day would greatly diminish the turn-of-the-century charm of Pleasant Pastures. If they all couldn't come to an agreement, the project could be tied up in court for years with appeals. And that, of course, would eat away at the funds that should be going to run the house, not lining the lawyers' pockets. Besides the money, the bigger question concerned the picture that endless court battles would give the people of Pleasant Pastures. Would they have a front row seat to all the wrangling? And in the process, would they wind up with a bad taste in their mouth concerning Safe Haven, as well as the church?

Both John and Wendy decided that whatever happened, they were going to make sure that the Lord would be honored in the midst of this whole mess. This looked insurmountable to them right now, but it wasn't the least bit overwhelming for God. He had an answer for this dilemma – they knew that for sure – but now it was their job to figure out what the answer was. How was God going to fix this? What was His part? And even more baffling, what was their part? When they figured out the answer to those two questions, everything else would fall into place.

The other thing that was weighing heavily on their minds was what The Tanks had told them about Nick. When they saw him walk out of church, he was obviously not feeling happy. It could very well be that Nick had thought that they'd have a last-minute change of heart and begin to see the value of his plan to make a ton of money by multiplying themselves, several times over. If they would agree to his plan, they'd all become wealthier. But it was obvious to Nick that they had rejected his ideas and instead had gone with the original plan that centered on Safe Haven and the ministry. Did that upset Nick enough that he had actually torched the place and then beat it out of town? That thought bothered them greatly because they felt they had come to an understanding and walked away on good terms. If Nick did this, obviously he'd have to answer for it, but neither John nor Wendy wanted that to happen. They were still praying for Nick, that he would come to know the Lord and, in the process change his ways. He may not be the big-time gangster he tried to convince everyone he was, but he was in the lifestyle nevertheless, and only the Lord could help him change. All John and Wendy could do was pray for him; there was nothing they could do *physically* because he was no longer in Pleasant Pastures, and so they left Nick and his future in God's hands... both of them acknowledging that it was the safest place he could be.

Three days after the fire, Chief Stewart Nagel called John at the church and asked if he could meet with him and Wendy. Wendy came right over to the church and Stu showed up five minutes later. After investigating the fire, they had come to the conclusion that it wasn't arson after all. Both John and Wendy breathed a collective sigh of relief. That meant that there wasn't some deranged person out there who was bent on destroying Safe Haven if they rebuilt. They wouldn't have to worry about that, at least. It also gave them a cause to rejoice, because it took Nick off the hook. It would have broken their hearts if Nick had been the culprit. But now, with this new revelation, they felt as if one huge burden had been lifted off their backs.

The next thing they had to look at was where to go from here. The dream of Safe Haven was still alive, but how exactly to get there was a daunting challenge. Because Wendy had quit her job to be the project manager, most of the details, of course, landed in her lap. After much prayer, Wendy felt that she had a pretty good handle on how to proceed.

There were several elements to her plan. One of the major hurdles would be finances. Money was always a major issue. With the added expense of finding another place, or rebuilding on the original site, the cost had suddenly gone up significantly. They'd have $50,000 from the insurance company, in addition to the money that had been pledged in one-time gifts. But by initial estimates they'd still be about $100,000 short for rebuilding and refurbishing, so money was indeed an issue.

The second element was the actual facility itself. Would they have to try to find someplace else or would they rebuild? Even if they had the money necessary, what would be their plan to go forward? If they rebuilt, would they be able to somehow duplicate the look of the original house? It was important to have continued good relationships with the city's "movers and shakers" if they hoped to have any kind of community support. Would it even be possible to rebuild in the turn-of-the-century style?

The third element was the furnishing of the house once it was built. That, of course, was a ways down the line, but Wendy knew she had to put a plan together for that also. They wouldn't have a lot of money to work with but they needed to make sure that Safe Haven was furnished beautifully. It was important to the overall philosophy of the ministry that they were attempting with the women - they are loved and they are valuable. The care taken in furnishing the home would go a long way toward instilling that message in each resident.

And of course, the fourth element of the plan was to design the program itself. The program needed to be Christ-centered, even though the women coming there may not have much of a faith, if any at all. But it would still be understood by every potential resident, that the program was based on Christian principles. And part of their successful escape from the sex industry would be learning about and, in time, hopefully embracing the spiritual element. Nothing would be forced. It would simply be offered as a proven, alternative path, away from the direction their life was taking before.

The fifth element was finding a House Mother. Wendy was going to be the project manager who oversaw the finances and facility, as well as volunteer staffing. Wendy would oversee it all. But there had to be that one very special lady who would live on site and help the women stay focused on the program. She would also have the job of making sure that the house rules were maintained by all the residents. The house rules were there for everybody's safety and for the ultimate success of the program.

Wendy reviewed her list of responsibilities and took a deep breath, realizing that each one was a huge challenge in itself. But as intimidating as that list was, she knew that God had placed her in the position of project manager for a reason. He knew that with His help, she was up to the task.

Over the next couple of weeks, things began to fall into place. It was decided that the best course of action was to rebuild on the newly cleared site. The land had been bulldozed and all the debris had been hauled away. Wendy had found a contractor from Ken and Barbie's church who was up to the challenge of rebuilding Safe Haven. He couldn't do it for free, of course, but Wendy knew that whatever he charged for the project would be fair and the work would be first rate. When she told him that she wanted it to look just like the original Sinclair mansion, that threw him off a bit, but he told Wendy to give him a couple days and he'd come back with a plan. Sure enough, three days later, he met with Wendy and showed her a set of yellowed architectural plans for the rebuild. He had contacted the Historical Society and told them his plans to rebuild the house, keeping it as close to the original as possible. He asked if they had any pictures of the house in its early days and they told him they could do better than that. They went to their archives room and came back with the original architectural drawings of the mansion - drawings that the Sinclair family had donated to the Society decades ago. They were going to rebuild to the exact specifications, but with the modern updates available today.

Wendy also had gone to the church finance team and told them about the latest developments. She was going to handle all the other issues of furnishings and programs and staff volunteers herself, but the finances had her stumped. She just wasn't sure how to go about it. She believed with all her heart that God was giving them the green light to proceed, but she wasn't sure how the people at the bank would view her faith. Yes, I'm sure they would appreciate her sincerity, but when push came to shove, sincerity didn't pay the mortgage. Could they take that part on and decide the best way to move forward? They assured Wendy that they were behind the vision all the way, and they'd figure out the best course of action.

Wendy breathed a sigh of relief when the financial burden was lifted off her shoulders. This team of financial people knew what they were doing. They came back a few days later and told her that they felt they had enough money to get the project started. They also knew that the bank would loan them the additional $75,000-$100,000 to complete the job, but they wanted to borrow only what was necessary. If the loan amount was too high, the monthly payment could exceed that which was pledged by the congregation. They needed to walk in faith and yet be fiscally responsible. They assured Wendy that they'd take care of the details, if she would manage all the rest.

The church broke ground on Safe Haven in the middle of October. The project was anticipated to take several extra months because of the winter weather which sometimes disrupted the work schedule. But, barring any major unforeseen disasters, Safe Haven would be up and running by early spring.

Over the next few months everything began to come together. Wendy had secured promises from several outlet stores for donated items of furniture, as well as appliances. If they couldn't donate the product out right, they offered her wonderful discounts. Every place Wendy approached was eager to help when they heard about the vision behind Safe Haven. She and Kathy also published a wish list in the bulletin each week, requesting certain kitchen items, as well as small household appliances.

Wendy also spent a lot of time with Barbie and her team, designing a program specifically geared to women coming out of the sex trade. The material emphasized reaffirming the value of each and every woman. Building self-esteem in these women was so important; Wendy knew that from personal experience. She'd never forgotten the curse that diner-guy had laid on her that first night. It had haunted her for years and she'd never been able to get beyond it until she met Jesus and walked with Him consistently. Wendy realized however, that though the latest catchphrase was self-esteem, it wasn't really that as much as it was Christ-esteem. That was absolutely crucial. Who are you in Christ? What does Jesus think about you? That's what really counts! And she wanted every woman who came through Safe Haven to know that Jesus thought they were great, that He deeply loved them, that He greatly valued them, that they were His lambs and He was their shepherd.

A few weeks later, after talking and praying with Barbie and Wendy, Jackie agreed to take on the role of House Mother. She was actually younger than some of the ladies who might come through Safe Haven, but her experience in the sex industry, as well as her success at escaping the life, made her the perfect person for the job. She could continue her college courses in Wenatchee during the day, and be at home in the evening to help guide the women and handle any bumps that might come along the way.

Things were going very smoothly on Wendy's end. It was marvelous to watch how God had worked over the months. They were getting close to the dedication and launch of Safe Haven. In just a short while women would begin to come, not realizing that this new shelter wasn't just going to be a place to lay their head at night; it was going to be a place where they were going to begin living, maybe for the first time in their lives. Safe Haven was going to be the home they'd never had.

Wendy was so grateful for all that God had done. But in spite of all she'd seen, she was still concerned over the finances. The team had secured a loan from the bank at a good interest rate, but the monthly payment was pretty high. It wasn't impossible, but it would definitely be a challenge each month. She would just have to continue to pray that God would keep the pledges coming in. The folks at church were so faithful in their giving, but like any household, there would always be extra expenses with furniture needing to be replaced, appliances needing repair, plumbing issues needing to be handled and on and on and on. All kinds of things could happen when you have 10 women and children all living in the same house. But then again, when your Father "owns the cattle on a thousand hills," I guess He can manage any financial crisis that comes along, Wendy mused. Faith is the key, and I have a feeling that my faith will be tested on a regular basis. But that's all right, she chuckled, testing just strengthens it anyway. When it comes to faith, Wendy realized, we can't lose – one way or the other, we just keep getting stronger.

"Oh God, give me faith for every woman who walks through the doors of Safe Haven. I know it's scary to make a move like that – to escape the lifestyle – but it's not half as scary as *not* moving. Women's lives are going to be changed. They're going to fall in love with Jesus and realize, for the first time in their life, what a real man is like. Jesus, thank you for showing me what I should expect to find in my husband. And Jesus, reveal that to every one of the ladies we'll encounter in the future. If they truly will love you with their whole heart, the rest of their life will fall into place. Not always perfect necessarily, not always easy, but safe and secure nevertheless. Overwhelm them with your love so that they are transformed into the women you created them to be."

Chapter 29

I T WAS A BEAUTIFUL SPRING DAY IN EASTERN Washington. The sun was shining bright and reflected off the majestic Cascades mountain range. It had been an exceptionally snowy winter; great for the ski resorts and those who were into winter sports of all kinds. Pleasant Pastures was the perfect place to live for those who wanted a little snow action in their lives such as skiing, snowshoeing, sledding, climbing or maybe just sipping hot chocolate at Snoqualmie Lodge.

It had been absolutely breathtaking to look out the parsonage windows and see acres and acres of snow-covered pasture land. Wendy and Travis particularly had enjoyed their first winter in this beautiful part of the country. They certainly had snow each year in Chicago, but it just wasn't the same. The snow would look pretty for a while, but it wasn't long before the pristine white would be destroyed by passing cars and pollution from the factories. All part of living in a major city, Wendy knew. But this! Oh my, what a beautiful area of the country. Wendy thanked the Lord every day for leading them here.

Wendy looked at the clock on the nightstand and realized that she had better get a move on it or she and her family would be late for church. And this was one day they wanted to be on time, for sure. This was going to be one of the most exciting days this church had experienced in a long time. Today was dedication Sunday. This was the day that they were officially going to launch Safe Haven. It had been a long six month building process. The weather had slowed them down a bit, as had the actual building challenges themselves. The contractor was trying to stay as close to the original architectural plans as possible, but certain things had to be modified to comply with present-day codes. And things like the three turrets were very time intensive to construct. The sweeping staircase that ascended to the second floor was dramatic in its effect, but had been somewhat of a challenge to build. Modifications had to be made in many areas of the interior, thus adding to the complexity of the overall project. But when it was completed, Safe Haven looked like an exact replica of the turn-of-the-century Sinclair mansion. It truly was a wonderful sight to behold. The design itself, with its three turrets and multilevel roof, gave the house an almost castle-like appearance. According to the archive pictures, the house had been originally painted white, with black trim on the shutters that enhanced every window. The exquisite gingerbread that outlined the house had been difficult to duplicate, but an artisan in Wenatchee, who specialized in turn-of-the-century wood-working designs, had done a wonderful job of re-creating the historical beauty of the home. It truly was exciting to watch the foundation being poured on a newly cleared patch of land. And now, step-by-step, six months later, the completed house stood as a beautiful monument, not only to history, but more importantly, to the future. Out of this home would flow life-changing miracles for decades to come.

The service was packed on this lovely spring day. The ushers had to bring in extra chairs and place them up and down the aisles, as well is in the foyer. It was a standing room only crowd, but nobody was complaining about the cramped conditions; it just added to the excitement and festive atmosphere of the morning.

Wendy was probably the most excited of all. As project manager for Safe Haven she had literally lived with every decision that had to be made for the entire six-month process. She had experienced moments of great joy, as well as moments of sheer agony. She could be riding high because of a victory one minute and the next minute find herself fretting over the difficult challenges that lay ahead. It was that way for the entire six months - six *long* months. But throughout the whole process she never gave up, she never lost the vision, she never stepped back and said, "That's it, I'm done!" Wendy weathered all the challenges of the project knowing, without a doubt, that God was in control. If He wanted Safe Haven to come into existence, He would make it happen one way or the other. And during the entire project, Wendy had seen God work many small, but amazing miracles. Now, maybe other people didn't recognize those miracles, but Wendy did. When you're that involved in a project, up close and personal, you witness things that other people don't. Wendy knew that her faith had been impacted on a much greater level than she had ever expected. When you see things that look like they might derail the entire project and you realize that you don't really have control over those things, you wind up on your knees, crying out to God in prayer. And then, when you see the blockades that were hindering a successful completion, come tumbling down before your eyes, the only thing you can do is give glory to God for His strength and His might in overcoming obstacles. To God be the glory!

It had been a wonderful service of worship. The congregation gathered there had sung with great exuberance at times, clapping to the music and shouting *amen* when a song had ended. But as the exuberance began to fade, there came a season of hushed worship, as people quietly and reverently expressed their love for Jesus. Hands were being raised across the sanctuary as people offered their praise to the Lord, in an expression that had been around for thousands of years. Raised hands - closed eyes - bended knees - whispered words - personal reflection - each person worshiping in the way that was personal to them. The atmosphere of worship was unlike anything Wendy had experienced in the short time she had walked with Christ. She found herself wiping her eyes and thanking God for His goodness and faithfulness.

As the worship time began to wind down, Wendy knew that she'd better get a grip and stop the waterworks. She was supposed to give a few words in preparation for the dedication and she had to get control of her emotions or she wouldn't be able to speak a word. And if there was any time that Wendy wanted to say something publicly, this was it.

John got up to the front in preparation for turning the pulpit over to Wendy. But just as he was getting ready to do that, he heard his name called from the back of the sanctuary. He looked up and he saw Maggie standing in the back, by the side door that led into the fellowship hall. She began walking down the aisle, looking like she was a woman on a mission. She asked if she could say something and John said, "Sure Maggie, what's on your mind?" Maggie took the mic and gave a short version of Wendy's story; a story that the entire congregation knew because Wendy had shared it months ago, very openly, and very honestly. The congregation had come around and embraced her fully, as Wendy put it, warts and all. It sounded as if Maggie just wanted to use that short story as a way to introduce Wendy and her remarks. Wendy figured that there must've been a last-minute change in the program that she knew nothing about. She looked at John and he looked at her, smiling. She'd seen that look before on her husband. Whatever was happening right now, John knew about it, but hadn't shared it with her. She had no idea where this was going, but she trusted these two precious people in her life and so she just relaxed, wondering what was next.

Maggie finished her little story and said, "We all know the story, don't we? And it's a marvelous story of grace and acceptance - of love and redemption - it's the gospel, pure and simple." Several amens erupted from the congregation. "You know the story," Maggie continued. "But today I want you to meet one of the characters from that story. I want to introduce you to Wendy's former boss. Come on in Nick." And with that, Nick Salerno stepped out of the side door and began making his way down the aisle towards the pulpit. Wendy was shocked and looked over at John, mouthing, "Did you know about this?" John smiled and nodded his head. Wendy looked at him with eyes that said, "I can't believe you didn't tell me." She wasn't mad, just surprised. She hadn't spoken to Nick since their lunch, six months ago. She just figured that he had gone back to Chicago and to his old ways. So if that was the case, what was he doing out here?

Nick got to the pulpit and gave Wendy a quick hug and shook hands with John. Nick took the mic and began to share a story that became increasingly more fascinating as it went on. Wendy found herself listening with rapt attention, as Nick poured out the story of his last six months. It was a story that Wendy never would have expected – not in a million years.

Chapter 30

"**F**ROM THE TIME I WAS A YOUNG KID ROAM-
ing the streets of Chicago, I knew I wanted to be somebody. I wanted to make a name for myself. I wanted
people to show me respect when I walked down the street. I wanted
a name for myself and I wanted to have money. We never had much
money when I was growing up and I always looked up to certain
guys who hung around the Italian section of town where I lived. They
dressed sharp, drove big cars, and always seemed to flash wads of cash,
wherever they went. That was really something to see, and as a young
boy I knew I wanted that too. I wanted to be known by my reputation and I wanted money - lots of money. I wanted to be able to buy

anything I desired, because if I could do that, then I'd know that I had arrived.

And over the years that dream of mine began to come together. I got involved in some business ventures that wound up making me a lot of cash. The two clubs I owned really took off, and within a short period of time the money was rolling in. But it was nothing compared to when I stepped out and decided to make the shift from go-go dancing to a topless venue. That's when things began to pop. I knew I had hit on something big, and at that time I was one of the few places in town that offered that form of entertainment. Not only that, my clubs weren't in the seedy part of town; they were in good locations where you didn't have to worry that you were going to get capped for just being down there.

My reputation was growing almost as fast as my bank account. But one day I came up with the brilliant idea of getting into the prostitution racket, and I thought I had just the dancer who I could maybe interest in helping me. It would be very lucrative for both of us. But to make a long story short, she paid attention to the voice she was hearing inside of her and ran away. This isn't new to any of you - you know the story. Wendy ran from me and from her life in Chicago. She came here to Pleasant Pastures and met her future husband. This little town became her home.

At one point in time, about six or seven months ago, I tracked her down and came out to make her pay back what I felt she owed me. I didn't want people to think I'd gone soft - that would've been bad for my rep - so I came out with every intention of making things right - at least right, by my standards.

When I got here, I saw something I wasn't expecting. I saw Wendy happily married and satisfied with her new life. It shocked me, to be honest. And as I observed from the shadows for a few days, I noticed that they were raising money for this home for women. I realized then, that Wendy had somehow come across a religious scam that had the potential to bring in some big bucks. But as I watched, I could tell that she and John just weren't making it what it could be.

I had already attempted to intimidate John the first Sunday I was here, but his two giant deacons backed him up and I wound up leaving, determined that I'd get to him at some point. I came into his office the next day, fully expecting that I'd teach him a lesson. Well, let me just say this: I don't know how many of you know this, but your pastor took only so much of my threats and after I'd swung at him twice, he hit me with a right cross that knocked me on my can. And judging from the gasp of the audience, my guess is that you didn't know that, did you? Your pastor can pack a punch and so my advice to you is: Don't get on his bad side. Nah…I'm just kidding. He wouldn't do that to you…he only does that to gangsters.

You might wonder how your pastor could do such a thing. But before you get all upset about that, just know that when I came to, I had a new respect for him. He wasn't the pansy I imagined all pastors to be. He had a strength about him that I came to find out later wasn't just physical, but also spiritual.

I suppose I should have just left town and headed back to Chicago with my tail between my legs, but this whole scene intrigued me. A tough-as-nails pastor, a beautiful wife by his side, money coming in every week. No doubt about it, I wanted in on the scam they had going. And so, on that next Friday, they invited me to lunch. I thought that was a little odd, given my history with Wendy, but I figured that maybe that would be the opportune time to present my idea to them on how to expand the operation and really see the bucks start rolling in. I could help them with the expansion, for a cut of the profits. I laid out for them what the potential take could be if they went with my plan and believe me, the numbers were impressive. They'd never have to worry about money again. But you want to know what your pastor and Wendy did? They turned me down flat. They said no to the gold mine I was offering them. And then they told me why. What they had going here wasn't a scam. It was the real deal. God was providing everything they needed and they knew that wouldn't stop. And to be honest, if they would've accepted my plan, I wouldn't be here today. I was shocked that they turned me down, but deep inside I had to admire that. But it wasn't just admiration that I felt. They had something in their lives that I had never experienced and it made me start to question. Is this whole God thing real? They talk like they're on a first name basis with the Lord. How is that even possible?

They invited me to church that next Sunday and I came. I almost skipped it, just so that I could get back on the road to Chicago. But I felt that maybe starting a few hours later wouldn't be a big deal, and so I came in and sat in the back. And what I heard that morning from these two ladies, I see them in the service today, by the way - what I heard from them really impacted me. Jackie's story of her life of abuse, beyond anything I could imagine, really got to me. And when I found out that all of that had set the stage for a life of prostitution, I found myself getting really angry on the inside. Angry at the pain that had been inflicted upon her. I was angry and trying to control myself. How could these men do that to her? But as I was growing more and more incensed over her story, a question came to me very clearly. And it was a question I'd hear over and over again in my mind as I drove back to Chicago, over the next three days. It just kept nagging at me: "How are you any different?" Finally, I couldn't take it any longer. The first chance I got during the closing prayer, I split as fast as I could and started driving back to Chicago where everything would be familiar and I wouldn't have to think about those things.

But that's not what happened at all. Running away from the church service didn't provide the relief I wanted, in fact, it was just the opposite. I was wrestling with anger and doubt all the way home - for three long days. And finally, when I was 100 miles outside of Chicago, it all began to come together. I prayed for the first time in my life - nothing fancy - just talking with God. And in essence I told Him that I'd been a jerk my whole life. I had done a lot of things that were wrong. I think that was called sin. I'd heard about sin in my Catholic school, but didn't pay much attention to it. But now, I was beginning to understand. And the more I thought about it, the clearer it became. Sin wasn't just something I did once in a while, sin was who I *was*: I was a sinner. And, whereas before, I wouldn't have really cared about that, right now it was bothering me greatly. I was frantic because I didn't know what to do with that revelation. How could I change it? What could I do to make it all right? I'd spent the last three days arguing back-and-forth with myself. One minute I figured I was good and I really cared about those gals who danced in my clubs. I even cared about the dancers who I'd take to the next step in prostitution. It would give them lots of money in their pockets and would open up a lot of new doors for them. I tried to convince myself that I was like a benefactor, giving them a wonderful opportunity. But every time I would start to convince myself that I was actually doing a good thing, I'd remember Jackie's testimony and the anger would start all over again. "How are you any different?" I grew to hate that question, with a passion.

So, as I said, 100 miles outside of Chicago I prayed for the first time. I admitted that I'd been a jerk my whole life. That was my way of admitting to God that I was a sinner and that I needed to change. I had no idea what to do about that and I was in a panic. But then a peace came over me and my frantic state of mine calmed down. It was almost like a wave of serenity had washed over me. I remembered part of the conversation I had with John and Wendy over lunch. When I talked about the religious scam they had going, they gently, but firmly told me that I had missed it completely. This wasn't a scam at all. This was about people finding real life in Jesus - forgiveness for their sins - a new pathway for life itself. I didn't know much about it, but I knew that whatever it was, I wanted it desperately. I *needed* it desperately. I was tired of the guy I had tried to be all my life. At that moment in time, something became crystal clear to me: it didn't matter if people knew the name Nick Salerno. What mattered now was if *God* knew my name. I told Jesus that I didn't know what I was doing exactly. I just knew that I needed Him in my life. And He could have all of me but He'd have to clean up the messes, because I had no idea how to do that.

In the last 50 miles of my journey home, He gave me a plan. And I knew that as I would work His plan, my life was going to change significantly. I rolled into town and went straight home to shower up and hit the sack early. I was exhausted, not so much from three days of driving, but from the emotions of the battle I'd been through. I hit the sack and slept for 11 hours straight. I hadn't slept like that in years; maybe never. I woke up refreshed and the first thing I did was to go to my old Catholic Church and talk with the new priest, Father Angelo. I discovered in that first meeting that he was young and energetic. I also could tell that his faith was real to him, as real as what I'd seen in John and Wendy. I told him my story and asked if he would be willing to spend some time with me, teaching me the things I needed to know about being a Christian. I was like a sponge and soaked up everything Father Angelo had for me over the next six months. He didn't spend a lot of time on doctrine, but rather he spent the time, both teaching and demonstrating, what it means to have Jesus as the Lord of my life.

The next day I decided to put the new plan into effect. I called my head dancer, Amber, and asked her to meet me at the club in an hour if she was free. She and I met and I told her that I had made a decision. And that decision was going to impact a lot of people, including her. I knew, when she was wringing her hands, that she figured now that I was back, I'd want to start setting up dates for the dancers and some of our top- level customers. I could tell that this was a conversation she didn't want to have. And once again, I felt badly that this is what she had come to expect of me. But you can imagine her surprise when I told her that I'd had a meeting with God while on this trip, and I wasn't going to try to break into the prostitution racket. In fact, I said, I'm going to shut both of my clubs down, starting this very minute. When the customers came tonight, they were going to find the doors locked and a sign that says` Out of Business`.

She asked me about suddenly closing the business without giving notice to all the employees. That would be pretty tough on them and they'd have to scramble to find new jobs. That's when I told her that one major portion of the plan was to give every employee three months wages as a severance package. They should all be able to find other jobs in that period of time and if they found them soon, the extra three months' salary would be like a bonus.

Amber mentioned that she thought that was very nice and she would really appreciate the three months' severance. I looked at her and told her that I had a different plan for my dancers. I wanted to meet with each dancer personally and so I asked Amber to set up appointments in one-hour segments, starting tomorrow. She said she would take care of it and would have a schedule for me by the end of the day.

I began meeting with the six dancers from the two clubs the next day. Amber was my last appointment. At my face-to-face meeting with each of the gals, I started out by telling them that I'd had a meeting with God and my life was in the process of changing. I also looked deeply into their eyes and apologized for putting them in front of a room full of leering men, night after night. I told them that I was so very sorry for simply seeing them as nothing but objects, whose sole purpose was to make me rich. I told them that they were so much more than just a body, but it took me all this time to understand their true value. I asked them to forgive me for my selfishness, even though I didn't deserve it. And you want to know something? Every one of my six dancers got tears in their eyes and thanked me for what I had said - *everyone*. It really meant a lot to them.

I told them that I wanted to try to put some practical meaning to my apology, in a form that I hoped would help them out a bit. I wanted to give each of them a one-year severance package. I admitted that it didn't come anywhere near making up for my years of ignoring what I was really doing as their boss. I willingly put them in a position every night that ate away at their self-esteem and sense of personal value. My prayer was that they'd be able to use the money to accomplish some dreams, that otherwise might have seemed impossible. I knew that several of the gals were in college, while others were single moms. I hoped and prayed that all of them would find a better way. I encouraged them to seriously consider finding a good church, because faith in God could really change lives.

For the next six months I worked on all the legal aspects of shutting down the clubs and selling the properties. I wanted to make sure that somehow, I could legally insist that these two high-end properties would never be used for any business that was associated with the sex industry. Over the next few months, the buildings were sold: one to a restaurant and one to a culinary school. Each property had top-of-the-line kitchens and so the sales were a natural.

I also spent my time doing volunteer work for St. Anthony's parish. I tried to immerse myself in as many opportunities as possible, as well as taking advantage of the various Bible Studies they offered each week. I learned a lot about my faith as a Christian. I was kind of late in coming to the game and I had a lot of ground to make up.

But a couple of weeks ago as I was spending time in prayer, I sensed the Lord saying that He had a new assignment for me. In the past six months I'd learned to pay attention to those inner impressions, because they might really be from God. And if they were, I didn't want to miss it. He kept bringing Pleasant Pastures to mind and so I'd just pray for all of you and figure that was it. I hadn't really had much contact, other than the few times when John called me at first to see how things were going. I didn't tell him about the change that had happened because, to tell you the truth, it was so new to me I just wanted to make sure it was going to stick. So, I was pretty non-committal and played my cards close to the vest. I think John just figured that I was back in Chicago, business as usual. My clubs were shut down and my phones were disconnected and we just lost touch with each other.

But, like I said before, a couple of weeks ago God started bringing Pleasant Pastures to mind. And finally, the impression became so strong that I jumped in my car and started driving out here again. The trip was absolutely beautiful. It's amazing how gorgeous this country is when you're not full of anger and revenge. I pulled into town late last night and immediately went to Maggie's to see if I could get something to eat. The diner was closed, but when she saw it was me, she let me in and fed me like a king. And then, as only Maggie can do, she got me talking and I told her the whole saga of the last six months. I told her everything - no holds barred. And when she heard the story, she said that my being out here, at this particular time, was no coincidence. God has His timing and it's always perfect. She asked if I would be willing to share my testimony at the church service the next day. I said that it was fine, as long as John agreed to it. She called him and he said great, but he was going to save it as a surprise for Wendy. We made quick plans for a dramatic entrance…and here I am.

And Wendy, I want to apologize to you also for the way I treated you all those months ago. I know you've already forgiven me, because that's the kind of woman of God you are. I'm not going to give you a year's severance like I did the other dancers. I don't think you'd take it anyway. But if you would allow me the privilege, I'd like to pay the mortgage on Safe Haven. I'm not trying to be the big hero here, believe me. It's just that I feel that it's the least I can do. If it wasn't for guys like me, there wouldn't be a need for homes like Safe Haven. 'How are you any different?' That question made me angry every time I heard it. But then my heart began to soften and it made me cry buckets of tears between here and Chicago. That's who I was before, but that's not who I am now. I'm different, but it's because of you and John. You're the ones who gave me my first glimpse of Jesus and I know I'll never be the same again."

Nick finished his testimony and the congregation sat there in tears, quietly reflecting on this marvelous story. If Jesus could change Nick Salerno, He could change anyone. They all stood up and sang the hymn, "Great is Thy Faithfulness." And then, as one body, they marched down the few blocks to the beautifully restored Sinclair mansion and had a short service of dedication. Through those doors would come women from all walks of life. But no matter where they came from or what life had handed them, they were all going to someday walk away with the same lesson learned: you are God's child, greatly loved and marvelously cherished. In Christ, you are a woman of God and your value knows no bounds - either on earth or in eternity.

Epilogue

JACKIE OPENED THE DOOR AND GREETED TIFFANY with a warm smile and a quick handshake. She was just 16, but had been on the streets of Seattle, turning tricks, since she was 12. Her mother was in prison on a drug charge and wouldn't be getting out anytime soon. Her father had been killed in a bar fight, three years ago. It didn't matter much to Tiffany since she'd never really known him anyway, even though he had lived in the same city until he was killed. No brothers and sisters, no aunts and uncles, no family anywhere - at least none that would claim her.

Jackie looked into Tiffany's heavily made-up eyes and saw what she expected to see. Nothing. Totally dead. Lacking even a spark of life. Jackie smiled once again, knowing that would change. It would take a while, but there would be life in those eyes – perhaps for the first time since she was an innocent child – and who knew when that was.

She showed Tiffany through the house and then said goodbye to the social worker who'd been assigned to the case. She'd come straight from court where she had been given a choice. She could either go to the woman's prison in Purdy, or she could go to a home for women in Eastern Washington. Tiffany thought the name was a joke: Safe Haven? No place was safe. If such a place existed, she'd never found it.

Jackie showed Tiffany to her room and watched out of the corner of her eye as the young girl looked it over. Where are the other beds, Tiffany wanted to know? Jackie told her that there weren't any other beds. This was her room – her bed. Tiffany got that all too familiar look in her eye and Jackie could see she wasn't buying it. Others will come, she was thinking, and I'll be out on my ear, just you wait. She looked at the beautiful quilt that covered the bed and remarked that it looked homemade. Jackie was rather surprised that she knew that and Tiffany must've caught her puzzled look. She told Jackie that she remembered that her grandma did quilting. She remembered some of the patterns that she loved as a child. But grandma had died when Tiffany was four, thus ending the one stable relationship she had.

Jackie asked Tiffany if she had ever tried quilting before. Tiffany gave a little sarcastic chuckle and said, "Nope…grandma died and life happened – end of story." Jackie let her know that the lady who made the quilts came in once a week to give lessons. In fact, she was coming tomorrow. She also let her know that when Tiffany left, she could take the quilt with her, as a remembrance of her time at Safe Haven.

Quilting lessons? Take the quilt with her? Tiffany looked at Jackie and asked her how long she'd be staying. Jackie looked at her with compassion and assured her that she could stay for as long as she wanted to: there was no time limit. This is your home for as long as you need it - it's yours until you feel you're ready to spread your wings and fly. Tiffany's eyes grew round, but just as quickly narrowed, as she processed what Jackie had said.

"You mean, I don't have to move in 30 days?"

"Nope. You can stay as long as you like."

"Huh. We'll see."

Jackie looked at Tiffany, recognizing once again how life on the streets prematurely aged you and made you hard and distrustful of everybody. And for good reason. But she also knew that Tiffany would come around. It was going take time. It wasn't going to be easy, but she would come around. Jackie smiled knowing that eventually Tiffany, like so many others, would be set free by God's transforming love.